M. Findlay.
Heather Cottage;

1963 £3

ANN
AND HER
MOTHER

ANN AND HER MOTHER

BY

O. DOUGLAS

AUTHOR OF "THE SETONS"
"PENNY PLAIN," ETC.

THOMAS NELSON AND SONS, Ltd.
LONDON, EDINBURGH, NEW YORK
TORONTO, AND PARIS

THOMAS NELSON AND SONS LTD
Parkside Works Edinburgh 9
3 Henrietta Street London WC2
312 Flinders Street Melbourne C1
5 Parker's Buildings Burg Street Cape Town

THOMAS NELSON AND SONS (CANADA) LTD
91–93 Wellington Street West   Toronto 1

THOMAS NELSON AND SONS
19 East 47th Street New York 17

SOCIÉTÉ FRANÇAISE D'EDITIONS NELSON
25 rue Henri Barbusse Paris V^e

" IN this age of opulence and refinement whom can such a character please ?   Such as are fond of high life will turn in disdain from the simplicity of a country fireside.   Such as mistake ribaldry for humour will find no wit in this harmless conversation : and such as have been taught to deride religion will laugh at one whose chief stores of comfort are drawn from futurity."

OLIVER GOLDSMITH.

ANN AND HER MOTHER

CHAPTER I

MRS. DOUGLAS and her daughter Ann sat together in their living-room one November night.

It was a wonderfully comfortable room, brightly yet softly lit, and warmed by a noble fire. There was a pleasant space and emptiness about it, an absence of ornaments and irrelevant photographs; each piece of furniture, each of the few pictures, was of value.

Mrs. Douglas had a book in her lap and in her hand a half-finished stocking, for she considered that she was wasting time if she did not knit while reading.

Ann sat on a stool by the fire, poring over a seedsman's catalogue, a puzzled frown on her brow.

" I wish," she said, without looking up, " I do wish I knew more about gardening. I can't make out from this what will grow best with us. . . . Don't you think, Mother, it is almost *lèse-majesté* to call a rose Queen Mary, and describe it as 'a gross feeder'? Oh, and this! *Mr. Asquith,* 'very compact in form, rosy in colour.' What humorists the compilers of seedsmen's catalogues are! And what poets! Where was it we read that article about catalogues? It said that the very names were like a procession of princes—' amber and carmine Queens, and Princes' Feathers, and Cloth of Gold.' The names tempt one simply by the glory of the sound. ' Love-in-a-Mist . . . Love-Fire, a rich cream with a faint suggestion of apricot primrose in petal '—and with a drop one learns that this beauty can be bought for the sum of tuppence! . . . Delphiniums we must have—dozens of them. I can picture us next summer lying on the lawn in deckchairs on hot, sunny days, looking between tall, blue delphiniums to green hilltops. Won't it be lovely, Mother?"

"H'm," said her mother in a dry voice, "at present you have only the hilltops. I haven't imagination enough to picture the hot sun and the lawn and the blue delphiniums."

"*Mother!*" said Ann, wheeling round on her stool and facing her parent, who was knitting with provoking calm, "there's nothing sporting about you at all. It always rains in November, but that's nobody's fault, and you might at least try to look as if you didn't mind. Nobody ever said a glen was a cheery place in winter, but, myself, I like it frightfully. When Uncle Bob left me the Green Glen for my very own I determined that somehow or other I would manage to build a house in it—a little white-faced house among the heather. Not big, but big enough to hold us all—six good bedrooms, one big living-room, a hall we could sit in, a smaller room to feed in. You all made objections—all except Charlotte, who encouraged me. You pointed out all the disadvantages : six miles from a station, a steep hill road, carting difficult ! You told me that building in these days was only the pastime of a millionaire, but—the house is built and, because the architect was a man of sense and listened to what I wanted, it is exactly the house I meant it to be in my dreams, so ' Dreams ' it will be called."

" I thought you hated new houses ? "

" So I do, except when it is my own house in my own Green Glen. And you will admit that it is comfortable."

" It's very bare," Mrs. Douglas said.

" Well, I like it bare. And your own room is far from bare. It is more like a museum than anything else, with so many mementoes of other days hung on the walls, and photographs of us all at every age and in every attitude, and shelves and shelves of devotional books, not to speak of all the little stucco figures you have cherished for years. Their heads have been gummed on so often they fall off if you look at them. Davie was always being entreated by you to mend them, and he found, finally, that Moses' head (or was it Eli ?) would only remain on if turned the wrong way about—so his beard was down his back! . . . To return to 'Dreams,' I admit the garden is still unmade, and the road a mere track, but wait and you will see it blossom like the rose. We shan't have any fences—there is no need for them among the hills, and the heather will grow to the edges of our shaven lawns, and we'll have herbaceous borders as gay as a carnation ribbon, and beds of mignonette . . ."

Mrs. Douglas laid down her stocking and looked at her daughter. " No fences ? And rabbits nibbling the mignonette—it's a thing they have a particular fancy for; and sheep eating the vegetables . . ."

" Go on with your stocking, Motherkin, and don't try to be crushing. We'll have fences then, and wire to keep out the rabbits, and we'll cover the fences with rambler roses—the bright red single kind ; I don't like Dorothy Perkins. And there's simply no end to what we can do with the burn ; it would make any garden fairyland, with those shining brown pools fringed with heather. *What* luck to have a burn ! Before the house we are going to have a paved bit, so that you can go out and take the air without getting your feet wet. There will be no ' gravel sweep,' and no one will be able to come to our door except on their own feet, for the road will stop a long way from the house."

Ann clasped her hands round her knees, and rocked herself in joyful anticipation.

" I remember," she went on, " hearing as a child some one praise a neighbourhood with the phrase,

' It is full of carriage people.' I wondered at the time what kind of people they were, and if they perhaps had their abode in a carriage, like a snail in its shell ! When ' motor people ' come to Dreams they will have to leave their motors and walk. We shall say to them, like True Thomas, ' Light down, light down from your horse o' pride.' . . . But, Mother, is this really going to bore you terribly ? Do you miss so badly the giddy round of Priorsford ? The pavements ? The shops ? The tea-parties ? ''

Mrs. Douglas gave a long sigh. " I don't want to grumble, but, you know, I always did say it was rash to attempt to stay a winter in the Green Glen. It's well enough in the summer (though even then I would prefer to be nearer civilization), and fine for the children, but in November, with the fields like sponges, and the road a mere Slough of Despond, and the hills covered with mist most of the time, and the wind coming down the glen howling like an evil spirit, and the station six miles away, and only a pony trap between us and complete burial ; Mark and Charlotte in India, and Jim in South Africa, and the children in Oxfordshire with their other grandmother, I feel like a pelican in the wilderness. I told you I would, and I do."

" Poor dear, but . . ."

" Through the day it isn't so bad. I admit the mornings are rather beautiful, and when it happens to be fine I can potter about outside, and Marget is always a divert. In the afternoon when it rains (and it has rained practically every day for three weeks) I sew and write letters and read, and there is always tea to look forward to. But in the evenings —and the curtains have to be drawn now about four o'clock—when there is no chance of a ring at the bell, no postman, no telephone-call, no stray callers, and the owls hoot, and my eyes get tired with reading, and one can't knit for ever even with four wild grandchildren to knit for, well——"

" But, my dear," said her daughter, " just think how you will appreciate Priorsford when you get back. We are very much alone just now—it was an odd chance that sent Mark and Charlotte to India and Jim to South Africa the same winter—but don't let's have to remember it as the winter of our discontent. . . . We must face facts. Neighbours we have almost none. Mr. Sharp, at the Manse, is practically the only one, and he is so shy that speaking to him is like trying to carry on a conversation with a very young rabbit in a trap. The Scotts aren't so very far away as the crow flies, only over the other side of the hill, but it is five miles round by road. It's an unpeopled world, but the great thing to remember is that any moment you please you can have a case packed, order the pony trap, drive to the station, buy a ticket, and in about two hours you would be in Glasgow, in the Central Station Hotel, among all the city gentlemen, feasting your eyes on people, forgetting the owls in listening to the Glasgow accent, eating large meals, frequenting picture houses. . . ."

Mrs. Douglas dropped both her book and stocking in her indignation.

" Ann, you know I *never* enter a picture house, and I haven't the least desire to go to Glasgow in the meantime."

" I tell you what," Ann cried, " go in for a course of reading and improve your mind. It's an opportunity that may not occur again."

" I'm too old to improve my mind ; besides, it isn't very nice of you to suggest that it needs improving."

Ann studied her mother with her head on one side. " You're sixty, aren't you ? Sixty's nothing. The late Mr. Gladstone learned Arabic when he was eighty. Besides, you are the most absurd person for sixty I ever saw. Your hair is as soft and brown as it was when you were thirty, and you have a complexion that is the envy of less fortunate women. And the odd thing is, I believe you hate to be told so. I believe you want to look old."

" Last summer," said Mrs. Douglas, " I overheard Rory say to Alison, ' Alis, Gran is nearly sixty ; I heard her say so,' and Alis, with a depth of pity in her voice, replied, ' Oh, *poor* Gran ! ' But when I think I'm only sixty I feel like pitying myself. In the *Times* last night there were six people among the ' Deaths ' who were over ninety. It frightens me to think that I may live to a great age, and, perhaps, see you all go before me—and I get so wearied sometimes for your father and the boys. . . ."

Ann laid her hand on her mother's. " I know," she said, " I know. But, Mother, are those who are gone so much more dear to you than we who are left ? As Pharaoh said to Hadad : ' What hast thou lacked with us, that, behold, thou seekest to go to thine own country ? ' "

" Ah, my dear, *nothing*, but . . ."

" The old answer," said Ann, " Nothing, nothing—' howbeit let me go in any wise.' . . . Well, we have wandered from our subject. What do you say, Mums, to reading Robert Louis right through ? We have the Edinburgh edition here. He will teach you to love the moorlands."

Mrs. Douglas recoiled in horror from the suggestion.

" Oh no ! No. No. The very name of R. L. S. makes me think of the eternal crying of whaups, and we are fairly beset with the creatures here. Really to appreciate Robert Louis you must read him immersed in a town with no hope of a holiday, or on the burning, shining plains of India, or on the South African veldt. To read there of ' a great, rooty sweetness of bogs ' and ' the infinite, melancholy piping of hill-birds,' and ' winds austere and pure,' is like water in a thirsty land. But when one is seated in the bogs, and deaved by the hill-birds, it's only an irritation. I'd rather read Ethel M. Dell, and warm myself with the thought of heroes whose eyes are like slumbering volcanoes, and heroines who generally manage to get a flogging from some one before they win through to happiness."

Ann laughed. "It's quite true. Here we must read books hot with life, full of intrigues and sensational developments. We have all the simplicity we want in the Green Glen."

Her mother sighed. "I'm not really discontented, Ann, though I'm afraid I sound so. But I seem to lead such a useless life here. A few letters to sick and sad people is all I accomplish. If there were some people about the doors whom I could visit, and, perhaps, help a little. Once a minister's wife always a minister's wife. I can't get out of the habit of trying to help. But there's only old Geordie's cottage, and he hasn't even a wife, and he wouldn't thank me for a visit."

"No," laughed Ann. "He is very proud of being able to fend for himself, and hopes to die without being beholden to any woman. He was telling me a sad tale the other day about an old friend of his who lived alone until he was eighty, and then fell ill and had to have the district nurse, who insisted on his remaining in bed. 'To think,' said Geordie, 'that a man should live to be aichty and be overpowered by a wumman in the end.' But I can quite see that the lack of people to comfort and help is a great lack to you—born minister's wife that you are."

"Ah, well, I made many mistakes, but my heart was in my job. It was a real pleasure to me to know every soul in the church, and to listen to all they cared to tell me of their trials and their troubles, and to be asked to share in their merry-makings; to have the right to laugh and cry with them. The wives used to say when your father intimated visiting, ' I wish the mistress wad come wi' the minister, she's a graund cracker.' Your father was sometimes ill-off knowing what to talk about in the different houses; he wasn't one of those glib men with a fund of easy phrases, but when they got to know him they liked him the better for his quietness, and valued his few words more than other people's eloquence. How he would have enjoyed this, Ann! He loved the Green Glen, and the burn, and the whaups crying."

There was a silence, and Mrs. Douglas sat looking into the fire. She was far away from the little house among the hills. She was young again, and the husband of her youth was once more at her side. Pictures, softened and beautified by time, unrolled themselves before her eyes. Children played in a garden among flowers, their laughter and shouting came to her ears, she could see their faces lifted to hers; but no beckoning could bring them to her, for long ago they had grown up and gone away; they were but dream children who played in that garden.

Ann watched her mother with a soft look in her grey eyes. " I've been thinking, Mums, you ought to write your *Life*."

Mrs. Douglas came back to the present with an effort. " Write my life? But I did—don't you remember? On that yachting cruise we went, when the sea never stayed calm except for a few hours. There was nothing much to do, so I wrote my life in a twopenny pass-book, with a pencil, and none of you were at all encouraging about it. I read it aloud to you somewhere about the Azores, when you were lying seasick in your berth, and you said it made you feel worse ; and Charlotte cried from the next cabin, ' Ann, what is wrong with Gran that she is making that curious, whining sound ? ' and Mark printed on the cover, ' The Life of auld Mistress Douglas written by herself,' and then it got lost."

" I remember," said Ann. " But this time it must be done properly. You'll tell it to me and I'll write it down, and we'll have it typed and perhaps printed, so that the children when they grow up will know what a queer little grandmother was theirs. Let me see—we'll be here alone until the Moncrieffs come about the middle of December ; that will give us a month to work at it. Two hours every night, perhaps more. Does that please you, Motherkin ? "

" Ann, you are trying to humour an old woman. I don't suppose the children would ever trouble to read my *Life*, except perhaps Alison—that child has a strong sense of duty ; but I must say I would enjoy remembering it all. . . . Here are Marget and Mysie."

The two servants came into the room accompanied by a large Persian cat, grey, the colour of a November sky. This beautiful creature had been named by Ann the " Tatler," because his genius for falling into photographic attitudes reminded her, she said, of those ladies, fair and fashionable, whose pictures adorn the weekly pages of that popular journal.

Marget seated herself majestically. She was a tall woman, with a broad, honest face, and hair pulled straight back and covered by a cap—not the flippant scrap of muslin with a bow generally worn, but an erection of coffee-coloured lace, with touches of crimson velvet, which she alluded to as a "kep," and which gave her almost a regal air.

Marget had been thirty-five years with the Douglas family, and was so thoroughly a Douglas that there was never any thought of keeping her in her "place." Mysie, who was her niece, she kept under iron control, but she allowed herself much latitude. No one knew Marget's age. It was a subject on which she had always been excessively touchy. When the Census came round she had said, "I'll no' pit it doon till a' the bairns are oot, an' naebody but the maister 'll ken, an' he'll no' tell."

She met all questions with "I'm as auld as ma little finger an' I'm aulder than ma teeth." In revenge the Douglases had intimated to their friends that they had inside knowledge that Marget was at least eighty.

After prayers Mysie left the room, but Marget generally remained for a "crack," delighting to bandy words with "Miss Ann"—a diversion which to-night ended in Ann being called "a daft lassie."

"*Lassie!*" cried Ann.

" Ye'll aye be a lassie to me," Marget told her ;
" but," turning to her mistress, " is it true, Mem,
that she's gaun to write yer *Life* ? I never ken
when Miss Ann's speakin' the truth and when she's
juist haverin'. . . . It wad be rale interestin'. Ye
wad need to pit in aboot thon daft man wha cam'
to see the maister and the pollis efter him, an' that
awfu' fricht we got wi' the big fire in the linoleum
factory, and aboot the man wha drooned hissel in
the Panny Pond and floatit. . . ."

" Yes, Marget," said Ann, " we'll need your help
to decide what is to be put in. One thing, of course,
must go in—your age."

Marget rose from her chair with a we-are-not-
amused look, put the Bibles back in their proper
places, dropped her delightful, old-fashioned curtsey,
walked to the door, and said before she closed it
behind her :

" Ye wadna daur. An', what's mair, ye *dinna
ken it*."

CHAPTER II

Two nights later, when the stars had come out to look down at the Green Glen and the curtains were drawn in Dreams, Ann sat down before a small table on which lay a pile of paper and a fountain-pen, and told her mother that she was now ready to write her *Life*.

" But how do you begin a *Life* ? " Mrs. Douglas asked. She was sitting in her favourite low chair, doing what she called her " reading." Beside her was a pile of devotional books, from each of which she read the portion for the day. Nothing would make her miss this ceremony, and she carted the whole pile about with her wherever she went.

" Shall I give you the date of my birth and say that I was the child of poor but honest parents ? I seem to remember that beginning."

" No," Ann decided, " we'll leave dates alone ; they are ' chiels that winna ding.' The point is, what style would you like me to write it in ? We might begin like *The Arabian Nights*—' It is related (but God alone is all-knowing, as well as all-wise and all-mighty and all-bountiful) that there was in ancient times a fair virgin, Helen. . . .' But I think, perhaps, your history is too tame and domestic for such a highly coloured style."

" I should think so, indeed," said her mother, as she laid down *Hours of Silence* and took up *Come ye Apart.*

" What about the Russian touch ? " Ann asked, waving her pen. " Like this : ' She turned upon her pillow, tearing at its satin cover with her nails, then, taking a spoonful of bromide, she continued——' "

" Oh, Ann—don't be ridiculous ! "

" Or shall I dispense entirely with commas, inverted and otherwise, and begin without a beginning at all, as the very best people do ? It does make Aunt Agatha so angry, that sort of book, where no explanations are offered, and you suddenly find yourself floundering among a lot of Christian names. Anyway, it's much too clever for me to attempt ! I'm afraid we must confine ourselves to a plain narrative, with no thoughts, only incidents. I think I'll begin : ' In my youth I wasna what you would ca' bonnie, but I was pale, penetratin', and interestin'.' How is that ? "

Mrs. Douglas shook her head. She had reached *From Day to Day*, and would soon be at the apex of the pile, *Golden Grain*. " If you are going to describe my appearance, you might at least be accurate."

" Well," said her daughter, " I only know you

from a very old photograph as a moon-faced child with tight curls, and then, later, with two babies and a *cap* ! What were you really like ? "

Mrs. Douglas sat very upright, with a becoming pink flush on her face and a little smile at the corners of her mouth. " I can see myself the day I met your father for the first time. I had on my first silk dress—royal blue it was—and a locket with a black velvet ribbon round my neck, and my hair most elaborately done in what was called a ' mane,' some rolled up on the top, some hanging down. My hair was my best point. It was thick and wavy, and as yellow as corn. Your father always said he fell in love with the back of my head. Who would believe it who saw me now ? "

" ' Faigs, ye're no' bad,' as Marget would say," Ann comforted her. " As one gets older looks are chiefly a matter of dress. When you take pains with your clothes no woman of your age looks better ; but when you wander out in a rather seedy black dress, with a dejected face under a hat that has seen better days, you can't wonder at what my friend Mrs. Bell said after meeting you one wet day : ' Eh, puir auld buddy ; she's an awfu' worrit-lookin' wumman ; it fair makes me no' weel to look at her ! ' "

" Yes, Ann, but you shouldn't have laughed. I don't like that Mrs. Bell. She's a forward woman, and you spoil her."

" Oh, I told her you weren't really old, but those women are so surprisingly young. They have grown-up families and hordes of grand-children, and you think they are at least seventy and they turn out to be fifty. Of course, it was rather disrespectful of her to call you ' puir auld buddy,' but the ' awfu' worrit-lookin' ' was such an exact description of you doing good works on a wet day in your old clothes that I had to laugh. But we're not getting on."

" It's absurd to talk of writing my life," Mrs. Douglas said. " There is nothing worth telling about. I asked Alison last summer what she was going to be, and she tossed back that yellow mane of hers, and said earnestly, ' Well, Gran, I did think of being a poet, but I've decided just to be an ordinary woman with a baby.' That's all I ever was. An ordinary woman with several babies and a man and a kirk to look after—a big handful for any woman. I'd better begin where, for me, the world first began, at Etterick. You remember the old house, don't you, with its white-washed walls and high pointed roof, standing at the end of the village ? When I think of it it always seems to be summer ; the shadow of the house falling black across the white road, a baker's van standing in the village, and one of the wives holding out her white apron for loaves, a hen clucking sleepily, the hum of the bees among the flowers in the old garden, the *clink-clink* from the smiddy at the burnside, my mother in a thin blue dress standing in the doorway with a basket on her arm—the peace of a summer afternoon !

And the smell of it! New-mown grass drying in
the sun, indescribable sweet scents from the
flower-thick roadsides, the smiddy smell of hot
iron sizzling on big hoofs, wafts from the roses
in the garden—those most fragrant, red, loose-
petalled roses that now I never see. Inside the
house was cool and dark, with drawn blinds.
D'you remember the parlour? I can tell you
where every bit of furniture in it stood. The
bureau behind the door, and along the wall the
old, wide sofa. I've often told you about the
upholsterer from Priorsford, who came to pre-
scribe for it when its springs began to subside?
He had a lisp, and after the examination was
finished he said simply and finally, ' The thofo's
done.' How we laughed over that, and the
' thofo ' held on for another twenty years, never
getting much worse. Yes, the piano came next
to the sofa, and then the wide window with all
the little panes. The tea-table stood there in
summer, and one could see all who passed by.
' The day the chaise and pair gaed through
Caddonfoot ' was a saying in the countryside, but
Etterick boasted carts and carriages in some pro-
fusion. I wonder if my mother's teas were really
better than any one else's? The cream so thick
that it had to be helped out of the jug with a
spoon! And the ' thin ' scones coated with fresh-
churned butter! My dear Robbie revelled in
them. He wrote from India, you remember,
that when camping they ran short of bread, and

the cook said he would bake some *chupattis*.
'And,' wrote Robbie, ' by the grace of God the
chupattis turned out to be my grandmother's
" thin " scones ! ' "

"I remember," said Ann. "He introduced
me to them when I went out. Wasn't the house
at Etterick an inn once ? "

"Yes, and all the rooms had numbers painted
on the doors. No. 8 was your nursery when we
used to spend the summer there. And the play-
room was called ' Jenny Berry '—why, I don't
know ; the reason for the name is lost in the mists
of antiquity. It was the first place you all rushed
to the moment you arrived, in a fever to see if your
treasures were safe, and you always found them
just as you left them. My mother was a very
understanding woman with children. She wasn't,
perhaps, a very tender grandmother as grandmothers go now, and you children held her in
some awe ; but you valued her good opinions, and
you knew her to be absolutely just. She seldom
praised, but, on the other hand, she never damped
your enthusiasms. ' Never daunton young folk '
was one of her favourite sayings. Yes. I'm
afraid she was somewhat intolerant, poor dear.
She had a great contempt for the gossiping,
crocheting, hen-headed female that abounded in
her day. ' A frivolous woman,' she would say
after a visit from such a one, ' fit for nothing but
fancy work and novelettes.' Good looks appealed
to her enormously, and she was glad all you

children had what she called 'china' faces;
swarthy people she could not abide. We took
Mrs. Alston to see her when she was staying with
us one summer at Caddonfoot—dear Mrs. Alston,
with her dun skin and projecting teeth and her
heart of gold! Your grandmother was the
frailest little body then, only her indomitable
spirit kept her going, and Mrs. Alston fussed over
her and deferred to her in the kindest way. But
the blandishments were all to no purpose; she
looked coldly at the visitor, and afterwards, when
I told her what a fine woman Mrs. Alston was, and
what fine work she had done in the mission-field,
all the answer I got was, 'Oh, I daresay, but I
never took my tea with a worse-looking woman.'"

"I remember that," said Ann. "I remember
how Father shouted when you told him. Granny
was often very amusing, but what I remember
most about her was her sense of comfort."

"Yes, if I've any notion how to make a house
comfortable I got it from my mother. She was
great in preparing for people. If we had only
gone to Priorsford for the day she made of our
return a sort of festival. Out on the doorstep to
meet us, fires blazing, tea ready, and such a
budget to tell us of the small events of the day.
Some women are so casual with their children,
they don't *thirl* them to themselves. They let
them go and come, and seem to take very little
interest in their comings and their goings, don't
even trouble to be in the house when the boys

come home for the holidays; suppose vaguely that this one or that one will be home to-day or to-morrow, never think of preparing a welcome. And then they wonder that their children have no love for their home; that when they go out into the world, they don't trouble to write except at infrequent intervals; that sometimes their lives drift so far apart that they cannot hear each other speak."

"Mother," said Ann, "you speak wisely, but how much of this is to go down in your *Life*? At present I have only got that you had yellow hair and a royal blue silk dress and a locket. Oughtn't I to say something about your childhood and what influenced you, and all that sort of thing? Do try to remember some thoughts you had; you know the sort of things these 'strong' novels are full of — your feelings when you found they had drowned your kitten—and weren't you ever misunderstood and driven to weep floods of tears in secret?"

Mrs. Douglas shook her head. "No, I never was clever enough to think the things children think in modern novels. And I don't remember being misunderstood, except that I was always considered rather a forward child when really I suffered much from shyness. One morning, with a great effort, I managed to say to old Sibbald, 'It's a fine morning,' as I passed him. 'What are ye sayin' noo wi' yer impertinence?' was his most uncalled-for response. I think my childhood was too happy to have any history. One of a big family, with freedom to roam, and pets in abundance, I never had a dull minute. And Etterick was a very interesting village, full of characters."

" Wasn't there somebody called ' Granny ' you used to tell us stories about ? "

" My mother's nurse. She died before you were born. The very wee-est woman that ever was—I used to pick her up and carry her about— and so bonnie, with a white-goffered mutch fram· ing her face. We all loved that little old woman. She lived in a tiny house at the top of the village with Tam, her husband ; all her family were up and married and away. ' Granny ' was our refuge in every kind of storm—indeed, she was everybody's refuge. And she had a great heart in her little body. It was told of her that when her eldest boy ran away to Edinburgh and enlisted, she made a pot of broth and baked a baking of scones for the children left at home, strapped the baby on her back, walked into Edinburgh, bought the boy off, and walked back again—fifty-six miles in all ! We have almost lost the use of our legs in these days of trains and motors. She never asked anything from anybody. I can remember her face when some well-meaning person offered her charity. ' Na, na, thank ye kindly. I may be sodger-clad, but I'm major-minded.' And there was old Peggy Leithen, who gave a ha'penny to every beggar that came to the door, murmuring as she did so, ' Charity covereth a multitude of sins,' and graphically described her conversion : ' I juist got the blessin' when ma knee was on the edge o' the bed steppin' in ahint Geordie.' And there was Jock Look-Up—but I could go on for hours. I think I was thirteen when I went to a boarding-school. I enjoyed that, too—all except the getting up to practise on winter mornings. I can feel now the chill of the notes on my numb fingers. I was going back to school for another year when I met your father and got married instead."

"Seventeen, weren't you ? "

"Seventeen, and childish at that. I never had my hair up till my marriage day. Your father was twenty-six."

"Babes ! " said Ann.

"It's odd how things come about," said Mrs. Douglas, as she put the last of the text-books on the pile, and took off the large, round-eyed, tortoise-shell spectacles that she wore when doing her " reading." " Dr. Watts, our own minister, was ordered to the South of France for the winter, and your father, who had just finished with college, came to take his place. We were used to fine ministers in Etterick. Dr. Watts was a saint and a scholar, and the parish minister was one of God's most faithful servants—both were men of dignity and power. But your father was so young and ardent ; he went through the district like a flame. He held meetings in lonely glens where no meeting had ever been held before. He kindled zeal in

quiet people who had been content to let things
go on as they had always gone ; it was a wonderful
six months.   Your Aunt Agatha, who, being older,
had left school before I did, wrote to tell me of this
extraordinary young man ; indeed, her letters
were so full of him that I made up my mind to dislike him at sight.   And after I did meet him I
pretended to myself and to Agatha that I thought
him a very tiresome young man.   I mimicked the
way he sang hymns and his boyish, off-hand
manner, so unlike Dr. Watts's grave, aloof ways.
I wish I had words, Ann, to give you some idea
of the man your father was in his youth.   As he
grew older he grew not less earnest, but more
tolerant—mellower, perhaps, is the word.   As a
young man he was like a sword-blade, pure and
keen.   And yet he was such a boy with it all, or
I never would have dared to marry him.   I had
absolutely no training for a minister's wife, but I
went into it quite blithely.   Now, looking back, I
wonder at myself.   At the time I was like the
little boy marching bravely into a dark room, his
bigger brother explaining the phenomenon with ' He
hasna the sense to be feart.' "

    " There's a lot in that," said Ann.   " But think
what a loss to the world if you had remained a
spinster—it hardly bears thinking of !   Well, we
haven't got very far to-night.   To-morrow you
must tell me all about the wedding.   I know Alison
would like to hear about the tiny, white, kid lacing
shoes with pale blue rosettes that I used to look

CHAPTER III

" Now that the visitors are gone," said Ann,
" we'll go on with our wedding number. Who
complained of the dullness of the Green Glen ?
Three visitors—the whole neighbourhood, you may
say—in one afternoon : first the parson, then the
two Miss Scotts. As I came down the burnside I
saw them go up to the door, and I said to myself in
the words of the old beadle who was asked what
sort of congregation was gathering : ' Graund !
Twa weemen pourin' in.' Didn't you like them,
Mother ? The Miss Scotts, I mean ? I thought
their weather-beaten faces very attractive, and
their voices so surprisingly soft and clear. Somehow
I had expected voices rather loud and strident,
to go with their workman-like clothes and heavy
boots. The younger one specially attracted me—
the way she beamed through her spectacles and
said ' Yes ' unexpectedly, whenever a pause
occurred in the conversation. They are going to
help me a lot with the garden ; their own place is
lovely. It's a nice happy way to end one's days—

at in a drawer. I believe they finished
jumble sale."

"Yes," Mrs. Douglas confessed. "It
first one we ever had, and you know the
madness that seizes you when you see people
to buy. I rushed home and looked out every
we could do without—my wedding slippers an
the lot. And poor old Mrs. Buchanan, in a sor
ecstasy of sacrifice, climbed up to her kitch
shelf and brought down the copper kettle that i
her saner moments she cherished like saffron, and
threw it on the pyre. The sale was for Women's
Foreign Missions, and when at the end of the most
strenuous evening any of us had ever spent the
treasurer and I lugged our takings home in a cab,
her husband met us at the door, and, lifting the
heavy bag, said, 'I doubt it's Alexander the
coppersmith.' But it wasn't; it was fully £100.
Dear, dear, the excitements of a ministerial life!"

living peacefully among growing flowers! Think of all the old women who live in hotels and boarding-houses, quite comfortable, I daresay, so far as fires and light and a good bed and well-cooked food go, but so barren of all interest except a morbid curiosity about their fellow-prisoners! How spacious a country life is! . . ."

"Oh yes," her mother broke in impatiently; "but hotel life can be very interesting, and there is nothing I enjoy so much as watching my neighbours. . . . I wonder why Mr. Sharp likes telling funny stories?"

"Shyness goads him to it," Ann said. "It's the same thing that makes me chatter like a swallow when I am with impressive people and ought to hold my peace. He's a decent lad, Mr. Sharp, but I wish that when I meet him outside he wouldn't treat me like a funeral. He doesn't look at me, but removes his hat when passing. Shyness again, I suppose."

"He has a housekeeper," Mrs. Douglas said, as she picked up a stitch. "It's a pity he hasn't a wife. In a quiet place like this the Manse should be a centre for the district. Don't you think, Ann, if we asked Nina Strachen, or——"

"Mother," said Ann solemnly, "I utterly refuse to have anything to do with your match-making efforts. Just let your mind dwell for a little on the result of your last."

Mrs. Douglas sighed. "Poor George Reid! But it wasn't marrying killed him. He couldn't have got a better wife than Jeanie Robb. The doctors said the trouble had been going on for a long time, and, anyway, the last months of his life were as comfortable as they could be made. If he hadn't married he would have been dependent on *fremt* women, for he hadn't a soul of his own ; and Jeanie gets the Widows' Fund, so you can't regret the marriage having taken place."

" Practical woman ! " laughed Ann. " But we must get on with your own wedding now—we are making no progress at all. When I think of what Hugh Walpole or Compton Mackenzie can make out of somebody's childhood, I blush for my few bald sentences. About your wedding—did my grandmother choose your things ? When I knew her she took very little interest in clothes, just wore whatever was brought to her."

" Ah, but she wasn't always like that. I remember Agatha and myself almost in tears begging her not to get a purple silk dress and bonnet which she much desired, as we thought them absurdly youthful for her years. Poor body ! I don't believe she was more than forty. Daughters can be very unfeeling."

" They can," Ann agreed, with a twinkle. " My poor grandmother ! What a shame to deprive her of her purple silk ! If you and Aunt Agatha could have looked forward forty years and seen grandmothers with dresses almost to their knees, dancing, playing tennis, frivolling, hardly recog-

nizable from the eighteen-year-olds, I wonder
what you would have thought. Well, who did
buy your trousseau ? Aunt Agatha ? "

" No, she was less sophisticated even than I
was. My stand-by was Miss Ayton. My mother
trusted her judgment and her taste and asked her
help, and Miss Ayton was only too willing to
give it ; for, spinster of fifty as she was, she loved
a marriage. She was one of those delightful
women who can be vividly interested in their
neighbours' business without ever being a nuisance,
and she presided like a stout, benign fairy over
my nuptials, getting things done, it seemed, by
a wave of her wand."

Mrs. Douglas let her knitting fall on her lap,
and lay in her chair, smiling.

" First I was whisked off to Edinburgh to have
some lessons in cooking (I knew absolutely nothing
about anything). *High-class* cooking it was
called, I suppose because nearly every recipe
called in the most casual way for a dozen of eggs
and a bottle of sherry. Not the sort of cooking
required for a manse, you will say. . . ."

Ann looked up from her writing. " Hadn't
you—I seem to remember—a cookery book
from that class, a fat green book ? It stood,
for some reason, on the nursery bookshelf, and
was a sort of Aladdin's Cave to us children. We
pored over it, reading aloud the rich, strange
ingredients, and lay on our faces gazing enraptured
at the picture of a dinner-table laid for about

sixty people, where each napkin was folded in a different way, and pheasants with long tail-feathers sat about in dishes, and brightly tinted jellies and creams and trifles made it blossom like a fairy garden. That picture always made us so hungry that we had to have 'a piece' all round after looking at it. . . . Why do I connect that cookery book with Communions ? "

Mrs. Douglas laughed. " Because at Communion times, when we had strange ministers assisting, we had puddings out of that book, at least expurgated editions of them. I have that book in my room now. It is too much a bit of my past for me ever to part with it. It has been with me since the start. At first it was all that stood between me and blank ignorance, and now it is a reminder of the days that seem like a happy dream. Well, the book and the cookery lessons were due to Miss Ayton. Or, was it Mrs. Watts first suggested I should learn cooking ? I believe it was. There was never any one so practical as Mrs. Watts, dear woman. I always regret that she was gone before you grew up, Ann ; you would have delighted in her. She was a daughter of the great Dr. Grierson—that mighty preacher and statesman—and she had much of the Grierson charm. Her husband, Dr. Watts, was laird as well as minister, and they didn't live at the Manse, but at their own place, Fennanhopes. It was about the greatest treat we had as children, to be invited to Fennanhopes, and I can't think why we liked it so much, for whenever we arrived Mrs. Watts would say, ' Now, friends,' and in a trice she had us all working hard. Some picked currants, some went to bring in the eggs, some weeded—but we all did something. We wouldn't have done it for any one else, but we liked to please Mrs. Watts. She kept everybody busy : visitors (the house was always full), village, the whole countryside, and there is no doubt that the state of being pleasantly busy is the best we can attain to in this world. Mrs. Watts was a noted house-wife, and servants trained by her were eagerly sought for. I remember going, during one Assembly time in Edinburgh, to a meeting at which Mrs. Watts was to speak. One knew what to expect as a rule—a rather gasped-out, tepid little homily from the wife of one or other well-known divine ; but I rather thought Mrs. Watts would be different. I waited with interest, and presently she stepped on to the platform, looking so big and fine and of the open air, spoke for a few minutes in her clear, round voice, and then, looking round the meeting with friendly eyes, she said, ' Now, friends, I am going to tell you how to make *really good coffee.*' "

Ann laughed. " What a dear ! I wish I had known her. I can just remember Dr. Watts. It seemed to me, standing somewhere about his knees, that his head must be dangerously near the clouds, and I remember his gentle voice saying to me, ' It will take you a long time to grow as big as I am.' . . . Yes, and so between Mrs. Watts and Miss Ayton you learned something about cooking. And who chose your trousseau, and all your ' providing ' ? "

" Miss Ayton, really, but of course my mother was there too, and I was there, though I don't think I was supposed to have an opinion. You would laugh at my things now, but they were considered very handsome—the best that could be had at Kennington & Jenner's."

" What ! Was Jenner's in Princes Street in those days ? " cried Ann, astonished.

" Dear me, why shouldn't Jenner's have been in Princes Street then ? Really, Ann, you talk as if it were before the Flood. I assure you my clothes caused something of a sensation in the country-side."

" I'm sure they did. I knew you had a sealskin coat, for it ended its long and useful existence as capes for Robbie and me. I liked mine, but Robbie wept bitterly, and said only coachmen wore capes. And you had a bonnet, hadn't you ? A bonnet at seventeen ! "

" A prune-coloured bonnet," said Mrs. Douglas, " high in front, and worn with a prune-coloured silk dress and the sealskin coat. Those were my ' going-away ' things. But the dress your father liked best was navy blue, what was called a Princess dress, buttoned straight down with small brass buttons. I had a sort of reefer coat to wear with that, and a hat with a blue veil. And I had a black satin for evenings (no self-respecting bride would have been without a black satin) besides my bridal white satin."

" You must have looked a duck with those little white kid shoes with the big rosettes on the toes and the blue silk laces. I suppose you were married in the house ? "

" Oh yes. Church weddings were practically unknown then. I was married in the drawing-room. Do you remember it ? Rather a gloomy room, and not often used. The partition between the dining-room and the room next it was taken down, and the luncheon was laid on long tables. People came from Priorsford the day before and cooked and made ready. It had been a terrible storm, and the drifts were piled up high, but I don't think any of the invited guests stayed away, although many of them had long distances to drive. The preparations were very exciting. I remember the great rich cakes from Edinburgh being cut down with a lavish hand, and big, round, thick cakes of shortbread with white sweeties on them, so the guests must have had tea as well as luncheon, and been well warmed and fed. Rather unlike our modern weddings, with a crumb of bridescake and a thimbleful of champagne, followed by a cup of tea and a sandwich. Hare soup, and roasts of all sorts, and creams and trifles galore. I was child enough to enjoy it all."

Ann stopped writing and sat with her fountain-pen poised in her hand, looking into the fire.

" I can just imagine," she said, " how jolly it must

have been. The comfortable old house in the
village street, all the rooms with blazing fires, and
the kitchen with the flagged, uneven floor, hot and
simmering with good things cooking, and the snow
outside, and the horses stamping in the cold, frosty
air, and the guests coming in laughing and talking.
And Father so young and tall and blue-eyed, and
you such a nice little white and gold bride, blue-
eyed, too (no wonder there is such a lamentable lack
of variety in the looks of your children ; I do
admire a family where some are dark, and some fair,
and some red-haired—it isn't so dreadfully monoto-
nous), and the bridesmaids in white with scarlet
berries, and your little brothers all agape for good
things. It must all have been so young and merry.
A good send-off to a very happy married life, eh,
Mother ? "

Mrs. Douglas looked at her daughter without
speaking, the tears slowly gathering in her eyes.
Ann bent forward and laid her hand on her mother's.
" Just say to me as Marget says, ' Oh, lassie, haud
yer tongue ! ' I know that is what you are feeling
like. It breaks your heart to look back. There
has been so much happiness and such great sorrow ;
but the sad bits are as precious as the happy bits,
and they all help to make the pattern. On the
whole a gay pattern, Mother."

" Oh yes, yes. I have had far beyond my deserts.
For many years life was almost cloudless, except
for the clouds I made with my own foolish fears and
forebodings. Why did nobody shake me for my

silliness? Fussing over trifles, worrying about the congregation, feverishly trying to lay by for an evil day. I wonder now how I could ever have made a trouble of anything when I had your father with me and all my children about me. And I *knew* I was happy, but I daren't say it even to myself, in case I brought disaster. What pagans we are at heart—afraid of envious fates! And then Rosamund died. . . . We thought we could never be happy again—but we were. It was never quite the same again; we walked much more softly, for the ground seemed brittle somehow, and the sorrow of the world came closer to us, and we went with a different understanding to the house of mourning—but we were happy. I think I must often have been very trying to my friends during those prosperous years. They talked of 'the Douglas luck,' for everything the boys tried for they seemed to get. And the educating being over we had more money in our hands, and you got about to see the world, and we could all go abroad at a time, and I could spend some money on the house—I always made a god of my house. How proud I was of my drawing-room when we got the green velvet carpet that was like moss, and the soft blue walls and hangings, and the big Chesterfield with the down cushions! And the tea-table set out with plates and green knives, while the people round were still handing their visitors a cup in their hand, and cake and scones on a cake-stand! I was a queen and no widow. . . . Why, Marget, is it nine o'clock already?"

Marget gave her demure, respectful curtsey, which was so oddly at variance with her frank and fearless comments on things in general, and sat down on a chair beside Mysie.

"Ay, Mem, it's nine o'clock. It's juist chappit on the lobby clock." She directed a suspicious glance towards the table where Ann sat. "Is Miss Ann gettin' on wi' yer *Life*? Dinna let her put in ony lees aboot us. How faur has she gotten? Juist to yer marriage? Oh, that's a' richt. I wasna there then. But I can keep ye richt aboot what happened ony time in the last five-and-thirty years."

CHAPTER IV

" No honeymoon ! "

Ann's pen was held aloft in amaze, as she looked across at her mother seated at the other side of the fire in her very own chair that had stood by the nursery fireside in long past days. Well did Ann remember the comfortable squat legs of it from the time when she had lived in that world of chair-legs and the underside of sofas which we all inhabit at the beginning of things.

Ann's mother was knitting as usual, a stocking for a long-legged grandson ; but she knitted mechanically, not looking at her work, her eyes on the dancing flames, a little reminiscent smile turning up the corners of her mouth.

" No honeymoon ! " Ann again ejaculated. " What was Father thinking of ? Didn't you mind ? "

" Mind ? No. Where would we go in December but to our own little house ? You must remember that I had hardly ever left Etterick except to go to school, and the journey north seemed a wonderful adventure to me ; and your father was in such a hurry to show me the little Manse and all the new furniture that the train journey seemed all too long. We got to Inchkeld very late, and it was snowing hard. We looked about for the cab that had been ordered to meet us, but your father said, ' There's only a carriage and pair ; that can't be for us—let's walk.' So off we set, I in my sealskin coat and prune-coloured bonnet ! And the sad thing was that the carriage and pair was meant for us. It turned out that the carriage-hirer came from Priorsford, and when he got the order he said, ' It's for Mr. Mark and his bride ; I'll send a pair.' And the pair came, and we walked ! "

Ann laughed. " Too much humility doesn't pay. There's a parable there if I had time to think it out. Well, and did the house come up to your expectations ? "

" It was one of a row of houses," said Mrs. Douglas. " There was a gate and a strip of garden, and a gravel-path leading to the front door. On your right as you went in at the door was the dining-room—but before we got to that your father had to show me everything in the little entrance hall and tell me the price. Very ugly things you would call them—you who like crumbling Jacobean chests and gate tables ; but I was very well pleased with the brand new hall table (on which stood a large brass bell), the hat-stand, and the thing for umbrellas. I really liked them much better than the beautiful old things at Etterick ; they were new and they were mine. The dining-room had a bow win-

dow which held a green wire stand full of growing
ferns. (Isn't it odd that after forty years I remember every detail ?) The room was hardly big enough
to hold the huge mahogany sideboard with the
mirrored back, and all the other furniture."

" I remember the pictures," Ann said, " at least
I expect they were the same as at Kirkcaple and
Glasgow—big steel engravings ; one of a slave
market which I liked very much, and another that
the boys liked better, of fat priests looking at the
provisions brought by the country people for the
Monastery—ducks and fowls, and a large salmon,
and a slain deer. We made up stories about those
pictures."

" The drawing-room was the crowning glory of
the house," Mrs. Douglas went on. She was not
listening to her daughter ; she was living over
again that first enchanting peep at her own house.
" My father furnished it for us, and everything he
did was well done. It was midnight before we had
finished supper, but I couldn't have slept without
seeing it. The wall-paper was pure white with
bunches of gilt flowers ; it was your father's choice,
and I thought I had seldom seen anything so beautiful. How dull it must be for women who marry
men who take no interest in the house ! I'm thankful that I had a man who was interested in everything. It made doing things so much more worth
while. He was so innocent the way he showed
his belongings to people, taking their interest for
granted, like a child. I can see him now watching

my face as the full glory of the room burst on me.
It was lit by a glittering glass gaselier hung from
the ceiling ; I had known only lamps and candles.
The rosewood suite was covered with bright crimson
rep, there were crimson rep curtains at the bow
window, a chiffonier with a marble top stood against
one wall, our shining new piano against another, a
round rosewood table in the middle of the room, and
an ottoman covered with bead work in the window.
Really, Ann, I can hardly forgive you when I think
that when you grew up you made me part with the
chiffonier and the rosewood table, and the ottoman,
and that *comfortable* couch."

" What a vindictive mother ! " said Ann.   " But
why did you do it ?   Surely my eighteen-year-old
yearnings after a high-art drawing-room could have
been quelled."

" Oh, I suppose they could, but I didn't want to
' daunton ' you, and you didn't see how you could
live unless you got at least one room in the house
made what you called artistic.   You said our drawing-room walls were just a network, and perhaps I
had too many things hanging from the picture-rail
(it used to be a puzzle to get them all up again at
spring-cleaning times), but they had all a reason for
being there—the plaques framed in plush that
Mark painted, your water-colours, and all the en-
larged photographs of people I was fond of.   You
put them all ruthlessly away, and had the walls done
with brown paper and hung up a few dreary-looking
pictures in dark frames.   And you chose a dull blue

carpet, and orange cushions, and all my cheerful
red rep chairs were covered with sad-coloured stuffs,
and you got green blinds and kept them pulled down
so that the room was almost quite dark, and people
who came to call just stotted over obstacles on their
way to shake hands. And you banished photographs——"

Ann's face wore a guilty look as her mother told
of her sins and faults of youth, and she broke in :

" But own, Mother, that the phase didn't last
long. I know it was dreadful while it lasted. I
had met some artists and they had fussed me and
my head was turned. I must have been a sore trial
to my family at that time. Father, losing patience
with me one night, said, ' Oh, go to bed, girl, and
don't sit attitudinizing there ! ' You should have
beaten me instead of giving in to me when I suggested putting away the things you were fond of.
Young people are heartless because they don't
think. I would know better now."

" Well," Mrs. Douglas gave a long sigh, " it's
only now I miss my things. I parted from them
light-heartedly—rather proud, I daresay, of being
so modern. I didn't know that I would live to
cherish every relic of my first married days because
I had lost the one who shared them. . . . Not that
I behaved well that first year in Inchkeld. Of
course, I was only seventeen, but I might have had
more sense. I cried half the time. What a damp
and disconsolate companion for any poor man ! No,
I had nothing to cry about ! *Au contraire*, as the

seasick Frenchman said when asked if he had dined
(to use Robbie's favourite jest) ; but I had never
been away from home before, and I missed Agatha,
and I missed the boys, and I missed all the stir of a
big family and the cheery bustle that goes on in a
country house.   I loved my little doll's house, so
new and fresh, but the streets, and the houses full
of strangers, oppressed me, and I was woefully homesick.   Your grandmother, my mother-in-law—she
died before you were born, and you missed knowing
one of the kindest women that ever lived—sent her
cook, Maggie Ann, a capable girl from the Borders,
to be my servant, and she was as homesick as I was.
One day we saw an old tinker body who visited
Etterick regularly on her rounds walking down the
road with her box of small wares slung on her back.
The sight to us was like cold water to a thirsty
man.   Maggie Ann rushed out and brought her in,
and we feasted the astonished old woman and
bought nearly all her wares.   The thought that she
would be seeing Etterick soon, that she would sleep
in our barn, would hear the soft Lowland tongue
and see all my own people, made that old beggar-
wife a being to be envied by me. . . . Poor Maggie
Ann was very patient with her inefficient mistress,
and was young enough rather to enjoy my effort to
housekeep.   She said it reminded her of when she
was a bairn and played at a wee house.   We tried
all sorts of experiments with food, but I don't remember that anything turned out very well.   I'm
afraid we wasted a good deal.   It was a very long,

cold winter, that winter in Inchkeld. The snow lay on the ground, and the frost held late into March, and even my sealskin coat could not keep out the cold. We grew tired of skating, and I took to moping in the house——"

"Really, Mother," said Ann, "it sounds frightfully unlike you as I have always known you—a little bustling hurricane of a woman, waking up all the dreaming ones, spurring the idle to work, a reproach to the listless, an example to all—and you tell me you sat in the house and moped and cried."

Mrs. Douglas shook her head. "I wasn't always a bustling hurricane. I think I became that because I married such a placid man; just as I became a Radical because he was such a Tory; just as I had to become sternly practical because he was such a dreamer. If we had both been alike we would have wandered hand-in-hand into the workhouse. Not that Mark spent money on himself—bless him— but nobody ever asked him for help and was refused; and he did like to buy things for me. I found I just had to take control of the money. Not at first, of course; it came to it by degrees. And your father was only too glad; money was never anything but a nuisance to him. I don't think I'm inordinately fond of money either, but I had to *hain* so that for years it had an undue prominence in my mind. Well, I sighed for the South Country, and one day, when I was miserably moping over the fire, your father said to me: 'Come on, Nell, I'm going to visit a sick girl about your own age. She's always asking me questions about you, and I said you would go and see her.'

" I didn't want to go, for I was shy of sick people —the being ill in bed seemed to put them such a distance away—but I put on my best clothes to make a good impression, and went. . . . We were taken into a clean, bright room, with a dressing-table dressed crisply in white muslin over pink. A girl was lying high up on the pillows, and I thought at first she couldn't be ill, she had such shining blue eyes and rose-flushed cheeks ; her yellow hair hung in two plaits over her shoulders. Then I saw that her hands were almost transparent, and that her breath came in quick gasps between her red, parted lips, and I knew that this pretty child was dying quickly of consumption. I couldn't speak as I took her hand, but I tried hard to keep the tears from my eyes as she looked at me—two girls about an age, the one beginning life at its fullest, the other about to leave the world and youth behind. I stood there in my wedding braws, hating myself almost for my health and happiness. Your father talked to her until I got hold of myself, and then she seemed to like to hear me tell about the little house and my attempts to cook. As we were leaving she held your father's hand, and said, in her weak, husky voice, ' Mr. Douglas, tell the folk on Sabbath that *Christ is a Rock.* . . .' I think I realized then, for the first time, what religion meant. A sentence in that book we were reading, *Green Apple Harvest*, reminded me of that girl. . . . You know when

Robert is dying and his brother Clem says to him :

" ' Oh, Bob, it seems unaccountable hard as you should die in the middle of May ! '

" And Robert replies : ' . . . I've a feeling as if I go to the Lord God I'll only be going into the middle of all that's alive. . . . If I'm with Him I can't never lose the month of May. . . .'

" I went home crying bitterly for the girl who was dying in the May morning of her days. I don't think I moped any more."

CHAPTER V

" INCHKELD was a most pleasant place in which to
have one's home—a city set among hills and watered
by a broad river ; and surely no young and witless
couple ever had a kinder and more indulgent congregation than we had.

" The first Sunday I appeared in church I was
almost dead with fright. I had to walk through the
church to reach the Manse seat, and every eye
seemed to be boring into me like a gimlet. As if
that weren't bad enough, I was accosted on my way
out by a tall, bland elder, who said he supposed I
would want to teach a class in the Sabbath school.
As a matter of fact, he supposed quite wrong, for
it had never entered into my head that such an
awful duty would be required of me. Think—
until a short time before I myself had been a
scholar (and a restless, impertinent one at that !),
and the very thought of trying to control a class
made my brain reel. But I was as clay in the hands
of this suave Highland potter, who went on to tell
me that the last minister's wife had carried on a

most successful class for older girls. ' She, of course,' he added, ' was a niece of the late Lord Clarke,' as if that fact explained any amount of talent for teaching the young. He led me away—I was now in a state of passive despair—and introduced me to a class as their new teacher. There were seven of them, girls about fifteen—always, I think, the worst and a most impudent age (you were a brat at fifteen, Ann !), and they fixed me with seven pairs of eyes, round brown eyes, rather like brandy-balls— I suppose they couldn't all have had brown eyes, but the general effect was of brandy-balls—silently taking me in. I heard the elder telling them how honoured they were to have the minister's wife as teacher ; then I was left with them. Later on, when I got to know the girls, I sometimes laughed at the terror of the first Sunday. They were the nicest girls, really, gentle and kind ; but that day they seemed to me inhuman little owls. They told me the lesson—one of the parables—but my mind was a blank, and I could think of no comment to make over it. I stumbled and stuttered, every moment getting more hot and ashamed, and finally went home, feeling, in spite of my sealskin coat and prune bonnet, the most miserably inadequate minister's wife that had ever tried to reign in a manse, scourged as with whips by the thought of the late Lord Clarke's niece. What a comfort your father always was ! He made it seem all right in a twinkling, assured me that I needn't teach a class unless I liked, but vowed that if I did no one could teach it half so well; and as for the late Lord Clarke's niece, he had never seen her, but he was sure she was a long-faced woman, with no sense of humour."

"I know," said Ann. "Father was always singularly comforting. When we hurt ourselves, you and Marget invariably took the gloomiest view, looked up medical books and prophesied dire results. Once I got my thumb badly crushed and the nail torn off while swinging on a see-saw. Marget at once said 'lockjaw!' I hadn't a notion what that was, but it had an eerily fatal sound, and I crept away to Father's study to try and lose my fears in a book. Presently Father came in, and I rolled out of the armchair I had cuddled into and ran to show him my bandaged hand.

"'Oh, Father!' I cried, 'will I take lockjaw and will I die?'" I can see him now, all fresh from the cold air, laughing at me, yet sorry for me, lifting me up in his strong arms, saying, 'Poor wifie, were they frightening you? Lockjaw? No. Let's look at it. Yes, I see the nail's off. Had we better get a celluloid one till the new one grows? Try and keep a cloth on it, like a good lassie, and it will soon be well.' And then peace slid into my soul, and I sat on his knee and he told me a story. I can quite see what a wonderful minister my father was. It was that air of surety, of steadfastness, that gave people such a lift, and that firm, comforting hand that touched things so gently. Robbie had the same; so had the little lad. . . .

But to go back to Inchkeld and the congregation——"

"Yes. It was a very flourishing congregation. Every Sunday it crammed the little church, and sometimes forms had to be brought in. The goodness of the people was almost destroying. They wanted to share everything they had with us. Constantly such things as a hare, or pheasants, or a ' black bun,' or several cakes of shortbread would arrive—and we had so few to eat them. Inchkeld was a sociable place, and I had lots of callers and no lack of opportunities for wearing my wedding finery. Those weren't the days of afternoon tea. Cake and wine were served in the drawing-room with the white and gilt wall-paper and the red rep furniture—neat squares of wedding-cake in the brand new silver cake-basket."

" Oooh ! " groaned Ann. " Can't I see those squares of wedding-cake ! I hope no hungry children ever came to see you. Do you remember taking me as a small child to call on some newly married people in Burntisland ?—I think I was taken because I was a firebrand at home—and tea came in on a silver tray, all prinked out with ruffly d'oyleys—scones about the size of half-crowns and a frightfully newly married shining cake-basket, holding inches of wedding-cake. I was passionately hungry, and could have eaten the whole show and never known it ; but I sat on a stool and nibbled a scone, and tried not to make any crumbs, and then I was handed the cake-basket.

We had been taught always to take the bit nearest us, and the bit nearest me—alas !—was the smallest bit in the basket, with only the minutest fragment of almond icing and sugar attached. I would fain have snatched two bits, but my upbringing was too strong for me, and I took the fragment. It was far the most delicious thing I had ever tasted. Surely, I thought, this must be what angels eat, and for the first time in my faulty life I wished to be an angel. It was over in a second, though I ate it crumb by crumb and kept the sugar for the last ; and then I sat and gazed hungrily for another bit ; but no one noticed me, no one brought the shining cake-basket again within my reach. I don't think that newly married wife could ever have come to any good—a woman who hadn't the sense to feed a hungry child ! You think I spoil our children, but it's because I remember the awfulness of having a very little of a good thing."

"I remember that visit to Burntisland," Mrs. Douglas said. "I had to take you into a shop on the way home and buy you biscuits. Your father wanted some, too—a handed-round tea was no use to him ; he liked a breakfast-cup filled several times. I don't think I was ever guilty of starving children of wedding-cake. I got surfeited with it myself, and a big family from across the way used to come in to help us away with all that was left over from our parties. We were glad to get things eaten up in those days. Both my own mother and your father's mother constantly sent us boxes of eatables

as if we had been on a desert island instead of in a
city of shops—great mutton-hams, and haggis, and
noble Selkirk bannocks ; I was afraid of them coming to our little household. How glad I would have
been to see them in later years, when I had growing
children to feed ! But the kind hands that packed
them were still. . . . We could entertain only in a
very small way in our very small house, but we
were asked to quite a lot of dinner-parties. They
were evenings of dread to me. I was so shockingly
bad at making conversation. I blushed fiercely
when any one spoke to me, and must have presented
an appearance of such callowness that I provoked
pity in the hearts of kindly people. One dear old
lady said to me, ' My dear, have you cut your wis-
dom teeth yet ? ' . . . In September Mark was born.
It was prayer-meeting night, and Maggie Ann care-
lessly let the cat eat my canary. They didn't tell
me about it until I asked why I wasn't hearing him
singing. Mark was a tiny, delicate baby, but he
was perfect in our eyes. We looked with distaste at
large fat children, who made poor little Mark look
so puny and fragile, and told each other that they
were ' coarse,' and that we were glad our baby
wasn't like that. When I was able to travel we set
off with our precious new possession to Etterick.
Agatha had been with us most of the summer, but
my mother didn't come ; she liked to stay in her
own house and welcome us there."

" A most detached woman, my grandmother,"
said Ann.

" You are rather like her, Ann," said Mrs. Douglas.

" Yes, I have the same aversion to staying in other people's houses, and I share her dislike to the casual kissing that so many people indulge in—people who are mere acquaintances. You should only kiss really great friends at really serious times, and then it means something."

Mrs. Douglas laughed. " Nobody ever took a liberty with your grandmother. My father was utterly different, the most approachable of men. People were always asking favours from him ; he liked them to. He didn't care how much he went out of his way to help any one, and his hand was never out of his pocket."

" You must be exactly like grandfather. I think you are one of the very few people left living in the world who do take trouble about their fellow-mortals. The rest of us are too selfish to bother."

" I like to be kind," said Mrs. Douglas, " but I don't take any credit for being kind. It's just my nature to want to give. The people who hate to give and yet make themselves do it are the ones who ought to be commended. It has always been my great desire to add a little to the happiness of the world, and I would never forgive myself if I thought I had added by one jot or tittle to the pain."

" I am very sure you haven't done that," Ann assured her. " You are the very kindest of funny little bodies, and when I call you ' Ella Wheeler

Wilcox' I don't really mean it. But you must admit that it is often very vicarious kindness, and the burden of it falls on your family. Oh, the deplorable people who have come to us 'for a stop' because you thought they were lonely and neglected! Of course, they were, but it was because it almost killed people to entertain them; there's a reason for everything in this world. But what a shame to laugh at your efforts! Never mind. There are those

> ' Who, passing thorough Baca's vale,
>   Therein do dig up wells,'

and you are one of them. But to go on with your *Life*. Didn't you leave Inchkeld quite soon after Mark was born? I know Robbie and Jim and I thought it very hard lines that he should have been born in a lovely old historic city, while the rest of us had to see the light first amid coalpits and linoleum factories. Mark never let us forget it, either."

" Mark was two months old when we left Inchkeld. When the Kirkcaple congregation called your father he felt he ought to go. Oh! but we were a thoughtless couple. It never gave me a thought to leave the people who had been so good to us. I just took everybody's kindness as a matter of course. I was too young to realize how rare such kindness is, and their interest in the baby, and their desire to have us stay in Inchkeld, seemed to me no

more than natural. I was amused and pleased at
the thought of going to a new place and a new house.
You can hardly get changes enough when you are
eighteen. In middle life one's most constant prayer
is that God will let things remain as they are.
What was that you were reading me the other
night ? I think it was from Charles Lamb."

Ann leant back in her chair and pulled a little
green book from a bookshelf. "This, I think it
was," she said, and read :

"'I am content to stand still at the age to which
I am arrived ; I, and my friends, to be no younger,
no richer, no handsomer. I do not want to be
wearied by age, or drop like mellow fruit, as they
say, into the grave. . . .'"

"Poor Charles Lamb !" said Mrs. Douglas,
shaking her head. "There *are* times when one
would like to stand still, where we seem to reach
a pleasant, rich plain and are at our ease, and
friends are many, and life is full of zest. . . . I
don't know whether it was wise to leave Inchkeld.
Your grandfather Douglas always regretted it.
When he visited us at Kirkcaple one remark he
always made was : 'A great pity Mark ever left
Inchkeld.' We used to wait for it and the funny
way he had of clearing his throat after every
sentence."

CHAPTER VI

" November is a poor time to go to a new place, and Kirkcaple certainly looked a most unattractive part of the world when we arrived on a cold, wet afternoon. ' The queer-like smell ' from the linoleum factories, the sea drearily grey and strange to my inland eyes, the drive through narrow streets and up the steep Path, past great factories and mean houses, until we reached the road, knee-deep in mud, where the Manse stood, combined to depress me to the earth. It might have been infinitely worse. I saw that in the light of the next morning. There was a field before the Manse, and though there was a factory and a rope-work and a bleach-field and a coal-pit all in close proximity to it, there was also the Den, where hyacinths grew in spring, and where you could dig fern-roots for your garden. The Manse itself stood in a large garden, and in time we forgot to notice the factories. The people were very unlike the courteous Inchkeld people—miners and factory workers, who gave one as they passed a Jack's-as-good-as-his-master sort of nod. We grew to understand them and to value their staunch friendship, but at first they were as *fremt* as the landscape.

" When the cab lurched through the ruts to the Manse gate and I got out and saw my new home I quailed. From the front it was a gloomy-looking house—one window on each side of the front door, and three windows above, and the kitchen premises on one side. There was a wide gravelled space in front, with a small shrubbery to shelter us from the road. It was a sombre and threatening place to enter on a dark night, and when alone I always made a mad rush from the gate to the front door. One night when I reached my haven I found a tall man standing against it. I had hardly strength to gasp, ' Who are you ? ' and the man replied, ' Weelum Dodds. I cam' to see the minister aboot gettin' the bairn bapteezed, but the lassie wadna open the door.' I had told the servants, who were young girls, to keep the chain on the door at night, and the poor patient soul had just propped himself up against the door and awaited developments. . . . The back of the house, looking to the garden, was delightful. You don't remember the garden ? "

" *Don't* I ? " said Ann. " I was only about nine when we left Kirkcaple, but I remember every detail of it. Just outside the nursery window there was a bush of flowering currant. Do *you* remember that ? And jasmine, and all sorts of creepers grew up the house. There was a big square lawn before the window, rather sloping, with two long flower-beds at the top and herbaceous borders round the high walls. Our own especial gardens were at the top of the kitchen garden. Mark had a Rose of Sharon tree in his garden about which he boasted; it seemed to set him a little apart. I had a white lilac tree in mine; Robbie, severely practical, grew nothing but vegetables, while Jim, when asked what his contained, said simply and truthfully, 'Wurrums.' Rosamond was a tiny baby when we left Kirkcaple, and the little lad knew only Glasgow. It was surely a very large garden, Mother? The gooseberry bushes alone seemed to me to extend for miles, and in a far-away corner there was the pigsty. Why was it called 'the pigsty'? In our day there was never anything in it but two much-loved Russian rabbits with pink eyes, Fluffy and Pluffy. I have a small red text-book in which, on a certain date, is printed in large round hand:

'This day Fluffy died.
    ,,   ,,   Pluffy ,, '

A ferret got in and sucked their blood. What a day of horror that was! The roof of the pigsty sloped up to the top of the wall, and we liked to sit on the wall and say rude things to the children on the road, they retorting with stones and clods of earth. We were all bonnie fighters. You had no notion, you and Father, when we came down to tea with well-brushed hair and flannel-polished faces, of the grim battles we had just emerged from. The enemy was even then at the gate. We, with ears to hear, knew what sundry dull thuds against the front door meant. Marget, wrathful but loyal, wiped away the dirt and said nothing to you—lots to us, though ! . . . But I'm getting years ahead. You were just arriving with baby Mark to an empty, echoing Manse, through ways heavy with November mud. Sorry I interrupted."

"As to that," said her mother, "I was really just talking to myself. It is good of you to listen to my maunderings about the past."

"Not at all," Ann said solemnly ; and then, "You daft wee mother, now that courtesies have been exchanged, will you go on with that *Life* of yours ? It will take us years at this rate. What happened when you tottered into the Manse ? Did you regret the little sunny, bow-windowed Manse in Inchkeld ? "

"Regret ! I ached for it. I couldn't picture us being happy in this muddy mining place ; I couldn't see this bare barracks ever getting home-like. But it was a roomy house. The dining-room was to the right of the front door, the study to the left, and the nursery was on the ground floor, too. They were all big, square rooms : the dining-room was cosy in the evening, but rather dark in the daytime ; the study was a very cheerful room, with books all round the walls, and a bright red carpet, and green leather furniture."

"And a little square clock," Ann added, " with an honest sort of face, and a picture of John Knox, long white beard and all, above the mantelpiece,

and the carpet had a design on it of large squares;
I know, for I used to play a game on it, jumping
from one to another. Some deceased elder had
left to the Manse and to each succeeding minister a
tall glass-doored bookcase containing, among other
books, a set of Shakespeare's plays illustrated. It
was funny to see how the artist had made even
Falstaff and Ariel quite early Victorian—and as for
merry Beatrice, I think she wore a bustle! Not
that it worried us; we were delighted with his
efforts . . . and in that glass-doored bookcase there
stayed also a very little book dressed in fairy green,
with gilt lettering on its cover. I have tried for
years to find another copy, but I have nothing to
go on except that it was a very tiny book and that
it contained fairy tales, translations from the Ger-
man, I think, for it talked in one of a king lying
under the green lindens! I thought linden the
most lovely word I had ever heard! it seemed to
set all the horns of Elfland blowing for me. One
of the stories must have been *Lohengrin*, there was
a swan in it and ' a frail scallop.' How I wept when
it appeared for the second time and took the knight
away for ever! I loved Germany then because it
was the home of green lindens and swans with
scallops, and houses with pointed roofs and wide
chimneys where storks nested. Even in the war
I couldn't hate it as much as I ought to have done,
because of that little green book. . . . But we're
straying again, at least I am. . . . You got to like
the house, didn't you ? "

"Oh dear, yes. It was terribly gaunt at first, but before we left it I thought it was pretty nearly perfect. When we got fresh paper and paint, and the wide upper landing and staircase carpeted with crimson, and curtains shading the high staircase window, every one said how pretty it was. The drawing-room was always a pleasant room, with two sunny windows, and all my treasures (you would call them atrocities) in the way of gilt and alabaster clocks with glass shades, and marble-topped chiffonier, and red rep furniture. But the big night nursery was the nicest room of all, with its row of little beds, each with a gay counterpane! There was a small room opening from it where your clothes stayed, with a bath and a wash-hand basin—a very handy place."

"Yes," said Ann; "and in one corner stood a very tall basket for soiled clothes. I remember Robbie, after hearing of some one's marriage, coming to you and saying so earnestly, 'I'll stay with you always, Mums, and if any one comes to marry me I'll hide in the dirty-clothes basket.'"

Robbie's mother looked into the dancing flames. "That was always his promise," she said softly, "I'll stay with you always. . . . It wouldn't have been so bad beginning in a new place, with a new baby (and me so utterly new myself!), if Mark hadn't been so fragile. I daresay he suffered from my inexperience, I almost smothered him with wraps, and hardly dared let him out of the warm nursery, but he must have been naturally delicate

as well. He got bronchitis on the smallest provoca-
tion, and my heart was perpetually in my mouth
with the frights I got. I spent hours listening to
his breathing and touching him to see if he felt hot,
and I kept your father racing for the doctor until
both he and the doctor struck. I was so wrapped
up in my baby that I simply never turned my head
to look at the congregation; but they understood
and were patient. I really was very absurd. Some
people gave a dinner-party for us, and your father
said I simply must go. On the night of the party
I was certain Mark was taking croup, and I could
hardly be dragged from him to dress. I was determined that anyway I must be home in good time,
and I ordered the cab to come back for us at a
quarter to nine! We had hardly finished dinner
when it was announced, but I rose at once to go.
The hostess, astonished but kind, said on hearing
my excuses, ' Ah, well, experience teaches.' ' Finish
your proverb, Mrs. Smeaton,' my dinner neighbour
(a clergyman from a neighbouring parish) broke in,
' Experience teaches fools.' Now I realize that the
man was embittered—and little wonder!—by having tried to make conversation to me for a dreary
hour, but at the moment I hated him. When we
left Kirkcaple he and his wife were our greatest
friends. . . . There were four houses in our road.
The large one nearest the Den belonged to one of the
linoleum people, we came next, and then there was
a low, bungalow sort of house where the Mestons
lived with their three little girls, and at the end of

the road lived one of the elders in the church—
Goskirk was the name—with his wife and eight
sons. How they all got into that small house I
know not, but it was always comfortable, and there
was always a welcome, and Mrs. Goskirk was the
busiest, happiest little woman in Kirkcaple, and a
great stand-by to me. ' How's baby to-day ? ' she
would come in saying, every word tilted up at the
end as is the accent of Fife. As rich in experience as I was poor, she could soothe my fears and
laugh at my forebodings. She prescribed simple,
homely remedies and told me not to fuss. She gave
me a new interest in life, and kept me happily engaged by teaching me how to make clothes for
Mark. Her little boys trotted in and out, coming
to show me all their treasures, and going away
pleased with a sweetie or a sugar biscuit ! They
did much to make me feel at home. . . . When I
went back to Etterick in summer I thought Mark
was a lovely baby, and that he had a wonderful
mother ! He wore a pelisse I had made him (under
Mrs. Goskirk's eye), cream cashmere, with a wide
band of lavender velvet, and a soft, white felt hat
with a lavender feather round it. I paid fifteen
shillings for the feather and thought it a great
price. . . . For three years we had only Mark, then
you and Robbie quite close together. But Mark
was never put in the ' stirk's stall '; for you were
a healthy, placid baby, and my dear Robbie was
just like you. I remember his coming so well. It
was a February morning, and Mrs. Penn, the nurse,

said : ' Another deil o' a laddie.' She much preferred girls. Robbie was such a *caller* baby, so fat and good-natured and thriving."

" My very first recollection of Robbie," Ann said, " is in the garden. I think it must have been an April morning, for I remember daffodils, and the sun was shining, and the wind tumbling us about, and Mark said to me that he thought Ellie Robbie meant to run away with Robbie, and that it behoved us to save him. As he told me his terrible suspicions Robbie came down the walk pulling behind him a large rake—a little boy with an almost white head, very blue eyes, and very chubby, very rosy cheeks. I remember we separated him from his rake and Mark dragged us both into the gooseberry bushes, where we lay hid until Ellie Robbie (the suspect) came to look for us, bringing us a treat in the shape of a slice each of brown scone spread with marmalade, and two acid drops. That closed the incident."

CHAPTER VII

On these winter evenings in the Green Glen, when the wind and the rain beat upon the house, and Ann by the fireside wrote down her mother's life, Marget made many errands into the drawing-room to offer advice.

"I think"—said Ann one evening—"I think I must have been horribly neglected as a baby. Every one was so taken up with Mark they hadn't time to look at me."

Marget was standing in the middle of the room with her hands folded on her black satin apron ; she would have scorned to wear a white apron after working hours. She had come in with a list of groceries to be ordered by post, and stood looking suspiciously at Ann and her writing.

"Ye were never negleckit when I kent ye, an' I cam' to the hoose afore ye kent yer richt hand frae yer left. You were a wee white-heided cratur and Maister Robbie wasna shortened."

"Ah, but were you there when Mark fell out of the carriage and was so frightfully hurt ? I've been told by Aunt Agatha that no one had time to attend to me, and I was just shut up in a room with some toys and fed at intervals. It's a wonder that the Cruelty to Children people didn't get you."

" Havers," said Marget.

" That was a terrible time," Mrs. Douglas said. " Mark was four, and beginning to get stronger. You were a year old, Ann. It was a lovely day in June, and Mr. Kerr, in the kindness of his heart, sent a carriage to take us all for a drive."

" I mind fine o' Mr. Kerr," Marget broke in. " He was fair bigot-ed on the kirk. I dinna think he ever missed a Sabbath's service or a Wednesday prayer-meeting."

" I mind of him, too," said Ann. " He had white hair and bushy white eyebrows, and a fierce expression and an ebony stick with an ivory handle. He used to give Mark presents at Christmas-time, but he ignored the existence of the rest of us. I remember we went to see him once, and he presented Mark with a book. Mark took it and said, ' Yes, and what for Ann ? ' and Mr. Kerr had to fumble about and produce something for me while I waited stolidly, quite unabashed by my brother's unconventional behaviour."

" Mr. Kerr was the best friend the Kirkcaple Church had," Mrs. Douglas said. " He ' joyed ' in its prosperity—how he struggled to get the members to increase their givings ! His great desire was that it should give more largely than the parish kirk of the district. People may talk about union and one great Church, but when we are all one I'm afraid there may be a lack of interest—a falling off in endeavour. St. Paul knew what he was talking about when he spoke of 'provoking' one another to love and good works. . . . At first I couldn't bear Mr. Kerr. If I let your father forget an intimation, or if a funeral was forgotten, or some one was neglected, he came to the Manse in a passion. I fled at the sight of him. But gradually I found that his fierceness wasn't to be feared, and that it was the sheer interest he took that made him hate things to go wrong—and one is grateful to people who take a real interest, however oddly they may show it."

"So Mr. Kerr sent his carriage," Ann prompted.

"Mr. Kerr sent his carriage," said her mother, "and we set out to have a picnic on the Loan. We were as merry as children. You were on my knee, Ann, and Agatha sat beside me, your father and Mark opposite. We were about Thornkirk, and Mark, who was always mad about flowers, pointing to the dusty roadside, cried, ' A blue-bell,' and suddenly made a spring against the door, which, to our horror, opened, and Mark fell out. . . . I don't know what happened next. The first thing I knew I was in a cottage frantically pulling at a chest of drawers and crying for something to cover the awful wound. By great good

fortune our own doctor happened to pass in his
dogcart just then. All he said was, ' Take him
home.' . . . He stayed with us most of the night,
but he could give us no hope that the child would
live, or, living, have his reason. For days he lay
unconscious, sometimes raving, sometimes piti-
fully moaning. Agatha and I knew nothing
of nursing, and there were no trained nurses in
those days—at least, not in Kirkcaple. What
would have happened to us all I know not if Mrs.
Peat hadn't appeared like a good angel on the
scene. It was wonderful of her to come. A fortnight before she had got news that her son in
India—her idolized only son—had been killed in
some native rising, and she put her own grief aside
and came to us. ' My dear,' she said, ' I've come
to take the nights, if you will let me. You're
young, and you need your sleep.' So every
evening she came and sat up—night after night
for four long weeks. I used to go into the night
nursery on those summer mornings—I was so
young and strong that, anxious as I was, I couldn't
help sleeping—and find Mrs. Peat sitting there
with her cap ribbons unruffled, her hair smooth,
so serene looking that no one could have believed
that she had kept a weary vigil. She was a born
nurse, and she possessed a healing touch. I
believe she did more than any one to pull Mark
through ; and all the time we were in Kirkcaple
she was a tower of strength to me. Always twice
a week she came up early in the afternoon and

stayed till evening, her cap in the neatest little basket in her hand—for she always took off her bonnet. I think I hear her saying, ' Eh, my dear,' with a sort of slow emphasis on the ' my.' She never made mischief in the congregation by boasting how ' far ben ' she was at the Manse. She had a mind far above petty things ; she dreamed dreams and saw visions."

Mrs. Douglas stopped and laughed. " Your father, who admired her very much, had been telling an old body troubled with sleepless nights how Mrs. Peat spent her wakeful hours, and she said to me, ' It's an awfu' job to rowe aboot in this bed a' nicht ; I wisht I had some o' Mrs. Peat's veesions.' "

" I mind Mistress Peat," said Marget, who had now seated herself ; " I mind her fine. She was a rale fine buddy. Miss Peat was a braw wumman. D'ye mind her comin' to a pairty we had in a crimson satin body an' her hair a' crimpit an' pearls aboot as big as bantam's eggs ? Eh, I say ! "

" I remember the pearls," said Ann. " I suppose they were paste, but I thought the Queen of Sheba couldn't have been much more impressive than Miss Peat. She had a velvet coat trimmed with some sort of feather trimming, and a muff to match—beautiful soft grey feathers. I used to lean against her and stroke it and think it was like a dove's breast. I overheard some one say that it was marvellous to think that the Peats had no servants and that Miss Peat could clean pots and cook, and then emerge like Solomon in all his glory. After that, when we sang the psalm :

> ' Though ye have lain among the pots,
> Like doves ye shall appear . . .'

I thought of Miss Peat in her velvet coat and her soft feathers. . . . Was she good to you, too, when Mark was so ill ? "

" I should think she was—but every one was good. At the time I took it all as a matter of course, but afterwards I realized it. For days Mark lay delirious, and I was distraught with the thought that his brain might be injured ; you see, the wheel passed over the side of his head. When he became conscious at last, the doctor told me to ask him some questions. I could think of nothing, and then I remembered that Mark had had a special fondness for Crichton, our butcher. Trembling, I asked, ' Darling, what is the butcher called ? ' and in a flash he answered ' Mr. Cwichton.' I wept with relief. But it seemed as if the poor little chap was never to be given a chance to get well. Three times the wound healed and three times it had to be opened again. No wonder our thoughts were all for him, and that you were neglected, Ann, poor child ! And you were so good, so little trouble, it almost seemed as if you understood. Mark had a great big wooden box filled with every kind of dry sweetie, and he would sit propped up with pillows, and weigh them, and

make them up in little ' pokes.' Sometimes he
would ask for you, and you were brought in, so
delighted to play on the bed and crawl about; but
very soon he tired of you (especially if you touched
his sweeties !), and ordered you away. He could
not be allowed to cry, and we had to devise things
to keep him amused. Opening lucky bags was a
great diversion. They cost a ha'penny each, and
he made away with dozens in a day. The great
difficulty was getting him to eat. At Etterick he
was accustomed to going to the milk-house and
getting new milk from the pail into his ' tinny,'
and when he was ill he wouldn't touch milk,
because he said it wasn't ' Etterick milk.' So
your father scoured Kirkcaple until he found a
' tinny,' and a pail as nearly as possible like the
milk-pails at Etterick, and we took them to the
nursery, and said, ' Now, then, Mark, is *this* real
Etterick milk ? ' and the poor little man held out
his thin hands for the ' tinny ' and drank greedily.
. . . He lay for six months, and when he got up
he had to be taught how to walk ! And even after
we got him up and out he was the most pathetic
little figure, with a bandaged head far too big for
his shadow of a body. But I was so proud of having
got him so far on the way to recovery that I didn't
realize how he looked to outsiders, until a very
cruel thing was said to me the very first time I
had him out. A man we knew slightly stopped
to ask for him, and said, ' It seems almost a pity
he pulled through. I'm afraid he will never be

anything but an object.' I don't think he meant
to hurt me; perhaps it was just sheer stupidity,
but. . . . It was a man called Temple who said
it. You never knew him, Ann."

"Temple," said Marget. "Dauvit Temple the
manufacturer? Eh, the impident fella'. Him to
ca' onybody, let alone Mr. Mark, an objec'. Objec'
himsel'. It wad hae been tellin' him if he had
fa'en on his heid an' gien his brains a bit jumble,
but I doot if the puir sowl had ony to jumble; he
hed a heid like a hen. He was fit for naething but
ridin' in a high dogcart an' tryin' to forget that
his dacent auld mither bleached her claes on the
Panny Braes an' his faither worked in the pit.
But ye needna fash yersel' aboot him and his
sayin's noo, Mem. He's gone to his reward—such
as it is."

"Indeed, Marget, it's a poor thing to bear
malice, and I believe that awful accident was the
making of Mark. He grew up as strong as a
Shetland pony. He was an extraordinarily clever
little boy. We were told not to try and teach
him till he was seven, but he taught himself to
read from the posters. He asked endless questions
of every one he met, and so acquired information.
There was nothing he wasn't interested in, and
every week brought a fresh craze. At one time it
was fowls, and he spent hours with Mrs. Frew, a
specialist on the subject, and came home with
coloured pictures of prize cocks which he insisted
on pinning round the nursery walls. For a long

time it was ships, and he and Mr. Peat, who was
a retired sea-captain, spent most of their time at
the harbour. Next it was precious stones, and he
accosted every lady (whether known to him or
not), and asked her about the stones she was
wearing."

"Yes," said Ann, "he was a wonderful contrast
to Robbie and me. We never asked for information on any subject, for we wanted none. We were
ignorant and unashamed, and we used to look
with such bored eyes at Mark and wonder how he
could be bothered. It was really disgusting for
the rest of us to have such a clever eldest brother.
He set a standard which we couldn't hope—indeed,
we never thought of trying—to attain to. What a
boy he was for falling on his head! He had been
warned that if he cut open the wound in his head
again it would never heal, so when he fell from a
tree, or a cart, or a pony, or whatever he was on at
the moment, we stood afar off and shouted, ' Is
it your wound, Mark ? ' prepared on hearing it
was to run as far as our legs would carry us. That
is a child's great idea when trouble comes—to
run away from it. Once Mark—do you remember ?
—climbed the white lilac tree in my garden on a
Sunday afternoon and, slipping, fell on a spiked
branch and hung there. Instead of going for help
I ran and hid among the gooseberry bushes, and he
wasn't rescued until you came home from church."

"That was too bad of you," her mother said,
"for Mark had always a great responsibility for

you. One day when there was a bad thunderstorm I found him dragging you by the hand to
the nursery—such a fat, sulky little thing you
looked.

" ' I'm going to pray for Ann,' he told me.
' She won't pray for herself.' "

CHAPTER VIII

" I DON'T know," said Mrs. Douglas, " when I first realized what was expected of me as a minister's wife. I suppose I just grew to it. At first I visited the people and tried to take an interest in them, because I felt it to be my duty, and then I found that it had ceased to be merely duty, and that one couldn't live among people and not go shares with them. It was the long anxiety about Mark that really drew us together and made us friends in a way that years of prosperity would never have done. There was hardly a soul in the congregation who didn't try to do us some little kindness in those dark days. Fife people are suspicious of strangers and rather aloof in their manner, but once you are their friend you are a friend for life. Ours was a working-class congregation (with a sprinkling of well-to-do people to help us along)—miners, and workers in the linoleum factories—decent, thrifty folk. Trade was dull all the time we were in Kirkcaple, and wages were low—ridiculously low when you think of the present-day standard, and it was a hard struggle for the mothers with big young families. Of course, food was cheap—half a loaf and a biscuit for two-pence, and 'penny haddies,' and eggs at nine-pence a dozen—and people hadn't the exalted ideas they have now."

"Well," said Ann, who was busy filling her fountain-pen, "I seem to remember rather luxurious living about the Mid Street, and the Nether Street, and the Watery Wynd. Don't you remember I made friends with some girls playing 'the pal-lals' in the street, and fetched them home with me, and when upbraided for so doing by Ellie Robbie in the nursery, I said, 'But they're *gentry*; they get kippers to their tea.' My 'bare-footed gentry' became a family jest."

Mrs. Douglas laughed, "I remember. To save your face we let them stay to tea, but you were told 'Never again.'"

"It was a way I had," said Ann. "I was full of hospitable instincts, and liked to invite people; but as I had seldom the moral courage to confess what I had done, the results were disastrous. Once I invited eight genteel young friends who, thinking it was a *pukka* invitation, arrived washed and brushed and dressed for a party, only to find us tearing about the garden in our old Saturday clothes. Ellie Robbie was justly incensed, as she hadn't even a sugar-biscuit to give an air of festivity to the nursery tea, and you were out. In private she addressed me as 'ye little dirt'; but she didn't give me away in public. And the dreadful thing was that I repudiated my guests, and looked as if I wondered what they were doing there."

" Poor Ellie Robbie ! " Mrs. Douglas said. " She was an anxious pilgrim, and you children worried her horribly. She came when she was sixteen to be nursemaid to Mark, and she stayed on till we left Kirkcaple, when she married the joiner. Do you remember her much ? "

" I remember one evening in the Den. We were getting fern-roots, and Ellie Robbie and Marget were both with us, and Marget said to Ellie, ' My, how neat your dress kicks out at the back when you walk ! ' Isn't memory an extraordinary thing ? I've forgotten most of the things I ought to have remembered, but I can recall every detail of that scene—the earthy smell of the fern-roots, the trowel sticking out of Mark's pocket, the sunlight falling through the trees, the pleased smirk on Ellie Robbie's face. I suppose I would be about five. At that time I was completely lost about my age. When people asked me how old I was, I kept on saying, ' Five past,' but to myself I said, ' I must be far more, but no one has ever told me.' . . . What was Ellie Robbie's real name ? "

" Ellen Robinson. Her father's name was Jack, and he was supposed by you children to be the original of the saying, ' Before you can say Jack Robinson.' Marget and Ellie got on very well together, although they were as the poles asunder—

Ellie so small and neat and gentle, Marget rather like a benevolent elephant. She is a much better-looking old woman than she was a young one."

" Did Marget come when Maggie Ann married ? "

" Yes. No — there was one between — Katie Herd. She stayed a month and was doing very well, but she suddenly announced that she was going home. When we asked her why, she replied with great candour, ' I dinna like it verra weel,' and off she went. Marget was a success from the first. We knew it was all right as soon as she began to talk of ' oor bairns.' When the work was over she liked to go to the nursery, and you children welcomed her with enthusiasm, and at once called on her to say her poem. Then she would stand up and shuffle her feet, and say :

> ' Marget Meikle is ma name,
> Scotland is ma nation,
> Harehope is ma dwelling place—
> A pleasant habitation.'

You delighted in her witticisms. ' Ca' me names, ca' me onything, but dinna ca' me ower,' was one that had a great success. Both she and Ellie were ideal servants for a minister's house ; they were both so discreet. No tales were ever carried by them to or from the Manse. There was one noted gossip in the congregation who was a terror to Ellie. Her husband had a shop, and of course we dealt at it—he was an elder in the church—

and Ellie dreaded going in, for she knew that if
Mrs. Beaton happened to be there she would be
subjected to a fire of questions. Marget enjoyed
an encounter, and liked to think out ways of
defeating Mrs. Beaton's curiosity. Not that there
was any harm in Mrs. Beaton and her desire to
know all our doings. I daresay it was only kindly
interest. I got to like her very much ; she was a
racy talker and full of whinstone common sense.
I was sorry for her, too, for no woman ever worked
harder, both in the shop and in the house, and her
husband and family took it all for granted. She did
kind things in an ungracious way, and was vexed
when people failed to appreciate her kindness.
Across the road from Mrs. Beaton lived another
elder's wife, Mrs. Lister, who, Mrs. Beaton
thought, got from life the very things she had
missed.

" ' Never toil yourself to death,' she used to
tell me, ' for your man and your bairns ; they'll
no thank you for it. Look at the Listers over
there. Willie Lister goes about with holes like
half-crowns in his heels, but he thinks the world
of his Aggie.' And it was quite true. I knew
that gentle little Mrs. Lister was everybody's
favourite, for she contradicted no one, ruffled no
one's feelings, while rough-tongued, honest, impudent Mrs. Beaton was both feared and disliked.
And yet there was no doubt which of the two
women one would have chosen to ride the ford
with. Had a tea-meeting to be arranged, a sale

of work to be organized, or a Christmas-tree to be
provided for Sunday school, Mrs. Beaton was in
it—purse and person.

" Mrs. Lister always took ' the bile ' when anything was expected of her. Once a year we were
invited to tea at the Listers' house, and as sure as
we found ourselves seated before a table groaning
with bake-meats and were being pressed by Mr.
Lister to partake of them because they were all
baked by ' Mamaw,' Mrs. Lister would say, ' Ay,
and I had a job baking them—for I was bad with
" the bile " all morning.' As Marget says, ' The
mistress is awfu' easy scunnered,' and after hearing
that my tea was a pretence. It was worse when
Agatha was there, for then we were apt to wait for
the announcement, and when it came give way to
painful, secret laughter. Agatha always laughed,
too, when Mrs. Lister capped her husband's sayings
with ' Ay, that's it, Paw.' She was a most agreeable
wife, but she was a mother before everything. She
would have talked all day about her children, burst-
ing out with odd little disjointed confidences about
them in the middle of a conversation about something else. ' He's an awful nice boy, Johnnie ; he's
got a fine voice,' would occur in a conversation about
the Sustentation Fund, and in the middle of a discussion about a series of lectures she would whisper,
' He's a queer laddie, our Tommy. When Nettie
was born he put his head round my bedroom door
and said, " Is she a richt ane, Maw ? " He meant
not deaf or dumb or anything, you know.' She

sometimes irritated her husband by her over anxiety
about the health of her children. If one coughed
in the night she always heard and, fearful of waking
Mr. Lister, she would creep out of bed and jump
from mat to mat (I can see her doing it—a sort of
anxious little antelope), and listen to their breathing, and hap them up with extra bedclothes. Nettie
was the youngest, and the delicate one, and had to
be tempted to eat. ' Oh, ma Nettie,' she would
say, ' could you take a taste of haddie to your tea
or a new-laid egg ? '

" She was afraid of nearly everything—mice,
and wind, and thunder, and she hated the sea.
One morning I met her almost distraught because
her boys had all gone out in a boat. ' Is their
father with them ? ' I asked. ' No, no,' she said,
' I didna let him go ; it was just the more to drown.'
Poor, anxious little body ! God took her first, and
she never had the anguish of parting with her
children. . . . What an opportunity ministers and
ministers' wives have of getting to know people
as they are—their very hearts ! "

" Yes," said Ann ; " but it isn't every minister
or every minister's wife who can make anything
of the opportunity. Just think of some we know—
sticks. Can you think of any poor stricken soul
going to them to be comforted ' as one whom his
mother comforteth ' ? What would they say ?
' Oh, indeed ! How sad ! ' or ' Really ! I'm very
sorry.' Some little stilted sentence that would
freeze the very fount of tears. You, Mother, I don't

think you would say anything. To speak to those who weep is no use; you must be able in all sincerity to weep with them. As for Father, his voice was enough. Isn't it in one of the Elizabeth books that some one talking of the futility of long, dull sermons, says, ' If only a man with a voice of gold would stand up and say, " Children, Christ died for you," I would lay down my head and cry and cry. . . .' Oh, it's a great life if a minister and his wife are any good at their job, and, above all, if they have a sense of humour ! "

" Well, I don't know about the sense of humour," Mrs. Douglas said doubtfully. " I have often envied the people who never seem overcome by the ludicrous side of things, who don't even seem aware that it is there. Do you remember Mrs. Daw ? I daresay not. My first meeting with her was in the Path on a hot summer's day. I saw an enormously stout woman toiling in front of me with a heavy basket, and as I passed her she laid down her load, and, turning to me a red, perspiring, but surprisingly bland countenance, said, ' Hech ! but it's a sair world for stout folk.' There was something so Falstaffian and jocund about the great figure, and the way she took me into her confidence, that I simply stood still and laughed, and she laughed with me. We shared the basket between us the rest of the way, and after that I often visited her. But I could never let your father come with me ; Mrs. Daw was too much for us together. Only once we tried it, and she told us that the doctor had advised her to take 'sheriff-wine and Van Hou-tong's cocoah,' and her genteel pronunciation was too much for us. She was never at her best when your father was there; she didn't care for the clergy.

" ' A lazy lot,' she called them. ' No wan o' them does a decent day's work. If it was me I wad mak' a' the ministers pollismen as weel, and that wad save some o' the country's siller.' She conde-scended to say that she rather liked your father's preaching, though her reason for liking it was not very flattering. ' I like him because he's no what ye ca' a scholarly preacher. I dinna like thae scholars, they're michty dull. I like the kind o' minister that misca's the deevil for aboot twenty meenits and then stops.'

" Mrs. Daw had me bogged at once when we started on theological discussions. She would ask questions and answer them herself as she knelt before the kitchen fire, engaged in what she called ' ringein' the ribs.'

" ' Ay,' she would say, ' I'm verra fond o' a clear fire. Mercy me, it'll be an awfu' want in heaven—a guid fire. Ye read aboot golden streets and pearly gates, but it's cauld comfort to an auld body wha likes her ain fireside. Of coorse we'll a' be speerits.' (It needed a tremendous effort of imagination to picture Mrs. Daw as a spirit !) ' Wull speerit ken speerit ? ' and then, as if in scorn at her own question, ' I daursay no ! It wad be little use if they did. I could get sma' enjoyment frae crackin' wi' a neebor, if a' the time I was lookin' through her, and her through me. An' what wad we crack aboot ? Nae couthy bits o' gossip up there—juist harps an' angels fleein' aboot. . . .'

"I would suggest diffidently that when we had gone on to another and higher life we wouldn't feel the want of the homely things so necessary to us here, and Mrs. Daw, shaking her head, would say, 'I dinna ken,' and then with her great laugh (your father used to quote something about a thousand beeves at pasture when he heard it) she would finish the profitless discussion with 'Weel, sit ye doun by ma guid fire and I'll mak' ye a cup o' tea in ma granny's cheeny teapot. We'll tak' our comforts so long as we hae them, for think as ye like the next warld's a queer turn-up onyway. . . .'"

CHAPTER IX

EVENING had come again to Dreams, but Ann, instead of being found at her writing-table, was stretched flat in the largest and softest of the many comfortable chairs the room contained, with the Tatler, a great, furry, sleepy mass, curled in her arms.

" Dear me, Ann ! " Mrs. Douglas said, looking up from her " reading." " You seem very exhausted. Aren't you going to write to-night ? "

Ann looked through half-closed eyes at her mother.

" Can't," she said lazily ; " too dog-tired. A tea-party in the Green Glen is too much for me. After such unwonted excitement I must sit all evening with my hands before me. Mother, did we ever really entertain people day after day—relays of them ? I can't believe to-night that we ever pre-sided at meetings, and read papers, and gave away prizes, and organized sales of work and cookery classes for the masses, and visited the sick, and talked for ever and did not faint—such feeble folk as we have become."

Mrs. Douglas sighed as she laid down *Hours of*

Silence. "I was of some use in the world then," she said, "not a mere cumberer of the ground."

Ann sat up and laughed at her mother. "I'm not going to rise to that fly, Motherkin. You remind me of the Glasgow woman we met in Switzerland, who was suffering from some nervous trouble, and who said, 'I would give a thousand pounds to be the Mistress Finlay I once was.' Perhaps you are not quite the Mistress Douglas you once were, but I can see very little difference."

Mrs. Douglas sighed again, and shook her head. "Oh—sic a worrit-lookin' wumman!" Ann quoted. Then, "I must say I enjoyed the tea-party. Mother, don't you like Mr. Sharp? I do. You needn't have rubbed it in about sermons being no use if they are read. He sat with such a guilty look like a scolded dog. I like his painstaking sermons and his sincere, difficult little prayers. He will never make a preacher, but he is a righteous man. Miss Ellen Scott cheered him by saying read sermons were generally more thoughtful. I do wish we could see the Scotts oftener. They have promised to come to luncheon one day, and go thoroughly into the garden question. They go south, they told me, in the early spring, so that the servants may get the house-cleaning done, and they weary all the time to get back. I wonder if they carry about them in London that sort of fragrance of the open air."

"They are nice women," said Mrs. Douglas, "and good, but they aren't my kind of people. We don't care about the same things. But Mr.

Sharp makes me feel young again ; he has the very atmosphere of a manse about him."

" The atmosphere of Mr. Sharp's Manse is chiefly paraffin oil," said Ann.

At that moment Marget came into the room, ostensibly to remind Ann of something needed at the village shop the next day, but really to talk over the tea-party.

" I think the minister enjoyed his tea," she remarked, "for there was an awful wheen scones eaten."

" He did, indeed, Marget," her mistress assured her. " He said he didn't know when he had tasted such good scones. He was asking me what I thought about him entertaining the office-bearers. He would like to, but his housekeeper is delicate and afraid of work ; and he's afraid to suggest anything in case she departs."

" Tets ! " said Marget. " That wumman fair angers me. She's neither sick nor sair, an' she's no' that auld aither, but she keeps that puir laddie in misery a' the time in case she's gaun to break doon. She never bakes him a scone, juist loaf breed a' the time, an' she'll no' bother to mak' him a bit steamed pudden' or a tert, juist aye a milk-thing, an' a gey watery milk-thing at that. She boasts that he carries trays for her and breaks sticks—the wumman should be ashamed to let the minister demean himsel'. If he wants to gie an Elders' Supper, what's to hinder me and Mysie to gang doon and gie a hand ? "

" Why, Marget," Ann cried, " I haven't heard

that expression since I was a child. It was at Kirkcaple we had Elders' Suppers, wasn't it, Mother —never in Glasgow ? "

" Only in Kirkcaple. They were held after the November Communions to purge the roll."

" *Purge the roll*," Ann murmured to herself ; " of all delicious phrases ! "

" If ye'll excuse me, Mem," said Marget, " I'll tak' a seat for a meenit. Mysie has just gone doon the road a step or two wi' the lassie Ritchie frae the cottages."

She seated herself primly on a chair and said :

" I think ye should pit in yer *Life* about the Elders' Suppers."

Ann nodded. " I think so, Marget. I can just recall them vaguely. We were all in bed before the elders actually came, but I remember the preparation, and how deeply I envied you and Ellie Robbie staying up, little dreaming, poor babe, how in after years I would envy the children who get away to bed before the party begins."

" They were terrifying occasions to me," said her mother. " Elders in the mass are difficult to cope with. When they arrived they were shown into the study, and when the business part of the proceedings was over they trooped into the dining-room for supper. To keep the ball of conversation going, to compel them to talk and save the party from being a dismal failure was my job, and it was no light task. They were the best of men, our Kirkcaple elders, but they let every subject drop like a hot potato.

It was from occasions like that I learned to talk
' even on,' as they say. I simply dared not let a
silence fall, for, from bitter experience, I knew that
if I did and caught your father's eye we would be
sure to laugh and bring disgrace on ourselves."

" Don't I know," said her daughter ; " will you
ever forget that night in Glasgow, when we invited
your class to an evening party, and they all arrived
in a body and in dead silence seated themselves
round the room, and none of us could think of a
single word to say, and in an agony we sat, becoming every moment more petrified, and my tongue
got so stiff I felt if I spoke it would break off, and
Father suddenly broke the awful silence with
' Quite so,' delivered in a high, meaningless voice,
and we simply fell on each other helpless with
laughter."

Mrs. Douglas laughed at the recollection. " Once
you let a silence fall," she said, " it's hopeless.
Nothing seems important enough to break it with.
. . . To go back to the Elders' Suppers—we always
had the same menu. Hot roast beef, hot beef-
steak pie, with vegetables, then plum-pudding and
apple-tart, and coffee. The oldest elder, Charles
Mitchell was his name, sat on my right hand, and
the next eldest, Henry Petrie, sat on my left.
Charles Mitchell was so deaf that any attempts to
converse were thrown away on him. Henry Petrie
was a man of most melancholy countenance, and
absolutely devoid of light table-talk. He was sad,
and said nothing, and might as well have been a

post. One night, having tried him on every subject with no success, I watched him being helped to vegetables, and said, in desperation, ' Potatoes are good this year, don't you think ? ' He turned on me his mournful eyes, his knife suspended on its way to his mouth, and said, ' They'll no' stand a boil.' "

" D'ye mind," said Marget, " thon awfu' nicht when the pie cowpit on the gravel ? We were gettin' it covered at Wilson's the baker's, for they made uncommon guid pastry, an' it didna come till the verra last meenit. I was oot lookin' for the laddie at the gate, an' when he came I took it frae him in a hurry, an', eh, mercy ! if the whole hypothic didna slidder oot o' ma hand on to the ground. I let oot a yell an' Ellie came runnin' oot, and syne she brocht a lamp, an' we fund that the pastry wasna muckle the waur, but the meat an' the gravy was a' amang the gravel. What could we do but juist scoop up wi' a spoon what we could get—meat, chuckie-stanes an' a'—an' into the hoose wi' it. I can tell ye I handit roond the plates gey feared that nicht. I tried ma best to get them to choose the guid clean roast beef, but there was nae takkers. Juist pie, pie, pie, one after another until I was fair provokit. Every meenit I expectit to hear their teeth gang crunch on a stane. I can tell ye I was glad when I got their plates whuppit awa' frae them, an' the puddens plankit doon. It was a guid thing appendicitis wasna invented then, or they wad a' ha' been lying wi' it, for an orange pip's a fule to a chuckie-stane.' "

4

" Ay, Marget," said her mistress, " we had many a fright. As old Mrs. Melville used to say, ' Folk gets awfu' frichts in this warld.' Well, well ! " Mrs. Douglas sighed as was her way. " We had many a successful party, too."

" Folk," said Marget complacently, " likit fine to come to oor hoose. They aye got a graund feed an' a guid lauch forbye. The maister wasna mebbe verra divertin' in company, being naitral quiet, but you were a great hand at the crackin', Mem."

Mrs. Douglas modestly waved away the compliment, while Ann said, " You must have had some very smart suppers, for I have a distinct recollection of eating ratafia biscuits and spun sugar from a trifle one morning after a party."

" The trifle evenings were few and far between," said her mother ; " but we had many a cosy little party among our neighbours."

Marget again broke in. " No' to mention a' the folk that juist drappit in. Oor hoose was a fair thro-gate for folk. A' the ministers that lived a bit away kent whaur to come to in Kirkcaple for their tea. Ye'll mind, Mem, that Mr. and Mrs. Dewar were never muckle away. When Mr. Dewar walkit in frae Buckie and fund naebody in, he wad say to me, ' I'll be back for my tea, Marget. Isn't this baking-day ? ' " (Marget adopted a loud, affected tone when imitating any one ; this she called " speaking proper.") " Then Mistress Dewar wad come hoppin' in—'deed she was often in afore I got to the door, for I wad mebbe be dressin' when the bell rang. I wad hae to put on my wrapper again, an' there she wad be sittin' on a chair in the lobby, knittin' awa' like mad. 'Always busy, you see, Marget,' she would say ; ' I belong to the save-the-moment society.' Then she wad gie that little lauch o' hers. Sic a wee bit o' a thing she wis, mair like a bairn than a mairret wumman."

"Once," said Ann, " I went somewhere to spend a day with Mrs. Dewar, and coming home we had to wait awhile for a train. Mrs. Dewar, of course, was knitting, and as the light was bad in the wait-ing-room she calmly climbed up on the table and stood, picking up a stitch, as near to the gas-jet as she could get. She made the oddest spectacle with her bonnet a little on one side, as it always was, her little blunt face and childish figure. And to make matters worse she sang as she knitted :

' Did you ever put a penny in a missionary box ?
A penny that you might have gone and spent like other folks ? '

It was torture to a self-conscious child to hear the giggles of the few spectators of the scene."

Mrs. Douglas laughed softly as if remembering something precious. " Little Mrs. Dewar cared who laughed at her. That was what made her so un-usual and so refreshing. The queer, dear, wee body ! There was no one I liked so much to come to the house. She was so companionable and so unfussy. If she could only stay ten minutes she was calm

and settled for that ten minutes, and then went.
I have seen people who meant to stay for hours
keep me restless and unhappy all the time by their
fluttered look. Whenever I got tired of my house,
or my work, or myself, I went to Buckie to Mrs.
Dewar. They had a delightful old manse, with
a charming garden behind, but in front it faced a
blank wall. Some one condoled with Mrs. Dewar
on the lack of view. 'Tuts,' she said, 'we've never
time to look at a view.'"

"Like old Mary Hart at Etterick, when a visitor
said to her, 'What a lovely view you have!' 'An'
what aboot it?' was the disconcerting answer. I
remember the Dewars' manse, Mother. I once
stayed there for a week. What a pity Mrs. Dewar
had no children of her own! She was a wonder
with children. I was only a tiny child, but she
taught me so much, and interested me in so many
different things and people. After breakfast I had
to help her to 'classify' the dishes; put all the
spoons together, and wipe the knives with soft
paper and make them all ready to be washed.
Then we saw that the salts and mustards were tidy,
and the butter and jam in dainty dishes. Then we
would take a bundle of American papers to a woman
who had a son in the United States, and on our way
home she would take me down to the shore and
point out the exact spot on the rocks where she had
once found a beautiful coral comb, and where the
next day she had found a mermaid sitting crying for
the loss of it. It was a long story, but I know it

finished with the grateful mermaid giving a large donation to the Sustentation Fund! Mrs. Dewar had an extraordinary number of relations, who all seemed to be generals and admirals, and things like that, and the tales of the Indian nephews who had come to her as babies were enthralling to me. They were grown up by that time, and, I suppose, on their way to become generals, too. There was always something rather military about Mrs. Dewar's small, alert figure. 'Mustard to mutton,' she would say to me at dinner; 'child, you would be expelled the mess.' She was really too funny. When Mr. Dewar would say, 'My dear, have you seen my spectacles?' she would reply, 'Seek and ye shall find, not speak and ye shall find.' And if the servants worried her she walked about saying the hymn beginning, 'Calm me, O God, and keep me calm.'"

"I likit Mrs. Dewar," said Marget; "she had queer ways, but she was a leddy. She was yin o' the Keiths o' Rathnay—rale gentry. Eh, Mem, d'ye mind the black that was preachin' for Maister Dewar, an' they couldna keep him in the hoose, for there was illness, and he cam' to us? Eh, I say!"

"Poor man! I remember your face, Marget, when I met you on the stairs the morning he left. You were holding some towels away from you and you said, 'I'm no verra sure aboot that black's towels.'"

"Neither I wis," said Marget; "I'm aye feared the black comes off."

CHAPTER X

"MOTHER," said Ann one evening, "do you realize that we are not getting on at all well with your *Life*? Marget has developed this passion for coming in and recalling absurd things—last night she wasted the whole evening with the tale of her grandfather's encounter with a bull; racy, I admit, but not relevant, and the night before she set me recalling mad escapades of our childhood, and I didn't write a word. Where we are, I don't know, but there are only three of us born—Mark and me and Robbie. Jim has got to be worked in somewhere—and Rosamund. We were all at Etterick recovering from whooping cough when Jim was born, so I don't remember much about him, but Rosamund's coming was a wonderful event. She was my birthday present when I was eight."

"In some ways Jim was the nicest of the babies," Mrs. Douglas said. "He was so pretty and sweet-tempered—quite a show child. Whenever we said, 'Sing, Jim,' he dropped on to the floor and began 'Lord, a little band and lowly,' and he was no age at all."

Ann laughed a sceptical laugh. "He ceased at an early age his efforts to entertain; he has no use for company now. I suppose it might be a re-action from his precocious childhood. But he still has the good nature."

"Indeed he has," said Jim's mother fervently. "The Fife people had a saying 'born for a bless-ing,' and Jim has been that. Rosamund"—she paused for a moment, then continued—"Rosa-mund was the most lovely child I ever saw. No, it wasn't because I was her mother; unprejudiced people said the same. I think, perhaps, it was the happiest time in my life, those weeks after Rosa-mund came. Not that I hadn't always been happy, but the years before had been rather a mêlée. Now I had found my feet, more or less, and church work and housekeeping and baby rearing no longer appalled me. It was in March she was born. We had got all the spring cleaning done well before-hand, and the Deacons' Court had papered and painted the stairs and lobbies, and we had afforded ourselves new stair and landing carpets, and the house was as fresh as it's possible for a house to be. I lay there with my baby, so utterly contented, listening to the voices of you and the boys playing in the garden in the spring sunlight, with pleasant thoughts going through my mind about my healthy, happy children and a smooth-running church, and thanking God for the best man that ever woman had. And all the kind people came flocking to see the new baby. Mrs. Dewar came with a dainty frock made by herself and an armful of books and magazines. 'These are George's choosing,' she said, 'and he says you will enjoy them all. I think myself they look rather dull, so I've brought you one of Annie Swan's—she's *capital* for a confinement.' And Mrs. Peat sat by the fire with Rosamund on her knee and said, 'Eh, my dear, she's a beauty,' and blessed her. And you children came running in with celandines from the Den, and grubby treasures which you tried to thrust into the baby's tiny hand—I often look back on those days. It seems to me that my cup of happiness must have been lipping over. Rosamund grew like a flower. There was always something special about her, and we felt it from the first. It wasn't only her beauty, it was something fine, aloof. You remember her, Ann ? "

"Yes, I remember her, Mother. She was always different; even at the beginning she wasn't red and puckered and squirming like most babies, but faintly pink like a rose. Father worshipped her. Of course, you know that you made far more of her than of any of the rest of us, and we were glad and willing that it should be so. We were never rough with her. She never lived the tumbled puppy-like life that I lived as a child."

Mrs. Douglas nodded. Presently she said :

" You had a happy childhood, Ann ? "

"Hadn't we just ? No children ever had a happier ; we were so free. When I see children dragging along dreary daily walks with nurses, I do pity them. We hated being taken walks by Ellie Robbie, and generally ran away. We used to meet the Johnstons with their Ellen, and then we big ones dashed off together on business of our own, leaving the poor nurses tethered to the prams. We were marauders of the worst type. Having always a great hunger for sweets and being always destitute of money, we had to devise schemes for getting them. In Nether Street there stood a little sweetie shop owned by one Archibald Forbes, a good-natured man who had once (in an evil moment for himself) given us a few sweeties for nothing. With the awful pertinacity of children we went back continually in the hope that he might do it again! (What you and Father would have thought if you had seen us, I know not!) Sometimes he ordered us away, but, when in a more forthcoming mood, he would make us say recitations to him, and then reward us. He must have been a very patient man, Mr. Archibald Forbes, for I can see him, his spectacles on the end of his nose, and his bushy eyebrows pulled down, standing behind his counter, listening without a movement to Mark relentlessly getting through ' The scene was changed '—you know that thing about Mary Queen of Scots ? "

" Indeed I do. If Mark was asked to recite when Mrs. Goskirk was present, and she heard him begin, ' The scene was changed,' she gave a resigned sigh and took up her knitting ; and there was another about Henry of Navarre that was almost as bad. The things you did were short and harmless."

"Oh, quite," said Ann. "There was one about a little girl called Fanny, a child for whom we had a deep distaste. She had a dream about being in heaven, I remember :

> ' I thought to see Papa's estate,
>   But oh ! 'twas far too small, Mamma ;
>   The whole wide world was not so big
>   As William's cricket ball, Mamma.'

And she finished :

> ' Your pretty Fanny woke, Mamma,
>   And lo ! 'twas but a dream.'

We thought the said Fanny was an insufferably sidey child, first of all for mentioning ' Papa's estate,' then for saying ' And lo !' and, worst of all, for alluding to herself as ' pretty Fanny '— that was beyond pardon. Talking about money, some one once gave me a sixpence, which I took, contrary to rule—we weren't allowed to take money. Feeling guilty, I ran into a little shop in the Watery Wynd, a fish shop that sold fruit, and demanded sixpennyworth of pears. Ellie Robbie was hard behind, so, with great presence of mind, I said, ' Give me one just now and I'll get the rest another time.' That sixpennyworth

of pears was a regular widow's cruse to me.   For
weeks I called nearly every day at that shop to
demand a pear due to me, until they said if I
came again they would tell my father! We can't
have had any decent pride about us, for I don't
think we minded being snubbed. When we ran
away from Ellie Robbie the harbour was generally our destination—a fascinating place where
Norwegian sailors strolled about in a friendly way
and could sometimes be persuaded to let us go on
board their ships, where they gave us hot coffee
out of gaily painted bowls. The harbour was
the only romantic thing in Kirkcaple. Time
meant nothing to us in those days, and, so far as
we were concerned, the King still sat in Dunfermline
town calling for a ' skeely skipper ' to sail his
ship to ' Norroway ower the faem ' ; and many an
hour we stood looking out to sea and watching
for the gallant ship ' that never mair cam' hame.'
Next to the harbour we loved the coalpit, and
felt that we were indeed greatly blessed to have
one so near the house. There was no romance
about a coalpit (except the romance that brings
in the nine-fifteen) ; but there were glorious opportunities for getting thoroughly dirty. We had
many friends among the miners, and they gave
us rides on trolleys, and helped us to make see-
saws, and admitted us into lovely little outhouses
containing, among other treasures, the yellow
grease that trains are greased with. And there
was the Hyacinth Den only a stone's-throw from

our own door, and the bleach-field beyond, and beyond that again the Wild Wood. And our own Manse garden was not to be despised, for did it not look into a field owned by the Huttons—a clan as wild and lawless as our own, and many a battle took place between us. They had a friend known to us as 'Wild Scott of the Huttons,' a truly great and tireless fighter, and if he happened to be visiting them we never knew when a head would pop up over the wall where the big pear tree grew, and challenge us to mortal combat. Did you hear that Mark came across a man in France, tremendously decorated and of high rank, who turned out to be our old enemy 'Wild Scott of the Huttons'? Besides the permanent feud with the Huttons, we had many small vendettas with boys from the town, who stoned Mark on Sundays because they didn't like his clothes."

Mrs. Douglas laid down her stocking, and said in a bewildered tone:

"I never could understand why you were so pugnacious. You were a dreadfully bad example to the other children in the place. They say that ministers' children are generally worse than other people's—on the principle, I suppose, that 'shoe-makers' bairns are aye ill shod,' but I never saw children more naturally bad than you were—well, not bad, perhaps, but wild and mischievous to a degree. Your father sometimes said that no one could doubt the theory of original sin after seeing our family. Alison sometimes comes to me in her wheedling way and says, ' Gran, do tell me about your bad children,' and I have to tell her of the time when you celebrated the Queen's birthday at the coalpit by setting fire to a lot of valuable wood and nearly burned the whole place, and the day when we lost you and found you all in the Panny Pond—literally ' in ' it you were, for you had made a raft and sunk with it into the soft, black mud."

" Yes," said Ann, " I was always sorry after that for ' The Girl who trod on a Loaf,' for I knew the dreadfulness of sinking down, down."

" I think my dear Robbie was the worst of you all. You others showed faint signs of improvement, but he never deviated into good behaviour. He was what is known in Priorsford as ' a notorious ill callant,' and in Fife as ' an awfu' steerin' bairn.' When I went away for a day or two I had always to take him with me, for I knew if I left him at home it would be sheer ' battleation,' and yet he had the tenderest heart among you, and Rosamund said, ' Robbie's the one who has never once been cross to me.' I remember the first time I took him to church. He disliked the look of the woman who sat in front, a prim lady, and he suddenly tilted her bonnet over her eyes. Then he shouted to a well-behaved child in the next seat, ' Bad boy make a face at me,' and before I could stop him, hurled his shoe at him ; and he announced at the top of his voice, ' Mark and Ann's away to Etterick, but I don't care a wee, wee

button,' and had then to be removed. 'Wheep
him,' Mrs. Beaton used to counsel; but Mrs. Peat
always said ' Robbie's a fine laddie.' "

Ann nodded. " So he was, always. Though
he was so turbulent and noisy, he was so uncunning
you couldn't but think nobly of the soul. Mark
and I thought of the mischievous things to do, and
Robbie threw himself into them so whole-heartedly
that generally he was the one caught and blamed.
The rest of us were better at wriggling out of
things. Father was never hard on us unless we
cheated or told lies. He wasn't even angry when
the policeman complained of us—do you remember
the one, an elder in our church, who said in despair
to his wife, ' I'll hae to jail thae bairns and leave the
kirk ' ? One of the few times I ever saw Father
really angry was when he was holding a class for
young communicants, and we crept into the cubby-
hole under the stairs, where the meter was, and
turned off the gas. Father emerged from the
study like a lion, and caught poor Jim, who had
loitered. The rest of us had gained the attics and
were in hiding. It must have been a great day
for the young communicants."

" Ann ! It was a shocking thing to do ; it would
have roused the mildest-mannered man."

" Father was very good-natured," said Ann,
kneeling on the rug to put a log on the fire ; " but
it was never safe to presume too much on his
mildness. He was subject to sudden and incom-
prehensible rages. One day I innocently remarked

that somebody had a 'polly' arm. I didn't know
that I meant a paralysed arm; I was only re-
peating what I had heard others say, but Father
grabbed me suddenly and said, 'You wretched
child! Where do you pick up those abominable
expressions? Go to the nursery.' I went weeping, feeling bitterly the injustice with which I had
been treated. But for every once that Father
made us cry, a hundred times he filled our mouths
with laughter. All our best games were invented
by him. Whenever he put his head round the
nursery door, we knew we were going to have good
times. There was a glorious game about India,
in which the nursery became a trackless jungle,
and Father was an elephant with a pair of bellows
for a trunk. Sometimes on a Sunday night, as a
great treat, we were allowed to play Bible games.
Then we would march round and round the nursery
table, blowing lustily on trumpets to cause the
walls of Jericho to fall, or Robbie as Jeremiah
would be let down by Mark and me into the pit
(which was the back of the old sofa), with 'clouts
under his armpits'; or, again, he and Mark lay
prostrate on the sofa (now the flat roof of an
Eastern house), while I, as Rahab, covered them
with flax. I have the nicest recollections of
winter evenings in the study, with the red curtains
drawn, and you sitting mending, when we lay on
the hearth-rug, and Father read to us of Bruce, and
Wallace, and that lonely, lovely lady, Mary of
Scotland; but my most cherished memory is of

a December day in Glasgow. It was a yellow fog that seemed to press down on us and choke us. You were out when we came in from our walk, the fire wasn't good, and everything seemed unspeakably dreary. We were quarrelling among ourselves and feeling altogether wretched, when the door opened and Father looked in on us. 'Alone, folkies?' he said. 'Where's your mother?' We told him you were out and that we had nothing to do, and that everything was beastly. He laughed and went away, and came back presently with a book. It was *The Queen's Wake*, and for the first time we heard of 'bonnie Kilmeny' who went away to Fairyland. We forgot the fog, we forgot our grievances; we were carried away with Kilmeny. Then Father got a ballad-book, and that was even better, for the clash of armies was ever music in our ears. We sprawled over him in our excitement as he read how 'in the gryming of a new-fa'en snaw' Jamie Telfer of the fair Dodhead carried the 'fraye' to Branksome ha'. Our tea was brought in, but the pile of bread-and-butter was hardly diminished, for Father read on, sometimes laughing aloud in his delight at what he read, sometimes stopping for a moment to drink some tea, but his eyes never leaving the printed page. How could we eat when we were hearing for the first time of Johnnie Armstrong going out to meet his King in all good faith, only to find that death was to be his portion? We howled like angry wolves when father read:

' To seek het water beneath cauld ice,
  Surely it is a great folie—
  I have asked grace at a graceless face,
  But there is nane for my men and me.'

When you came in, we only looked at you vaguely,
and said, ' Go on, Father, go on,' and he explained,
' These benighted children have never heard the
Border Ballads, Nell,' and then you sat down and
listened too. . . . D'you remember people in
Glasgow, who owned big restaurants all over the
place—Webster, I think, was the name, and there
was a fat only son who sometimes came in to
play with us ? I don't know what Mr. Webster
was like in his home life, but that fat boy said to
me very feelingly, ' *Yours is a jolly kind of father
to have.*' It was generous of him, for only that
morning he had taunted me with the fact that my
father played a penny whistle, and I, deeply
affronted, had replied with a tasteful reference to
the restaurants, ' Well, anyway, he doesn't sell
tuppenny pies like your father does.' "

" Oh, that penny whistle ! " said Mrs. Douglas,
with a laugh and a sigh. " He made wonderful
music on it. There was always something of the
Pied Piper about your father. Down in the district
the children used to come up and pull at his coat
and look up in his face ; they had no fear of him ;
and whenever he entered the hall on Band of Hope
nights the place was in an uproar with yells for a
story. He would get up on the little platform
and, leaning over the table, he would tell them

' Jock and his Mother,' or ' The Bannock that
went to see the World,' or ' Maya '—fine stories,
but not a moral to one of them."

"That was the best of Father's stories: they
never had morals," said Ann. "The real secret
of his charm was that at heart he was as much a
child as any of them. Once I was down in the
district with him, and we saw a very dirty little
boy sitting on a doorstep. He greeted Father with
a wide grin, and beckoned to him with a grimy
forefinger. Father went obediently, and very
slowly and mysteriously the little fellow drew
from his ragged pocket a handful of marbles (very
chipped and dirty ones) and said, ' Thae's whit ye
ca' *bools*,' and Father, bending over the small
figure, replied, ' So they are, sonny, so they are ! '

"Yes, the fat boy was right: he was a jolly
kind of father to have ! "

CHAPTER XI

" . . . When Rosamund was six months old we left Kirkcaple. It was a great uprooting. You don't live thirteen years in a place in close touch with the people without becoming deeply attached both to the place and people—and in the last year of our stay at Kirkcaple we had a wonderful experience. There was a great awakening of interest in spiritual things—a revival—and we saw many enter into life. . . ."

Mrs. Douglas stopped abruptly and regarded her daughter.

" Ann," she said, " why do you begin to look abashed and miserable if I mention the word revival ? Does conversion seem to you an improper subject ? "

Ann screwed her face uncomfortably. " Oh, I don't know, but I confess I do dislike to hear people talking glibly about that sort of thing. It somehow seems rather indecent. You didn't realize, you and Father, how miserable it was for us children going to so many evangelistic meetings. We liked shouting Sankey's hymns,

and the addresses were all right, but oh! those
'after-meetings,' when we sat sick with fright,
watching earnest young men working their way
down the church to speak personally to us. How
could we say we were on the road to heaven?
And we were too honest—at least the boys were
too honest—simply to say Yes, when asked if we
were saved. I shall never think it right or proper
that any casual person should leap on one and ask
questions about one's soul. I should object to
any one, other than a doctor or intimate friend,
asking me questions about my bodily health, and
why should I be less select about my immortal
soul? And it seemed to us so dreadful that they
should count the converts. I remember with
what abhorrence we once heard Mrs. Macfarlane
tell how she and her husband had both talked to
a young man about his soul. 'And when we had
shown him the light'—you remember the sort of
simper she gave—'and he had gone on his way
rejoicing, I said to Mr. Macfarlane, "George dear,
is it your soul or mine?"' In other words, 'My
bird, sir.' I suppose she was out for stars in her
crown, but I would rather have none than cadge
for them like that."

"Oh, Ann," cried her mother, "you don't know
what you are saying. It hurts me to hear you
talk in that flippant way about——"

"Mother, you needn't make a mournful face
at me." Ann's face was flushed, and she looked
very much in earnest. "You've simply no idea

how difficult it is for a minister's family to be anything but mere formalists. You see, we hear so
much about it all. From our infancy we are
familiar with all the shibboleths, until they almost
cease to have any meaning. I used to think as a
child that it was most unfairly easy for the heathen.
I pictured myself hearing for the very first time
the story of Jesus Christ, and I thought with
what gratitude and love I would have fallen on
my knees to thank Him. . . . As it was, we knew
the message so well that our attention was chiefly
directed to the messengers, and you must admit,
Mother, we had some very queer ones. You
can't have forgotten the big, red-haired evangelist,
as rough as the heather, who told us a story of a
pump being ' off the fang,' and finished remarkably
with ' Ah, my friends, God's pump's never off
the fang.' I think it was the same man who said
we were just like fagots, ' fit for the burning.'
Oh, but do you remember the man in Glasgow who
illustrated the shortness of life with a story about
' Gran'papaw ' who . . ."

" *Ann !* "

Mrs. Douglas had finished her daily reading and
sat with the pile of devotional books on her knee,
eyeing her daughter with a mixture of disapproval
and unwilling amusement. " Ann, you turn everything into ridicule."

Ann protested. " There's no ridicule about it.
It is a very good, serious tale. ' Gran'papaw he
gae two . . .' "

Again her mother interrupted her.

" I'm sure your father would be sorry to hear you laughing at evangelists. He revelled in evangelistic work."

Ann gave a squeal of rage. "*Mother!* D'you know what sort of picture of Father you would give to any one who didn't know him? Some one with a smug face and a soapy manner, and a way of shaking hands as if he had a poached egg in the palm. Could there be anything less like my father? There was nothing unctuous about him, nothing of the professional religionist. He was like a Raeburn portrait to look at . . .

> ' A face filled with a fine old-fashioned grace,
>   Fresh-coloured, frank——'

and he never thought that because he was virtuous there should be no more cakes and ale. He was a minister simply because the great fact of his life was Christ, and he desired above everything to bring men to Him. I never read of Mr. Standfast but I think of Father, for he, too, loved to hear his Lord spoken of, and coveted to set his feet in his Master's footprints. . . ."

Ann stopped and looked in a shamefaced way at her mother.

" And now I'm preaching! It's in my blood— well, you were beginning to tell me about the revival in Kirkcaple when I started to blaspheme. Please go on."

" Well, you may laugh at evangelists. . . ."

" *Who's* laughing ? " cried Ann.

Her mother went on calmly. " But I assure you that was a wonderful time in Kirkcaple. Night after night the church was crowded, and girls and young men went as blithely to those meetings as ever they went to a dance. You may talk as you like of ' emotionalism ' and ' the excitement of the moment,' but remember, this all happened nearly thirty years ago, and the young people who decided for Christ then are the chief support of the Church to-day. I am very certain they have never regretted staying to the after-meeting and throwing in their lot with Christ. How easy the church work was that winter ! The Wednesday prayer-meeting overflowing from the hall into the church, money forthcoming for everything—you may know conversion is real when it touches the pocket. We had a series of special meetings more or less all through that winter, and, of course, all the speakers stayed with us. Marget never grumbled at the extra work. One night, at a meeting where testimonies were asked for, to my utter amazement she got up and stammered out a few words. Long afterwards, in Glasgow, when she lost her temper about something, she said, ' Eh, I say, I'll need to be speakin in the kirk again.' She had evidently found it beneficial. We had all sorts of ministers, and evangelists staying with us, some delightful, others rather difficult. One week-end the great

Dr. Bentley came to preach, a very godly but a
very austere man. Your father was preaching
somewhere, and I had to bear the brunt of him
alone. Immediately he had had tea he suggested
that we should have a little Bible-reading and
prayer. It was a dreadful ordeal for me, for he
kept asking me what passage I should like read,
and my mind went blank and I couldn't think of
any ! Finally I managed to slip out of the room,
leaving him to rest, and not noticing that Robbie
was playing quietly behind the sofa. Shortly
after that we heard an uproar in the study, Dr.
Bentley's voice in trumpet notes and yells of rage
from Robbie. With Ellie Robbie at my heels, I
rushed to the rescue. . . . Dr. Bentley met me
with the words : ' I have had dealings with your
son.' It turned out that, seeing the old man
sitting alone, Robbie had gone to the bookcase,
pulled out as large a volume as he could manage,
and carried it to him. Dr. Bentley told him to
put the book back on the shelf and bring no more.
Robbie brought another and another, and Dr.
Bentley whipped him. Full of fury at the results
of his well-meant efforts to entertain him, Robbie
kicked Dr. Bentley—kicked the great Dr. Bentley
—and was carried out of the room in Ellie Robbie's
arms quite unrepentant, shouting as he went,
' Abominable gentleman ! ' ' "

Ann laughed with much enjoyment. " It isn't
one of the duties of a guest to beat his
host's children, but he met his match in Robbie.

You must have had a dreadful week-end, poor Mother!"

"Oh, dreadful! Everything went wrong. Dr. Bentley told me that he didn't like a fire in his bedroom, but that he liked a fire in his bed. This, he explained very solemnly, meant two hot-water cans and six pairs of blankets. Marget put in one hot-water can (a 'pig' one) and had gone to fill an india-rubber one, when Ellie Robbie, wishful to help, and unaware of one 'pig' in the bed, slapped in another. They met, and each halved neatly in two. The bed was a sea, and we were looking despairingly at it when Dr. Bentley appeared in the doorway and announced that he would like to retire for the night! . . . Some time afterwards Dr. Bentley was again in the neighbourhood and called, but found no one at home. Marget, telling us about his visit, said, 'It was thon auld man, I dinna mind his name; the yin the mistress is fear't for.'"

"With reason, I think," said Ann. "What an orgy of meetings you must have had that winter!"

"Yes, but I can't remember that there were any bad effects, or that we sank into indifference when the stimulus of the meetings was removed. Rather we went on resolved to do better than we had ever done, for the Lord had done great things for us. . . . Then came the call to Glasgow, and it was very difficult to decide what was for the best. We didn't love cities, and we had no friends in the West; on the other hand, we had to think about the education of you children. Your father was going on for forty, and he felt, if he ever meant to take a call, now was the time. You children were delighted. Any change seems a change for the better to a child ; you never gave a thought to the big, sunny garden you were leaving, or the Den, or the familiar friendly house, or the kind people. The day your father and I went to Glasgow to look for a house you all stood on the doorstep and shouted after us, ' Be sure and get one near a coalpit.' "

" Yes," Ann said; " the thought of a flitting enchanted us, and we began at once to pack. Where was it Robbie had inflammation of the lungs ? Before we went to Glasgow, wasn't it ? "

" The year before—in spring. He had got hot playing football and stood in the east wind. He was very ill, poor darling, and for long he needed great care. I got to know my wild boy in a different way in those days and nights of weakness."

Ann left her writing-table and sat on the fender-stool. She pushed the logs together and made them blaze, and, reaching over to the big basket that stood by the fireplace, she threw on log after log until the whole room was filled with the dancing light.

" Now, that's something like a fire," she said. " A dull fire makes one feel so despairing. . . . Robbie was so very proud of having had an illness ; he always called it ' my inflammation,' and when he broke his arm his conceit knew no bounds. I'm afraid I broke it for him by falling off the see-

saw on to the top of him. We didn't know what
had happened, but we saw that his arm looked very
queer, and Mark and I brought him home and
helped him to take off his boots, and were quite
unusually attentive to him. He didn't say a
word about it hurting until he heard that it was
broken, when he began to yell at once, and said,
' Will I die?—will I die?' Reassured on that
point, he was very pleased about his broken arm."

"Two days later," said Robbie's mother, " he
escaped from the nursery and was found on the
rafters of an unfinished house (how he managed to
climb with his arm in splints, I know not) singing
' I'm the King of the Castle.' "

Ann laughed softly. " He never let us forget
his achievements, dear lamb. If we quarrelled
about the possession of anything, Robbie was sure
to say, ' Give it to me, for I've had the inflammation.' Mark made a poem about him, which ran:

' And if in any battle I come to any harm,
  Why, I've had the inflammation, I've had a broken
      arm.'

It must have been no light task to remove us all
from Kirkcaple to Glasgow."

Mrs. Douglas shook her head. " A terrible
undertaking. But we were young and strong.
Mrs. Peat came up one day and found me crying
as I packed. ' Eh, my dear,' she said, ' you're
vexed to go, and I'm glad to see you're vexed to

leave us all, but you're taking all your own with you. You don't know what it means to leave a grave. . . .' Everybody made farewell parties for us, and we departed in a shower of presents and good wishes. That was nearly thirty years ago, and only the other day I met one of our Kirkcaple people in Edinburgh, and she said to me, with tears in her eyes, ' Hardly a day passes in our house without a mention of your name, and never a Sabbath comes but we say, " If only we could hear Mr. Douglas's voice again ! " Who says the ministry is not a repaying job ? ' Well, we got to Glasgow—I think you children all went to Etterick, didn't you ? "

" Only the boys," said Ann. " I went straight to Glasgow with you and Baby Rosamund. It was a great experience for me. I boasted about it for long. I was allowed to attend the Induction Soirée, and heard you and Father praised by every one. It was my first experience of Glasgow humour, and very funny I thought it. I remember one old elder who spoke told us of what a fine speech he had made the night before in his bed. ' My,' he said, beaming round on the company, ' what grand speeches ye can make in yer bed ! ' but it turned out he had forgotten it on the platform. I thought the Glasgow accent fascinating, and I liked to be told that I was a ' good wee Miss.' I began to like Glasgow people that night, and I've gone on liking them better and better ever since."

CHAPTER XII

" AND now," said Ann, " we're done with Kirkcaple
and must tackle Glasgow. And the Tatler is sitting
on my MS., and that won't improve its appearance.
Odd the passion that cat has for paper ! Perhaps
in a previous existence it was an editor. If the soul
of my grandam might haply inhabit a bird, the soul
of an editor—now he's done it ! . . ." She flew to
rescue the sheets that the Tatler had scattered on
the floor, while her mother put on large tortoise-
shell spectacles and knelt down to help.

" Don't you think," Mrs. Douglas said, when the
sheets had been rearranged in order, " that you'd
better read me what you've written ? "

Ann shook her head. " I think not. It's very
majestical and not quite true. You see, if you're
writing a *Life*, it's no good making a bald narrative
of it. One has to polish it up a bit for the sake
of posterity. I'm making you a very noble
character, I assure you. As old Mrs. Buchanan
said to me, after seeing me in some *tableaux vivants*,
' My, you were lovely. I didna ken ye.' The

children will be proud to think you were their grandmother."

Mrs. Douglas turned to take up her stocking, with a bored look.

" I wonder," she said, " that you can be bothered talking so much nonsense."

" I wonder, too," said Ann, " with the world in the state it is in. But I do agree, there is nothing so trying as a facetious person ! I wish I hadn't such high spirits. No wonder, Mother, that you are such a depressed wee body : to have had a husband and family who were always in uproarious spirits was enough to darken anybody's outlook on life. The first thing I remember about Glasgow is that you had a curly yellow coat and a sort of terra-cotta bonnet."

Mrs. Douglas's face lit up with a smile that made her look almost girlish. " That coat ! I do remember it well. It was ' old gold ' trimmed with plush of the same shade. My father bought it for me. I met him one day in Princes Street, and I must have looked very shabby, for he looked me up and down and said, ' Nell, surely the Sustentation Fund is very low,' and he took me into Jenner's, and got me that coat and bonnet. He got you a coat, too, and a delicious little astrakhan cap like a Cossack's. You were the prettiest thing in it, for your hair curled out under it like pure gold."

" I must have been a picturesque child," said Ann complacently, " for several times, you remember, artists asked me to sit for them." Then she laughed. " But I needn't boast about that, for my pride once got a severe fall. One day, at Etterick, we came on an artist (he turned out to be some one quite well known) sketching up the burnside. I obligingly posed myself in the foreground, and—he gave me sixpence to go away. *And I took it!*"

Mrs. Douglas smiled at the reminiscence, but her thoughts were still with the " old gold coat."

" It always pays to get a good thing. That coat wore and wore until everybody got tired of seeing me wear it, and it never really got very shabby—the bonnet, too."

" I suppose you would be about thirty," Ann said. " You said to us walking down to church one day that you were thirty, and then you said you would need to get a new bonnet. I looked at you and thought to myself : ' I shan't say it, but I'm quite sure it isn't worth while for Mother to get a new bonnet ; she *can't* live much longer.' I was shocked to hear that you had attained to such a great age, for I thought at thirty one was just toppling into the grave. Wasn't Glasgow a great change from Kirkcaple ? ' East is East and West is West, and never the twain shall meet.' "

" Oh, we hadn't much time to worry over East and West ; we had our work to do. We were very fortunate in getting a suitable house in a nice district. We might have been miles from a city in that road of decent grey houses, each in its own quiet garden. And the gardens all opened into an avenue of beautiful trees that had once been the entrance to the big house of the district. We couldn't have been more happily situated, and it was a comfortable house with good-sized rooms and—what your father specially prized—a well-placed staircase with shallow steps. It also contained what we had never had before, a basement flat ; but it wasn't as bad as it sounded, for the house was built on a slope, and the kitchen, though downstairs, was on a level with the garden."

" We children didn't mind the basement," said Ann ; " it was a joy to us, full of funny corners, excellent for hide-and-seek. One door had the legend *Dark Room* painted on it, and was an endless source of speculation. Could the former tenant have been a Nihilist ? or a murderer ? In the bright hours of the morning we liked to dally with those thoughts, but when the shadows lengthened we told each other that he was only a man who tried to develop his own negatives. We never felt in the least cabined or confined in Glasgow. It was a joke against me for long that when we first arrived I reproved Mark and Robbie for walking on the garden wall, saying, ' We must be very genteel now that we live in Glasgow.' "

" You didn't live up to that counsel of perfection, my dear. Anything less genteel than your behaviour ! One of the first things you and Mark did was to attend a wedding in the avenue—and when I say ' attend,' I mean you stood outside the gate of the house with a lot of other abandoned

children and shouted, ' Hard up ! ' when the bride
and bridegroom left without scattering pennies.
Jeanie Tod nearly wept with shame when she told
me of it."

"I remember Jeanie Tod," said Ann. "She
was small, but very determined. She had a brother
a sailor, and used to let me read his letters. One
of them described the writer riding in a rickshaw,
and finished : ' By Jingo, dear sister, you should
have seen your Brother that Day.' . . . It must
have been difficult for you, Mother, to leave
friendly Kirkcaple and go to a great city where
you knew almost no one. Weren't you lonely at
first ? "

"Never for a moment ; we just seemed to
tumble in among friends."

"The church people, you mean ? "

"Oh no—well, of course, they were friends—
very dear friends—but you need outside friends,
too. I found three very good ones waiting for
me in Glasgow."

"One was Mrs. Burnett ! " said Ann.

"Yes. Mrs. Burnett was my first friend. The
day we arrived in the avenue—we were next-door
neighbours—was the funeral day of her eldest
daughter. With most women that would have
been an excuse not to come near us for months,
but she came almost at once. She said that it
made a link between us, and that, in a way, our
coming helped a little to fill the blank left by the
dear daughter's death. Her kindness and interest

5

were very grateful to me, a stranger in a strange land, or, as Marget put it, 'a coo on an unco loan.' It was a great pleasure to run in for an hour to the Burnetts'; it was such a big, comfortable, perfectly kept house (the servants had been with them for twenty and thirty years, and had grown into Mrs. Burnett's dainty ways), and there was always a welcome awaiting one at any time."

"They had a splendid garden," said Ann, "with a swing and all manner of amusing things; and I think they really liked having children to tea. I remember their Hallow-e'en parties!"

"Mrs. Burnett looked like an abbess," Mrs. Douglas said. "She always wore a soft black dress—cashmere or silk—and a tiny white lace shawl turned back over her white hair. The style of dress suited her perfectly, for she was very tall and graceful, and glided rather than walked. I admired her very much, being so far from dignified myself, and I used to wonder how she kept so perfectly tidy and unruffled when I always looked as if I had been in the heart of a whirlwind."

"Oh, Mother!" laughed Ann, "just look at the difference in the two lives! Mrs. Burnett with her family grown up, a household running on well-oiled wheels, and a serenity partly natural and partly gained through long years' experience; you in the very forefront of the battle, with an incredibly wild and wicked family, a church to run, small means, and not an ounce of serenity anywhere in your little active body."

" Well, but now that I have leisure I'm not any more serene," Mrs. Douglas complained. " But it was comfort unspeakable just to see Mrs. Burnett, to know that she was near. We used to think that she sat and wondered what she would send us next, she loved so to give."

" I never smell a hyacinth," said Ann, " but I think of Mrs. Burnett. She always sent us the very first pot of hyacinths that came out in the greenhouse."

Mrs. Douglas nodded. " Mrs. Burnett would like to be remembered by spring flowers. She loved them as she loved all young things. Her one little grandson, Jimmie, was the same age as Davie. Her great regret when she was dying was that she wouldn't see the two boys grow up. Ah, but if she could have known—they didn't grow up very far. Jimmie was killed at the landing in Gallipoli, and Davie at Arras, when they were still only little boys."

" You have always been well off for friends, Mother," Ann said, breaking a silence. " In Inch-keld, in Kirkcaple, Glasgow. It's because you are such a friendly person yourself."

" Oh, me ! I often feel myself a poor creature, with little to give in return for treasure-houses opened to me."

Ann laughed unbelievingly and said, " I'm bound to admit we have had some wonderful friends— Miss Barbara Stewart for one. She was one of your three friends, wasn't she ? "

"Indeed she was! Miss Barbara—to say her name gives me a warm feeling at my heart."

"Miss Barbara," Ann repeated. "What a lot the name conjures up! I don't know any one who made more of life. She might have been a lonely, soured old woman, for she was the very last of her family, wasn't she? but to the great family of the poor and the afflicted she said, ' You are my brothers and my sisters.' I wonder how many men in Glasgow owe their start in life to Miss Barbara? I wonder how many lonely women died blessing her that it was their own and not a workhouse roof that covered them at the end? I wonder how many betrayed souls sinking hopelessly into hell had a succouring hand held out to them by that sharp-tongued spinster? How did you know Miss Barbara so well? She didn't belong to the church."

"Not in our time, but all her people had belonged. Miss Barbara had gone to the other side of Glasgow, and it was too far for her to come. She always took a great interest; but what good work was she not interested in? She sat there in her vast, early-Victorian dining-room, wrapped in innumerable shawls and woolly coats, for she suspected draughts from every quarter, a tall woman, broadly made, with a large, strong face. What would I not give now to go into that room and see those whimsical, shrewd, kind eyes, and feel the wealth of welcome in those big soft hands as she rose to greet me, with shawls falling from her like leaves in Vallombrosa. She generally received me with abuse. ' What d'you mean by coming out on such a day? You'll go home with a chill and bother your poor family by lying in bed. Here—see—sit down in that chair and hold the soles of your boots to the fire,' all the time doing things for one's comfort, ringing for tea to be brought in, kneeling down to make fresh toast. She hated to trouble any one; it was almost an obsession with her, the desire not to be a nuisance. She had a very aged cook, who had been in the Stewart family all her life, and it was said that Miss Barbara, herself nearly eighty, got up every morning and carried tea to her before she would let her rise to her duties."

"Dear Miss Barbara," Ann said, stroking the Tatler's smoke-grey fur, "she wasn't only good, she was delightfully funny. Her passion for cats!— not for well-fed, comfortable cats, but for poor, lean, homeless ones. She used to send me into a butcher's shop to buy a quarter of a pound of mince-collops, and then down area steps carrying it (the horrid stuff oozing clammily through the paper) after some terrified animal that fled from me, paying no attention to my blandishments. She was utterly unlike the ordinary rich old woman, flattered and kotowed to for her money until she thinks she isn't made of ordinary clay. I don't think Miss Barbara ever gave a thought to herself; she hadn't time, she was so busy looking after other people."

"In her youth," said Mrs. Douglas, "Miss Barbara was a great worker in the slums of Glasgow, but when I knew her she wasn't able for that, and people had to go to her. The clergy waited on her by the dozen, and every one else who wanted money for good works, not to speak of many who were mere cranks and charlatans. Every one who came was admitted, and Miss Barbara wouldn't have listened to a word against any of them."

"No," said Ann; "she would have said with Falstaff, 'Tush, man, mortal men, mortal men'; or, rather, she wouldn't, for she had probably never heard of Falstaff, and thought that any one who could read Shakespeare for pleasure was eccentric almost to madness. If you told her of a book you had enjoyed, she would say, 'Is it true? No? Well, then——' But every one who went to No. 10 got a hearing."

"Every one got a hearing," said Mrs. Douglas, "and whatever else they got, you may be sure a good tea was never wanting. Many a tired and hungry voyager on life's ocean found sanctuary at No. 10. You remember when I had that bad breakdown, and you were all worn out with me, how Miss Barbara took me to No. 10 and coaxed and scolded me back to health! And I was too miserably ill and weak even to pretend gratitude, and, driving with her, I used to envy all the happy people walking on their own feet, and one day she said to me, with an amused twinkle in her eyes, 'Ay, and you never thought to pity the poor folk in their carriages before.'"

"I think she was funniest at Etterick," said Ann. "She kept regretting all the time the street lamps and pavements, and the sight of Tweed winding in links through the glens vexed her practical soul. ' What a waste ! ' she said ; ' couldn't it be cut straight like a canal ? ' Father's face ! How Miss Barbara would have hated the Green Glen ! " She jumped up to open the door for the Tatler. " He's tired of us. He wants to try Marget and Mysie. Who was your third great friend, Mother ? You had so many. I'm interested to know which you considered your greatest."

" Mrs. Lang."

" Oh, of course—Mrs. Lang. She's been dead for a long time now."

Mrs. Douglas sighed. " Nearly all my friends are dead."

" Because," said Ann, " you always liked old people best, and made your friends among women much older than yourself. And now you mourn and say your friends are nearly all gone, and talk about the elect being gathered in—but, elect or not, people are apt to be gathered in if they are over eighty."

Mrs. Douglas sighed more deeply, and, ignoring her daughter's bracing remarks, said, " I can't care for new friends as I cared for the old ; they can't go back with me. I'm not interested in their talk. . . . Mrs. Lang was a very good friend to me at my busiest time. What a capable woman she was. There was nothing she couldn't do with her hands. When the boys went to Oxford she practically made their outfits, and made them beautifully. She used to say that it was a kindness to let her help, for she had had such a busy life, she simply couldn't rest. I know now what she meant."

"I remember Mrs. Lang very well," Ann said—"a stately woman who rocked a little when she walked. She had crinkly white hair parted in the middle, and keen, blue eyes in a fresh-coloured face. I always think of her as dressed in a sealskin mantle trimmed with skunk and a Mary Stuart bonnet."

Mrs. Douglas laid down her stocking. "Yes. I remember her best like that. I did like to see her come rocking in at the gate, though sometimes I was a little afraid of her. Your father used to say she was a typical Scotswoman of the old school—a type that has almost disappeared. There wasn't a trace of sickly sentiment about her. She was a stern, God-fearing woman, with a strong brain and a big heart and an unbending will. She lived to be nearly ninety, and to the end her mind was as clear as a bell. In the last letter she wrote to me: 'I go out for a walk every day, no matter what the weather is, and I am twice in church every Sabbath.'"

"Didn't Mrs. Lang come from Fife?" Ann asked. "I know there was always an east windy tang about her! She had nothing of the soft, couthy Glasgow manner. I was really very scared of her. When she discovered me hopelessly ignorant (as she was always doing) about something she thought I should have known all about, like jam-making, she had a way of saying: 'You amuse me very much,' which was utterly crushing. And she was very much given to contradicting people flat, generally prefacing her remarks with ' You will *pardon me* ! ' delivered like a sledge-hammer. Well, it's too late to write anything to-night. Marget and Mysie will be in for prayers in a few minutes, and I've an interesting book to finish. To-morrow I shall add another stone to the noble pile I am raising to you —but, no, it can't be to-morrow. To-morrow I go to Birkshaw for two nights. Mother, why did I say I would go ? I can't bear to leave Dreams for two whole nights."

CHAPTER XIII

FOR two days it was as if an enchantment had been thrown over Dreams, so great a quiet held the house. Marget and Mysie went about their work hardly speaking at all; Mrs. Douglas sat alone with her stocking and her books of devotion; the Tatler slept for hours together on chairs that he knew well were prohibited; the very fire did not crackle, but lay in a deep glow; the wind was hushed, and moved softly round the white-faced house among the heather.

The enchantment lifted when the pony-cart bringing Ann back was seen coming up the hill. Mrs. Douglas at once began to pile the fire high with logs and coal; the Tatler, as if aware of an impending upheaval, awoke, stretched himself, and stalked out of the room, while in the kitchen Mysie flew to make hot toast and Marget gave a final polish to the already glittering silver.

"Hear till her," Marget said to Mysie, with a broad grin on her face, as Ann's voice was heard greeting her mother.

"She was aye like that; aye lauchin', an' aye

fu' o' impudence, the cratur! It's like a death in the hoose when she's oot o't. Awa' ben wi' the tea, Mysie woman; she'll want it afore she tak's off her things."

"Well," said Mrs. Douglas, some time later, "it is good to have you back."

She had got her "reading" over early, the pile of books was put away, and she was ready to listen to Ann's news.

"After two days!" said Ann, "you remind me of Davie when he was once in bed with a bilious turn till lunch-time. The moment he got up he rushed to the window and said, with a gasp of thankfulness, 'It's good to see the green grass again.' You must have enjoyed the rest from my long tongue. I needn't ask if any one called."

"Mr. Sharp came to tea with me yesterday."

"Did he? Good man! You've got a very attentive pastor, Motherkin."

"Yes," Mrs. Douglas agreed. "I must say I'm fond of that young man, though he does read his sermons and his theology isn't as sound as I would like. We had such a nice talk, and he told me all about his people. They are evidently not at all well off, and he says they had a great business getting the Manse furnished. But everything is paid for. His father and mother are coming to visit him about New Year time. We must try in every way we can to make their visit enjoyable. He is so young, and there is something very innocent about him—he reminds me a little of Davie."

" And were you favoured with much of Marget's conversation ? " Ann asked.

" Oh yes. She came in and out ; but Marget is very dull when you are away. She used to say, when you were all at Etterick and the house was peaceful and the work light, ' It's a queer thing : I like faur better when oor bairns are a' at hame.' Well, and was Birkshaw nice ? Tell me all about it."

Ann had seated herself on her favourite stool in front of the fire, and she now turned round facing her mother, and nodded happily.

" Birkshaw was very nice, and the Miss Scotts are exactly the kind of hostesses I thought they would be. When I saw my room I was sure of it. Some people's spare rooms are just free-coups full of pictures that nobody else will allow in their rooms, chairs that are too hard for anything but a guest to sit on, books that no one can read. And in these spare rooms you generally find a corner of the wardrobe reserved for somebody's parasols, and a fur coat in camphor occupies the only really good drawer. My room at Birkshaw was a treasure. There was a delicious old four-post bed, with a little valance of chintz round the top, and all the rest of the furniture in keeping. A nosegay on the dressing-table, a comfortable couch drawn up to a blazing fire, a table with a pile of most readable-looking books, and absolutely unencumbered drawers. There were only three other people staying in the house—a man and his daughter—Barnes was the name—English. Mr. Barnes was very sprightly, and looked about fifty, and so, oddly enough, did his daughter. Either she looked very old for her age or her father looked much too young for his. She was a dull little lady with protruding eyes and unbecoming clothes, and she appeared to me rather to have given up the unequal contest. I have noticed — haven't you ? — that very vivacious parents have often depressed offspring, and vice versa. Mr. Barnes, though English, was a great lover of Scotland, and an ardent Jacobite. He confused me a good deal by talking about Charles III. I found him very interesting, but I had the feeling that he thought poorly of my intelligence. And, of course," Ann finished cheerfully, " I am almost entirely illiterate."

Mrs. Douglas looked mildly indignant. " Ann, when I think of the money spent on your education——"

" Oh, you spent money all right, but no one could make me learn when I didn't want to. I don't know whether I was naturally stupid, or whether it was sheer wickedness, but, anyway, it doesn't matter now, except that intelligent people are bored with me sometimes——"

" Who was the other person staying at Birkshaw ? Didn't you say there were three ? "

" Yes, a bachelor nephew of the Miss Scotts'— Mr. Philip Scott."

" Young ? "

Ann screwed her face. " Youngish. Forty or

thereabouts—forty-five, I should think. Oh yes, because he told me he was thirty-eight when the war came. He looked quite young because he was slim, and he wasn't bald ; rather a good-looking man."

" Did you like him ?   Was he nice ? "

Ann laughed as if at the remembrance of something pleasant.

" Oh yes, I liked him.   He was very companionable, and it turned out we had a good many friends in common. The Miss Scotts are extraordinarily good company. There is no need to make conversation at Birkshaw ; the talk was so entertaining that we sat an unconscionable time over our meals. And they never worry you to do things. If you prefer an armchair by the fire and a book—well and good. You know how I hate visiting, as a rule, but I really did enjoy my two nights away, and I learned a lot about gardening."

" Did you wear your new frock ? " Mrs. Douglas asked.

" Oh yes. You were quite right to advise me to take it. You never know about people now. Some have never got over war-habits and still wear sort of half-and-half things in the evening—rather tired-looking afternoon dresses or jumpers ; but the Miss Scotts came down charming in lace and jewels and beautifully done hair. I do like that. Heaviest of tweeds and thick boots in the daytime, but in the evening perfect in every detail—so I was glad I had a pretty fresh frock to do them honour."

Ann stretched out her feet to the blazing fire. "But it's fine to be back in this dear room, wearing slippers not quite in their first youth, and a dress that no amount of lounging will hurt. Birkshaw doesn't come up to Dreams, though it is several centuries older, and at least three times bigger and full of priceless treasures in the way of pictures and furniture and books——"

Ann stopped to laugh at her own absurdity, and her mother said, "You're like your father, child. He never saw anything to equal his own house. He didn't know the meaning of envy——"

"Ah, but I'm not like that. Envy! I'm some-times chock-full of it——"

The door opened and Marget came in. She was primed with an excuse for her appearance, but Ann didn't give her time to make it.

"Come away, Marget, and hear all about Birk-shaw, and tell me what has been happening since I went away. I've just been saying to Mother that I'm very glad to be back."

Ann pulled forward a chair, which Marget accepted primly.

"I daresay ye are. We 'gree fine, the fower o' us."

"And yet, Marget," said Ann, "I have just been reading a book by a very clever woman in which she says that women cannot live together with any profit. They fester. That is the ugly expression she uses."

Marget gave a disgusted snort. "Mebbe thae

saft scented weemen, aggravatin' and clawin' at each other like cats, no' weemen wi' self-respect an' wark to do. A' the same, I'm no' sayin' I'll no' be glad when Maister Jimmie comes hame. I like a man aboot the house. It's kin' o' hertless work cookin' for weemen; hauf the time they're no' heedin' what they're eatin'."

"Ah, Marget," said her mistress, "it's not like the days when the boys were all home from school and you couldn't make a pudding big enough."

Marget shook her head sadly. "It is not, Mem," she said, and then, turning suddenly to Ann, she asked, "Hoo's the *Life* gettin' on?"

Ann jumped up and went to the writing-table. "That reminds me I've no business to be sitting roasting my face at the fire when I haven't written a word for nights."

She found a notebook and pencil and came back to the fireside. "The Moncrieffs will be on us before we are half finished. We've got to Glasgow, Marget. Tell me your first impression of that great city."

Marget sat forward with one hand on each knee.

"Eh, I thocht it was an awfu' place. D'ye mind, Mem, thon day you took me awa' into Argyle Street to see the 'Poly'—a place mair like a toun than a shop? I was fair fear't."

Mrs. Douglas, picking up a stitch, stopped to laugh.

"That was a great day, Marget. You suddenly found yourself looking into a long mirror, and you turned to me and said, ' Eh, I say—there's a wumman awfu' like ma sister.' "

" Didn't you know yourself, Marget ? " Ann asked.

" No' me. I had never seen the whole o' masel' afore, an' how was I to ken I was sic a queer-lookin' body ? "

" I know," said Ann. " I've had some shocks myself." She turned to her mother. " I always sympathized with Trudi in *The Benefactress* when she looked into a mirror and was disgusted to find that she wasn't looking as pretty as she felt. But, Marget, what else struck you besides the size of the ' Poly ' and its mirrors ? "

Marget was chuckling to herself. " I aye mind how affrontit I was in the ' Poly.' I wanted to buy something, but the only thing I could mind I wanted was a yaird o' hat elastic. A young man, like a lord, leaned over the counter and says, ' What can I do for you, Madam ? ' "

Here Marget became convulsed with laughter, and had to wipe her eyes before going on. " ' Aw,' says I, ' a yaird o' hat elastic,' an' says he, ' One penny, Madam.' I thocht fair shame to see a braw man like that servin' me wi' hat elastic. I telt the mistress I wadna gang back there till I needed a new goon or something wise-like. Ay, there was a heap o' queer things in Glasgae that we hadna in Kirkcaple, but I likit it fine. We a' settled doon rale comfortable, an' a'body that cam' to Glasgae frae Kirkcaple cam' to oor kirk, so we never felt far frae hame. Oh, I likit Glasgae rale weel when once I fund ma way aboot."

" It's odd," said Ann, " to think of Glasgow as the ' Scottish Oxford ' of the seventeenth-century traveller. How pretty it must have been, with gardens going down to the Clyde, a college in the High Street, an old cathedral on a hill overlooking the city, and with so clear an air that a mountain called ' Ben Lomond ' could be seen by the shop-keepers of King Street. Alack-a-day ! the green places have been laid waste. . . . Mother, do you remember on winter nights as we sat round the fire how we sometimes used to hear men calling ' Call-er oy-sters ' ? That is the most vivid re-collection that has remained with me of those Glasgow days—a November evening with a touch of the fog that frost was apt to bring, a clear fire burning in the nursery grate, books and games scattered about, and through the misty stillness outside the cry, ' Call-er oy-sters.' I used to lift a corner of the blind to look out, wondering if I would see some wandering sailor-man with a pokeful of oysters on his back—but there was nothing, nothing but the strangely mournful cry."

" Glasgae folk," said Marget, who had not been listening, but thinking her own thoughts, " are awfu' easy to ken and rale nice, but they're no' so hospitable as they get the name for bein'."

" Why, Marget," cried Mrs. Douglas, astonished, " Glasgow people are considered the very essence of hospitality."

Marget set her mouth obstinately. "Weel, Mem, it's mebbe as you say, but I've sat whole nichts in their hooses an' they never so much as said to me, 'Collie, wull ye lick?' When ye went into a hoose at Kirkcaple the first thing they did was to pit on the kettle. Glasgae folk made a great fuss aboot ye, but they're no' great at offerin' ye meat."

"This," said Ann, sharpening a pencil, "is quite a new light on Glasgow people. They are accused of many things, but seldom of inhospitality."

"Well, I must say," said Mrs. Douglas, "that I missed in Glasgow the constant interchange of hospitality that we had in Kirkcaple. For instance, when your father exchanged with another minister it was always a question of staying the week-end; and, if the minister who came to help at the Communion was a friend, his wife (if he had one) was always invited with him. And then we had endless parties, and people dropping in casually all the time, as is the friendly country way. In a big city everything is different. Ministers came to preach, but we only saw them for a few minutes in the vestry; they had no time to come out to us for a meal. Everything was a rush; we had all so much to do that there was little coming and going between the different ministers' wives. Almost our only meeting-place was the house in which the Clerical Club was held once a month, when papers were read and we had tea."

"I liked when the Club was at our house," said Ann, "but I thought ministers had very poor taste in jokes : they laughed so much at such very poor ones. I remember one facetious minister saying to me, ' It would be a grand job ours if it weren't for the Sabbaths,' and looked startled when I cordially agreed with him. To a child of twelve the writing of sermons does seem a waste of time. But, Mother, you knew lots of ministers' wives in Glasgow. Why, Mr. Johnston is still a bosom friend of yours. Oh, do you remember how you used to tease Father by holding up Mr. Johnston as an example of what every minister should be ? "

" I didn't mean it ; your father knew that very well, and he didn't care a scrap who was held up to him—but I wish now I hadn't done it. But the Johnstons were really the most exemplary couple in every way, almost provoking in their perfection. Their church was quite near Martyrs, and their house was quite near ours, and we were very good friends ; but sometimes I couldn't help being envious a little. In Inchkeld and Kirkcaple we had had prosperous, well-attended churches, but in Glasgow that was changed. Our new field, so to speak, was a difficult one. Martyrs was in the heart of the town, in a district full of Jews and Roman Catholics, which meant that we had a very small population to draw from, and most of our people came from distant suburbs. When we came to Glasgow, Martyrs was known as ' the scrapit kirk ' because of its white, unpainted seats. No hymn had ever been sung in it ; rarely, if ever, a paraphrase. A precentor in a box led the people in the Psalms of David. Everything was as it had been for the last hundred years. The congregation looked a mere handful in the great church, and I must say I quailed in spirit when I saw the wilderness of empty seats."

"Jeanie Tod, the nursemaid," said Ann, "always let me read not only the letters she received, but the letters she wrote, and in one I read: 'The church is very *toom*, but Mr. Douglas will soon fill it.' It was indeed *toom*, but every Sunday we expected quite suddenly it would fill up and we would go in and find a crowd. It did fill up a little, didn't it, Mother?"

"Oh yes, a lot of new people came; but it was never anything like full. Mr. Johnston, with the very same difficulties to contend with, had his filled to overflowing. He was a splendid organizer, and very wise and prudent; and his wife was just as good in her own way. She was a miracle for cutting-out—I was no good at that—and her sewing-classes and Mothers' Meetings, and indeed everything she attempted, were the best in the district, and she was so pretty and neat that it was a pleasure to look at her. If I held Mr. Johnston up to your father, I held Mrs. Johnston up to myself."

"But Father worked just as hard as Mr. Johnston," Ann said.

"Oh yes, but he hadn't Mr. Johnston's business capacity. He was the despair of those who look for the reality of things in minute-books and financial statements. A small audience never troubled him. Every one was there that the message was meant for, he sometimes told me. For what the world calls success he never craved. I could see that it was fine, but it was rather annoying, too."

Ann laughed, and Marget said reminiscently, " It was a braw kirk when we got it a' pentit and the seats widened, and a choir and organ and hymns . . ."

"Yes," said Mrs. Douglas; "gradually the service was brought into line with present-day ideas. I confess I was rather sorry, and your father would have been very pleased to leave it as it was. He infinitely preferred the Psalms of David to mere ' human ' hymns."

"I should think so," said Ann. "Imagine singing a chirrupy hymn when one might sing ' O thou, my soul, bless God the Lord,' to the tune of ' French.' "

"'Deed," said Marget, "a buddy never gets tired o' the psalms; they're wonderfu' comfortin', but some o' the hymns are ower bairnly even for bairns. I've a fair ill-will at that yin aboot ' What can little eyes do? ' but I like fine to sing ' There is a happy land far, far away.' We aye sung that on Sabbath nichts when ye were a' wee."

"There's a lot in association," Ann said. "Words you have loved as a child have always a glamour over them. I liked the sound of the

psalms, but I got dreadfully tied up in the hymns.
I always sang :

> ' Can a woman's tender care
> Cease towards the child she-bear ? '

with the picture in my mind of a dear fubsey
bear being petted. D'you remember Robbie
always chose hymns that mentioned Satan ? "

"Aye," Marget said seriously. " Puir Maister
Robbie had aye an awfu' wark wi' Satan when he
was a wee laddie."

Ann laughed, and, getting up from the fender-
stool, went over to the bureau.

"Mother," she said, " I promised to ask Mr.
Scott over to see our funny little house. Would
luncheon on Thursday be a suitable sort of time ? "

CHAPTER XIV

ANN had been writing steadily for nearly an hour.

Her mother, watching her, said :

" I'm afraid, if you write so hard, your brain will go."

Ann, as if glad of the interruption, laid her pen in a china dish, pushed away the sheets of paper, sighed deeply, and, rising, came over to the fire.

" I know it will," she said. " I can feel it doing it. It's that old *Life* of yours—I can't make it sound right. Sir Walter Raleigh talks somewhere of men whose true selves are almost completely obscured beneath their ragged and incompetent speech. I'm afraid I'm concealing you completely under my ' ragged and incompetent ' words. If you live to be ninety, as you threaten, it will be all right ; the children will be able to make their own estimate, but, if they have to depend on my *Life*, I don't quite know what they'll make of you."

Ann began to laugh in a helpless way. " It's funny. I know so well what impression I want to give, but when I try to write it down it's just nothing—stilted, meaningless sentences. I want to make a picture of Dr. Struthers. I've been trying for the last hour, labouring in rowing, covering my brow with wrinkles, with no result. How would you describe him?"

Mrs. Douglas thought for a minute. "It would be difficult to make a true picture of him. If you simply told of the views that were his, how he wouldn't sing a paraphrase, let alone a hymn, and held the Sabbath day as something that must not be broken, you would give an impression of narrowness and rigid conservatism that wouldn't at all be the Dr. Struthers that we knew. When we heard that the Glasgow church had a senior minister, we thought it was a drawback; your father rather wondered how he would comport himself as a 'colleague and successor,' but we didn't know Dr. Struthers then. Sometimes, in Glasgow, when we were inclined to regret Kirkcaple and the flourishing congregation, and the peaceful time we enjoyed there—but when I say peaceful I mean only comparatively; no minister's wife ever attains to peace in this world!—your father would say, 'But if we had stayed in Kirkcaple we would never have known Dr. Struthers,' and that closed the matter. When I first met him I thought he was more like some fresh, hearty old country laird than a parson. But he was really very frail, and to walk even a short distance was a great effort. He had a place about fifty miles from Glasgow,

Langlands, and as long as he was able he came to preach in Martyrs about once a month. The old congregation adored to have him come, but the new-comers, who had no romance about the old man, thought his sermons much too long. And they were too long as sermons go now. We are not the patient listeners our forefathers were. Dr. Struthers once said to me that no man could do justice to a subject under fifty-five minutes, and we used sometimes to think that he was done before his allotted time, but he just went on."

"We children dearly loved Dr. Struthers," said Ann; "but we did not appreciate the length of his sermons. My friend, Mrs. Smail—the butcher's wife, you remember?—used to sit with a most forlorn face while he preached; thinking, I expect, that she would be half an hour late, and that the numerous young Smails would have fallen in the fire. Dear me, it's a long time since I thought of Mrs. Smail. I liked her very much. There was a sort of bond of sympathy between us, and she invited me sometimes to tea-parties where we got tea and cookies and penny cakes and hot roast beef. I never learned to appreciate the combination, but the rest of the company seemed to enjoy it. I sat beside one gentleman who, after doing full justice to the meal, wiped his forehead with a red silk handkerchief, and, turning to me, said, 'A grand house this for flesh.' After the 'flesh' we all contributed songs and recitations—great evenings. Well, what I mean to say is that Mrs.

Smail represented the new people who were impatient of Dr. Struthers and impatient of all the old traditions of the church which the original members clung to with such pathetic loyalty."

" But in time," said Mrs. Douglas, " the newcomers got to see how very fine the old man was, and everybody was sorry when he got too frail to preach. It was quite extraordinary how fond you children were of him, for he never told you stories or played with you."

" No," said Ann thoughtfully, " he never did anything to make himself popular. We didn't expect it any more than we would have expected a god from Mount Olympus to jest with a mortal. They say we needs must love the highest when we see it, but that isn't true ; often the highest simply irritates. I think it was his simple goodness that made us fond of him, and a certain understanding and sympathy that he had for bad children. And he never talked down to us or became facetious."

Mrs. Douglas nodded. " I know. Children like to be taken seriously, and Dr. Struthers was certainly not given to making fun of them."

Ann clasped her hands round her knees and looked into the fire.

" One thing we liked about the Glasgow Sundays was that we stayed down in the vestry for lunch. It was our weekly picnic, and the fact that it was eaten in the church premises gave a touch of solemnity to the occasion. When Dr. Struthers was preaching, we had a more elaborate meal. Strong beef-tea was made at home and brought down in a bottle to be heated, for he was often very exhausted after preaching. One never-to-be-forgotten day I was told to watch the pan of beef-tea heating, and I had evidently begun to dream, for the pan fell into the fire and the contents were lost. I felt as badly about it as any of you, but I only made a sulky face. I knew it was a real deprivation for the old man, though he made light of it, and said cocoa would be a nice change, and I felt very unhappy all through lunch. There was a particularly fine orange among some apples on a plate, and you asked Dr. Struthers to take it, but he looked across at my small sullen face and said, with that most delightful smile of his, ' I think we must give this orange to Ann.' I never forgot the way he did it; the ' pretty and sweet manner ' of it quite conquered me and made me far sorrier for my carelessness than any scolding would have done. I don't believe scoldings ever do any good, only harm."

" Some children," said Mrs. Douglas, " are the better of scoldings. Mark always ' took a telling,' but the more you and Robbie were scolded, the worse you got. . . . Generally Dr. Struthers stayed with his daughter, but now and again he stayed with us. We liked having him, but it made rather an upheaval in our modest establishment. You see, he had to bring his man, Samuel Thomson, with him, and Samuel Thomson was such a

very superior, silver-haired, apple-cheeked gentleman's gentleman, we could hardly ask him to take
his meals in the kitchen, so the boys' study had
to be given up to him. Davie was very fond of
sitting with him, and I once overheard Samuel
Thomson reading aloud to him from the Bible
some Old Testament story, and commenting on
what he read. ' Those were grand angels, Master
David,' he was saying. It was the time when
Davie cared for nothing but to be like a jockey."

" ' Angels ! ' he said, ' I thought you were
talking about horses,' and he straddled away in
deep disgust."

Ann laughed. " Davie was very much against
all things religious at that time, and he wouldn't
even say his prayers. Marget use to toil up
from the kitchen to reason with him, and when he
heard her coming he would give a wicked wallop
in his bed and say, ' That's Marget comin' to convert
me.' You know, Mother, in some ways Davie
was a much more abandoned character than we
were as children. We reverenced the Covenanters,
but Davie said he preferred Claverhouse, and
most blasphemously said of John Brown, of
Priesthill—he must have got the expression from
Marget—' I think John Brown was a *gey lawd*.'
Speaking of conversion, I think Dr. Struthers was
the only person we didn't mind ' speaking personally ' to us. We realized that he, like Nehemiah,
' feared the Lord above many.' When Mark
told him he meant to go to Oxford and then

to the Bar, he said, ' Look higher than the Wool-
sack, Mark.'   He spoke kindly to Jeanie Tod
about her home in Kirkcaple, and said, ' Do you
ever think where you are going ? ' and I shall
always remember how one day he laid his big
soft hand on my unruly head and said, ' Little
Ann, *take Jesus*.'   Do you remember one day
when he was preaching I announced that I had a
sore throat and couldn't possibly go to church,
and was allowed to remain at home ?   Dr.
Struthers missed me, and asked why I wasn't
there, and you—not greatly believing, I daresay,
in the excuse—said I had a sore throat.   Mark
rushed home between services to tell me that
Dr. Struthers had prayed for me in church,
prayed that my bodily affliction might pass from
me !   Guiltily aware of perfect health—my sore
throat hadn't kept me from eating apples and
reading a story-book—I didn't know what awful
consequences the prayer might have.   Anyway,
I flew upstairs, flung on my coat and hat, and was
in my place for the afternoon service, determined
to ward off any more petitions on my behalf.
But I was never frightened for Dr. Struthers
after I found he liked adventure books and didn't
even mind the swear words.   He was surely a very
rich man, Mother ?   Ministers don't as a rule
have places like Langlands, and man-servants
and maid-servants.   A house and a wife, and
a stranger within the gates, are about all they
ever attain to.''

" Yes, he was rich, but I never met any one who gave one so little an impression of great possessions. Having his treasure laid up where thieves cannot break through and steal, he cared little for the gold of this world. He gave largely, but so unobtrusively that it wasn't until his death that we realized the extent of his givings. He was the humblest of men, lowly and a peace-maker."

" Once," said Ann, " Robbie and Jim and I went from Etterick to spend the day at Langlands. It was after Mrs. Struthers died, and Miss Calder kept house. I somehow think we weren't ex-pected. There was something queer about it, anyway, and Miss Calder, although she was kind, as she always was, looked very worried. She had some engagement in the village that morning, so she sent us up the hill to play till luncheon. We went obediently up the hill, but as soon as we saw Miss Calder walk down the avenue, back we pranced. Samuel Thomson saw us, and, con-ducting us to the croquet lawn, advised us to have a game. He helped us to put out the hoops, and we began to play. Unfortunately Robbie and I soon fell into a discussion about the right and wrong way to play, and I regret to say I kicked Robbie, who at once retaliated, and the next thing the horrified eyes of Samuel Thomson saw was Robbie and me hitting one another with croquet mallets. It was only the beginning of a thoroughly ill-spent day, and if Dr. Struthers

and Miss Calder hadn't been the most patient
and forgiving of people we would never have been
asked back."

"It was odd," said Mrs. Douglas; "but you
and Robbie could never behave properly if you
were together. I wonder I was so rash as to let
you go away for a whole day, and to Langlands
of all places. Its beautiful tidiness seemed to act
on you in a pernicious way. It was always a treat
to me to go to Langlands. I enjoyed the beauty
and the peace of it, and it seemed exactly the right
setting for Dr. Struthers. I was thankful that,
when the end came, it came at Langlands, suddenly,
painlessly, and most fittingly on the Sabbath day.
'I am going,' he said to Samuel Thomson, and
in a minute he was gone, almost 'translated
unaware.'"

"What a beautiful way to die," said Ann.
"His task accomplished and the long day done.
Without weariness of waiting, with no pain of
parting, suddenly to find his boat in the harbour
and to see his Pilot face to face."

CHAPTER XV

THE arrival of the post was almost the only excitement at Dreams, and on the days that the Indian and South African mails came, Mrs. Douglas could do nothing but pore over the precious letters. She pounced on them when they arrived, and read them anxiously; after luncheon she read them again, and in the evening she read them aloud in case she or Ann had missed a word.

One evening she sat with a pile of letters on her lap, her large tortoise-shell spectacles on the top of the pile, and said, with a satisfied sigh:

"This has been a good day—news from all quarters. I am glad Jim is having this tour. He does love to see the world, and to be able to combine business and pleasure makes a holiday ideal. Charlotte and Mark seem to be enjoying their trip greatly, but I can see Charlotte's thoughts are always with the children. She says she knows they won't be missing her, but I think she is wrong. I daresay they are quite happy, but they must feel a lack. Charlotte has such pretty ways with her children, and I think they realize that they have got rather a special mother, though Rory says, 'Poor Mummy's English, but we're Scots.' I do wonder, Ann, when Rory is going to begin to write better. This letter is a disgrace, both in writing and spelling, and his school report said that he cared for nothing but cricket and food."

"What does it matter, Mother?" said Ann comfortably; "he is only nine. I'm glad he isn't precocious, and I like his staggering little letters. He said to me once, 'P'r'aps you notice that I always say the same thing in my letters?' I said that I had noticed a certain lack of variety in his statements, and he explained, 'You see, those are the only words I can spell, and I don't like to ask people.' It isn't in the least that he lacks brains. He knows all sorts of things outside his ordinary lessons: about the ways of birds and beasts you can't fickle him; and he reads a lot and has his own ideas about things. He hates Oliver Cromwell and all his works. One day at table some one mentioned that great man, and Rory's face got pink all over, and he said, 'I hate him, the sieve-headed brute.' It was funny to see Mark, whose admiration for Oliver Cromwell is unbounded, surveying his small son. A more unjust accusation was never made, but Rory is a born Royalist."

Mrs. Douglas shook her head. "He ought to write better than he does. I don't think children are taught properly now. Have they copy-books?

I used to write copperplate ; indeed, I got a prize for writing."

" I know," said Ann, " and one for spelling, and one for dictation, and one for composition, and one for French. You used to reel them off to me when I came home without a single one. The only prize I got was for needlework, and I fear it was more by way of a consolation prize than anything else. No wonder I feel for poor old Rory. Alis is more of your school of thought ; she is a clever child."

Mrs. Douglas refused to be optimistic. " Alis picks things up almost too easily. I'm afraid she will be a Jack-of-all-trades. Did you read Nannie's letter ? Rob and Davie seem to be thriving. Charlotte will find a great difference in the little pair." Mrs. Douglas put on her spectacles and took up a letter to read extracts, but Ann caught her hand.

" Not now, Mother, please ; we must talk of Glasgow now. I want to finish your *Life* this week and get begun to my Christmas presents. You'll read the letters to us when Marget and Mysie come in to prayers. . . . I wish you would give me your advice, for, after all, it is your affair. So far I have drawn your portrait as a very efficient, very painstaking, and, I fear, very dull minister's wife. You see, that side of you is so easy to draw. But the other side is so much more *you*. If I could only write about you as I remember you at home with us, anxiously doing your best for every one, slaving away with Sales of Work and Mothers' Meetings, incorrigibly hospitable, pretending deep and abiding pessimism, but liable at any moment to break into bursts of delightful nonsense and rash talking—the person who never talks rashly is a weariness to the flesh—a most excellent mimic—when you came in from visiting, you made us see the people you had been seeing— with a rare talent for living . . ."

Mrs. Douglas laid down her stocking and gasped at her daughter :

"*Ann!* I don't know what you mean. There never was a more ordinary woman, and if you try to make me anything else, you are simply romancing. I'm sure you have always said that you would know me for a minister's wife a mile away."

"In appearance, my dear lady, you are a typical minister's wife, but your conversation is often a pleasing surprise. And, oh! surely, Mother, all ministers' wives don't behave to congregations as you did. *Given to hospitality* should be your epitaph. I remember when we left Glasgow, Mrs. Nicol, bemoaning to me your going away, said, ' Well, we'll never get another like her. Who else would have bothered to have me and my wild boys in her house ? ' and I, remembering John and Mackenzie, could have echoed, ' *Who, indeed ?* ' "

Mrs. Douglas was about to speak, but Ann hurried on :

"No, Mother, don't defend them. You can't

have forgotten that black day when the Nicol
family arrived to spend the afternoon—John and
Mackenzie ripe for any wickedness. The house
had just been spring cleaned, and was spotless,
and those two boys went through it like an army
with banners. It was wet, and they couldn't go
out to the garden, and they scoffed at the very
idea of looking at picture-books. They slid down
the banisters, they tobogganed down the white
enamelled stairs, they kicked the paint off the
doors. They broke Davie's cherished air-gun, and
their mother, instead of rebuking them, seemed to
admire their high spirits. Utterly worn-out, I left
them to work their wicked will in the box-room—I
thought they would be comparatively harmless there;
but presently we smelt burning, and found them in
your bedroom with the towel-horse on fire. No man
knows how they accomplished it, for a towel-horse
isn't a particularly inflammable thing, but if I hadn't
managed to throw it out of the window, I believe
the house might have been burned down."

Mrs. Douglas laughed, and told her daughter
not to exaggerate.

" Mrs. Nicol was a particularly nice woman, and
there was nothing wrong with John and Mackenzie
except high spirits. Mackenzie came to see us at
Priorsford—I think you must have been away from
home—such a quiet, well-mannered young fellow.
Both he and his brother are doing very well. The
Nicols were mild compared to the Wrights—you
remember Phil and Ronald ? "

Ann threw up her hands at the mention of the names.

" The Wrights," she said, " were really the frozen edge. The only thing Mrs. Wright had ever been able to teach her offspring was to call her ' Mother dear,' which they did religiously. Davie was no model, but he sat round-eyed at the performance of the Wrights when they came to tea. They mounted on the table and pranced among the butter and jam dishes, and to all their mother's anguished entreaties to desist they replied, in the broadest of accents, ' We wull not, Mother dear—we wull not.' They thought Davie's accent rather finicking—Davie's accent, which at that stage was a compound of low Glasgow and broad Linlithgow picked up from the nursemaid—and asked, ' Is Davie English, Mother dear ? '

" ' No, no, darlings ' (Mrs. Wright's own accent was all that there was of the most genteel), ' he only speaks nicely.' Marget used to shake her head over the Wrights and say, ' Eh, I say, thae bairns need a guid skelpin'.' "

" Yes," said Mrs. Douglas ; " but the last time I saw the Wright boys they were the most glossy-looking creatures—you know the kind of young men whose hair looks unnaturally bright and whose clothes fit almost too well ; don't you call them ' knuts ' ?—with supercilious manners and Glasgow-English voices, and I rather yearned for the extremely bad but quite unaffected little boys they once had been."

" I know ; one often regrets the ' lad that is gone.'
Boys are like pigs, they are nicest when they are
small. Talking of the Wrights reminds me of a
children's party we once gave, to which you invited
a missionary's little girl, and two black boys. You
had never seen them and thought they would be
quite tiny, and when they came they were great
strong creatures with *pointed teeth*. Somebody told
us they had teeth like that because they were
cannibals, and, after hearing that, it was a night-
mare evening. We played hide-and-seek, and every
one screamed with terror when caught by the poor
black boys. It was terrible to see them eating
sandwiches at supper and reflect on what they would
have *liked* to eat."

" Oh, Ann ! The poor innocents ! They weren't
cannibals ; they were rescued by the missionaries
when they were babies. But I must say I was
rather alarmed when I saw how big they were.
They didn't realize their own strength, and I was
afraid they might hurt some of the little ones. I
spent an anxious evening, too."

" Mother," said Ann, leaning forward with her
elbows on her knees and her face supported in her
two hands, " you were dreadfully given to spoiling
the look of my parties. The boys didn't mind,
but I was a desperate little snob. It seemed
impossible for me to have the kind of party other
girls had, with all the children prettily dressed,
and dancing, and a smart supper. At the last
moment you were always discovering some child

who was crippled and didn't get any fun, or some
one who hadn't a proper party frock and hadn't
been asked to any parties. You told them it
didn't matter what they wore to our house, and
insisted on their coming—' compelled them to come
in.' Oh, you were a real ' highways and hedges
person ' ! As a matter of fact, it wasn't at all kind
to ask those children. They felt out of it and unhappy, no matter how much one tried. If you had
asked them when there wasn't a party, and they
could have had all the attention, it would have been
infinitely better."

" Oh, I daresay," said Mrs. Douglas. " I've
spent my life doing impulsive things and regretting
them. But, Ann, though you laugh at me about
having so many people to the house, the trouble
we took was nothing compared to the pleasure it
gave. In our church there were so many who
needed encouragement : single women fighting for
a living and coming home after a long day's work
to cook their supper over a gas-ring were glad at
times to get a well-cooked and daintily served
meal, with people to talk to while they ate ; and
mothers cooped up in tiny flats with noisy children
liked to walk to a green suburb, and get tea and
home-made scones and jam ; and it does make a
difference to boys from the country, living in lodg-
ings, if they know there is some house they can
go to whenever they like."

" True, my dear, true, and I don't suppose you
ever denied yourself to any one, no matter how

tired, or ill, or grieved you were feeling. You
welcomed them all with ' gently smiling jaws.' Do
you remember the only occasion on which we said
' Not at home ' ? We had been at the church hall
all afternoon preparing it for a church ' At Home '
and had just come in for tea and a short rest, with
the prospect of three hours' solid smiling later in
the evening. When I found the housemaid going
to answer the door-bell I hissed at her, ' Say not at
home,' and by sheer bad luck the caller turned out
to be a minister's wife from a distance, who had
depended on being warmed and fed at our house.
She had gone home cold and tealess and, as a conse-
quence, got a bad chill, and we felt so guilty about
it we trailed away to see her, and on hearing she had
a sale of work in prospect—when has a minister's
wife not a sale of work in prospect ?—we felt bound
to send her a handsome contribution. I sadly
sacrificed on the altar of remorse some pretty silver
things I had brought from India, feeling it an ex-
pensive pleasure to say ' Not at home.' But of
course you are right. Now that it is all over and
we have long hours to read and write and think long
thoughts, it is nice to feel that you helped a lot of
people over rough bits of the road and didn't think
how tired it made you."

Mrs. Douglas looked at her daughter with un-
smiling eyes. " Do you know what I feel ? " she
asked. " I feel that I have done nothing—*nothing*.
All the opportunities I was given, I can see now
how I missed them ; while I was busy here and

there, they were gone. And I grumbled when I
trudged down to the sewing-class on Monday
nights, leaving all you children. I used sometimes
to envy the mothers who had no kirk, and no
meetings, and could spend their evenings at home.
I had to be out so many nights of the week. No
wonder poor little Davie said, ' I wish I had a
mother who didn't go to meetings.' And it was
such a long way home. Standing shivering in the
wind and rain at the corner of Bridge Street,
waiting for a car, I wondered if there would ever
come a time when I would sit at my ease in the
evenings with no late meetings to bother about.
I didn't know how blessed I was. ' The Almighty
was still with me, and my children were about me.'
How could I know when I yearned for ease and
idleness that when I got them I should sit bereft,
and ask nothing better than the old hard-working
days back——"

Ann said nothing for a minute, but sat scribbling
on a corner of her paper ; then she looked at her
mother, and her eyes were half sad, half merry :

" It's an odd thing, Motherkin, that only very
good people feel their own shortcomings. Now, I,
covered as with a garment by sins of omission and
commission, am quite perky and well pleased with
myself. I walk on my heels and think what a
noble creature I am, and how much people must
admire me. Try being complacent, my dear, for
a change ! It's much more comfortable. You
know, Mother, you should have been a Roman

Catholic, then you could have worn a hair shirt, and done all sorts of little penances and kept yourself happy."

" Oh, Ann ! " Mrs. Douglas gave a laugh that was almost a sob. " You do talk such utter nonsense, but you look at me with your father's eyes. . ."

" Well, what I want is to get some information about the Glasgow part of your life. You started a lot of new things, didn't you, in connection with the church ? "

" Oh yes, a sewing-class and a mothers' meeting, and a fellowship meeting and a literary society —I forget what else, but they were all more or less successful. Martyrs people were delightful to work with—so appreciative."

" And very amusing," said Ann ; " I always enjoyed their remarks about things. I overheard one young man say, as he wiped his heated brow after a thoroughly unventilated evening spent looking at magic-lantern slides of various mission stations—' My ! I'm fair sweatin' comin' through thae Tropics.' We always called him ' Tropics ' after that. What they thoroughly enjoyed was being asked to our house. It wasn't till I grew up that I appreciated those parties, but I very distinctly remember some you gave at the time of your silver wedding to let every one see the presents. We tried to assort the people—young men and women in the evening, and matrons in the afternoon. It wasn't always easy to find suitable topics to converse on with the matrons, but one afternoon some one started the subject of washing clothes, and it called forth a perfect flood of eloquence. Every one had something to say, and we thrashed out the subject from the first stage of soaking the clothes until they were starched and ironed and put away. There didn't seem to be one more word that could be said about it when the arrival of some newcomers made rearranging the room necessary. As I moved about, I saw one woman hitch her chair nearer her neighbour and heard her say thrillingly, ' Speakin' aboot washing, Mrs. Law, did ye ever try——' It became a favourite saying with us. When Robbie wanted to change the subject he always began, ' Speakin' aboot washing, Mrs. Law——' "

CHAPTER XVI

WHEN Mr. Philip Scott came to lunch at Dreams he stayed a long time—so long that Marget remarked to Mysie in the kitchen, " That man is surely het at hame that he's sittin' here so long clatterin'."

He had had a good lunch, had been shown the house and what would be the garden, had walked with Ann a little way along the hill road and duly admired the view, and had then returned to the living-room, where he sat talking and listening till tea was brought in, stayed for an hour after tea, and even then had seemed loath to go away.

" Well," said Mrs. Douglas, when the guest had at last departed, " it's a blessing there is a moon—and that he knows the hill road well. It will take him all his time to be at Birkshaw in time for dinner."

" You shouldn't have made yourself so agreeable, Mother. He couldn't bear to leave your interesting conversation."

" As to that," said Mrs. Douglas, " it does one good to see a man sometimes and hear a man's talk."

"Mother," laughed Ann, "you dearly love a man, and you have all the Victorian woman's reliance on a man's opinion. You love doing things for their benefit; you positively *pander* to them."

Mrs. Douglas refused to be abashed by this accusation.

"Well, why not? I think men are the lords of creation, and I do like them to have the best of everything. I like the old-fashioned way of doing everything for one's men-folk—seeing that their bags are properly packed and their clothes kept in perfect order. I can't bear the modern way of letting a man look after himself; it is so nice to feel that one's men are dependent on one for their comfort."

Ann groaned and, sitting down on the rug, pulled the Tatler into her lap.

"Cat, d'you hear that? Lords of creation, indeed! Those are your sentiments, too, aren't they?"

The Tatler blinked sleepily, and stuck his claws into Ann's arm.

Ann pushed him away and got up. "Ah yes, Mother, I know you of old. I didn't mind running errands for Father when he came in tired, but I did resent being told: 'Run and pack Mark's bag.' 'Get Robbie a clean handkerchief——' That was 'fair ridiculous!'"

"Yes, but, on the other hand, the boys were always being told, 'Give it to Ann; she's the girl.' You were utterly spoiled, and there's one thing,

Ann, I must ask you. When I'm asking a blessing for tea, don't go on filling cups."

" But I don't," Ann said indignantly, " though what you want with a blessing for tea, I don't know. Nobody I ever heard of has a blessing for tea except Miss Barbara, and I generally had taken a large bite out of a scone before she began, and it lay on my plate and looked at me reproachfully. Poor Mr. Scott spoke right through your blessing to-day ; he didn't know what you were doing."

Mrs. Douglas sighed deeply. " Ah, well, Ann, I don't suppose I'll be with you very long to worry you with my old-fashioned ways."

" Oh, Mother, that's not fair. You're hitting below the belt."

" But you may be away first," continued Mrs. Douglas, " and then I shall be left to regret."

" Well, then," said Ann flippantly, " we'll arrange that neither of us will regret anything. You and Mr. Scott made great friends, Mother. He has very nice manners, hasn't he ? "

Mrs. Douglas laid down *Hours of Silence*, which she had taken up to begin her evening's reading, and removed the large spectacles which made her look like a little owl.

" I liked him, Ann. There is something very likeable about him. He reminded me just a little of Robbie."

" I wondered if that would strike you," Ann said.
" It isn't that there is any resemblance, but he has

some of Robbie's ways. . . . He was tremendously interested about your *Life*, Mother, so I gave him what I had written to look over. Oh, you needn't feel hurt about it. It's only that he may give me some advice. He writes himself, you know. As you say, it is nice to talk to a man again— one's own kind of man. Mr. Sharp is a dear, but it isn't much fun making conversation with him."

There was silence in the room as Mrs. Douglas began to read her evening portion out of each of her many volumes, and Ann sat watching the flames leap, and thinking, thinking.

"Mother," she said suddenly, "you said a little while ago that I was spoiled as a child, but I wasn't. Dear me, I was a regular burden bearer, and Mark christened me 'The Patient Cuddy'! You see, I was hampered with always having a small brother to lug about ; I could never harden my heart enough to leave them at home. An only girl in a family of brothers has really a harassed existence. It would have been different if Rosamund had lived. She was too tiny to come into our games, though she meant a great deal to us —much more than we realized."

Mrs. Douglas laid down her book. "She loved being allowed to play with you," she said, "and you were good about making games that she could join in. But, somehow, she was more a companion to her father and me than your playfellow. For one thing, she shared your father's love of gardening.

The rest of you helped sometimes in the garden, but you always let it be seen that it was a penance. You hardly knew one flower from another, and you sped like arrows from a bow whenever you were released. But Rosamund trotted about happily for hours, utterly contented to be with her father and the flowers. We used often to say to each other, your father and I, how different she was to you and the boys. You were healthy, ordinary children who never thought of saying pretty things to your parents or any one else. You found the world so full of a number of things that your days were passed in a sort of breathless investigation. Rosamund was a revelation to us. She was rather dignified and aloof with strangers, but for her own people her heart was a treasure-house of love. I never knew of so young a child having such strong yet discerning affections. She wasn't in the least priggish; indeed, she could be naughty in a peculiarly impish way, and you children were always teaching her rude expressions, which she used to Marget, who adored her, but all Marget said was, ' D'ye think I'm gaun to quarrel wi' you, impident little thing that ye are ? ' She and Marget were great friends, and there was nothing she liked better than to help Marget work, and bake little dough rabbits with currants for eyes. The big black cat—christened by Mark, ' William Tweezer, Earl of Scullery '— superintended operations, and Marget would say to him when he got in the way, ' Awa' oot and play yersel', Weellum, like a man.' We had a game that the fairy Whuppetie Stourie hid in the nursery chimney and when little girls were good laid a present on the hearth-rug. I didn't realize it was all real to her until Jeanie Tod set the chimney on fire, and Rosamund, with a white face, sobbed, ' Jeanie, you forget I've a friend up there.' I can hear her voice now.''

" How you remember, Mother. I wish I could! I can see her still, but I can't hear her voice. You see, I was only about thirteen when she died, and children forget so soon. I can remember looking down into her face and thinking that her eyes were like violets ; and I remember a little white dress trimmed with ' flowering,' and a blue cloak with a hood. I remember at breakfast-time she used to walk round the table and ask for tops of eggs. She only got a whole egg on Sundays, and she never forgot to pray, ' Bless my whole egg next Sabbath day.' She was a very happy child. I think she enjoyed the little short time she had in the world, but she was very shy and timid, wasn't she ? You remember, when Mrs. Lang asked her to a tea-party alone, it quite preyed on her mind ? The day of the party she summoned up courage to ring the Langs' bell, but when the servant came she had no words. Three times she rang the bell without being able to give a message, and the third time Mrs. Lang came herself and said, ' Now, Rosamund, you are a naughty child, and you must not ring the bell again until it is time for the party.' Poor little Rosamund crept away without ever being able to explain that

all she wanted to ask was that I might go with her !
Rather unlike Robbie, when Mark and I were invited to a party, and he called at the house to ask if
there had been any mistake that he hadn't been
invited."

"Dear Robbie," said Mrs. Douglas, then fell
silent. In a little she spoke again :

"Christmas to me, even now, always seems
Rosamund's time. It is odd to think that she was
only with us for five short years, and she has been
away more than twenty, and yet the thought of
her is always with me. She lives to me so vividly
that it seems only yesterday that it all happened.
As Christmas drew near, you were all excited, but
Rosamund seemed utterly possessed with the spirit
of the season. She wanted to give presents to every
one she knew, and couldn't understand why any
limit should be put to the size of our Christmas
party. She loved dolls—unlike you, Ann, who
never knew how to hold a doll !—and I dressed her
two great big ones for her fourth Christmas, a wax
one called Muriel, and Black Sam. Old Mrs. Hamil-
ton in the church made her a wonderful rag-doll,
as big as a baby, with arms and legs complete, only
the face had a gruesome lack of profile. I dressed
up like Father Christmas and brought all the
presents into the room in a big basket, and made
speeches as I gave them out, and Rosamund was
speechless with delight. She could hardly tell me
about it when I came into the room a few minutes
later, and her great regret was that I had happened

to be out of the room ; she thought it was such bad luck for me. When she was dying she said, ' When Father Christmas comes this year, tell him you have no Rosamund, and ask him to give my presents to Ann.' "

Ann moved quickly in her chair, and busied herself for a little in putting some papers in order. Then she burst out, " Why did she die, Mother ? What made her ill ? "

Mrs. Douglas shook her head. " Ah, my dear ! We have these treasures in earthen vessels. I suppose the time had come for us to give her back. It began so simply. She was a very healthy child and rarely ailed anything, but one day she got her feet wet playing in the snow, and that brought on a slight chill. It seemed to be nothing, and passed, but after that we noticed her droop a little. I didn't get the doctor at once, for I had so often got him on false pretences, and I knew he thought me an absurdly anxious mother, and when he came I was quite apologetic, expecting to be told I had been fussing again. But he didn't make light of it. He said it was slight gastric fever, and she must go to bed. That was in February. She seemed to get over it quickly, and was soon up and playing as busily as ever, but we noticed that she got tired. We had never heard the child own to being tired before, and it chilled our hearts to see her go and sit down quietly in her little chair. Then we found that her temperature had begun to rise in the afternoon. In the morning it was subnormal, but as the day advanced it crept up. We got one specialist after another, but no one seemed able to stop the horrible creeping fever. It was a very hard winter ; the snow lay on the ground well into March, and I used to sit with Rosamund on my knee at the window while you children built snow-men to amuse her. There were some li tle wild kittens that had been turned out of their home in a stable, and Rosamund worried about them, so you built a little house for them of orange boxes in the shrubbery and made it very cosy with a bit of old carpet. She could watch them creep in and get warm. On your walks you always went to the streets so that you might glue your faces to shop windows and decide what your scraped-together pennies would buy for Rosamund."

" I know," said Ann. " One day, to my joy, I found in a small grocer's shop tiny pots of jam and marmalade that cost one penny each, and Rosamund loved them for her dolls' tea-parties. If we could find anything to interest or amuse her, we were so proud. At first she was able to have us play quietly with her, then she began not to be able to walk about, and Mark carried her round the garden to look at the snowdrops and crocuses. We never owned to ourselves or each other that she wouldn't recover. We said, ' Rosamund will be all right when the spring comes,' but the spring came—— Mother, it must have been terrible for you to see the spring flowers come and your little Rose-of-the-world fade."

Mrs. Douglas covered her eyes for a minute with

a hand that shook, but when she spoke her voice
was steady.

" It was the most beautiful spring and summer
that I think I ever remember, and we all went away
to Etterick in April. It seemed that the sun and
the fresh winds and the quiet of the hills must heal,
and at first she did seem to improve. But it was
only for a little. The dreaded fever returned, and
every Monday, when your father came back from
preaching in Glasgow, he knew her to be losing.
She liked being out all the time, and our days were
spent by the burnside or on the hills. We had an
old pony and a low basket carriage which she found
comfortable, and we sometimes drove by the banks
of the Tweed until we came to some place which she
liked specially, when we would lift her out into a
nest of cushions and she could sit and listen to the
voice of the Tweed as it slipped past. And we had
lunch with us, and the boys fished, and you read
aloud fairy-tales, and we were almost happy in
spite of the cloud that covered us. . . . She had her
' well days ' and her ' ill days,' but she never complained ; indeed, I think her patience was almost
the hardest thing to bear. One day she said to
me, ' I'm talking to Whuppetie, Mother. I talk to
God when I'm ill and to Whuppetie when I'm well.'
The year before, her great joy had been to go to the
water meadow, where the banks of the ditch were
blue with forget-me-nots. I had always avoided
the place in her illness, and she had never asked to
be taken ; but one day, when we were driving past,

we heard the little Crichton girls say to their mother, ' Come after us when you're ready, Mummy; we're going down to the water meadow to get forget-me-nots.' Rosamund turned and looked at me, and there was such utter sadness in her eyes that my heart seemed as if it must break. . . . One very lovely day in June we had been out till quite late, for she wanted to see the sunset. It was so wonderful in its rose and gold and amethyst that Rosamund, looking with wistful eyes into the glory, said that she thought she could see the twelve gates, every gate a pearl. The beauty seemed to comfort her, but she said to me : ' Mother, if you could only go with me ! If there are twelve gates, how shall I know which one to watch for you at ? ' . . . Mark carried her up to bed that night, and you all sat about on the floor for a little, talking and laughing, and she smiled at you happily while she sipped her milk. It was a very hot night, and a corn-crake was calling in a hayfield near the window. Rosamund slept a little, and woke about three. I sponged her face and hands to cool her, and put lavender water on her pillows ; the windows were wide open, but she seemed to be breathless. Her father heard us moving, and came in from the dressing-room, and Rosamund held out her hands to him. The dawn was beginning to break, and he said, ' The night has passed, darling; it is morning.' She nodded. ' There's that corn-crake corn-craking yet,' she said, and then she gave a little cry. I caught her in my arms, and her head fell on my breast like a dead bird's. . . ."

CHAPTER XVII

WITH the last days of November winter descended with real earnest on the Green Glen. For thirty-six hours snow fell, blotting out the paths, piling great drifts in the hollows, making the high road almost level with the tops of the hedges. The carts from the shops, the butcher, the baker, the grocer, had to remain in the town, the postman could not come near, Mr. Sharp stayed snugly in his Manse, and Dreams was entirely cut off from the rest of the world.

When the frost came, hardening the snow, Ann got out her toboggan and spent glorious hours flying down the hillside and toilful ones dragging the toboggan up again. Glowing with health and self-satisfaction, she came in in the frosty twilight, to drink tea and upbraid her mother for electing to remain by the fire.

" How can you frowst by the fire, Mother, when you might be out looking at the most glorious sun-set and drinking in great draughts of air that is like champagne ? What ? Cold ? Not a bit, once you are out ; indeed, I was almost too warm. The mistake about tobogganing is that the rush down is so short and the toil up so long. I must demand like the Irishman, that all roads be either level or downhill. What a delicious muffin this is ! May I have the jam ? "

Ann rose to get herself another cup of tea, and looked out of the window on the way. " It's bitter hard to-night—you know the frost is very severe when the snow creaks. ' Hech, sirs, it's winter fairly.' Do come and look out, Mother. It's glorious being in Dreams in snow—like living in the heart of a crystal."

Mrs. Douglas shivered as she looked out at the waste of snow. " Draw the curtains, Ann, and shut it out. I never did like snow : cold, unfriendly stuff, making everything uncomfortable, blocking roads and killing sheep and delaying trains ; and when it goes away, burst pipes and dripping misery. But you children always loved it. At Kirkcaple, when it came, you were out before breakfast snow-balling the milkman."

Ann finished her tea and lay back in her chair regarding her mother, who was finishing her " reading " for the day, taking sips of tea and reading *Golden Grain* at the same time.

" Mother," said Ann, " did you ever give your-self good times ? You began your married life without a honeymoon, and I'm afraid you continued on the same principle. I don't seem to remember that you ever got rid of us all and had a real holiday alone with Father."

Mrs. Douglas finished what she was reading and laid the little book on the pile before she answered her daughter. Then she took off her spectacles and took up her cup of tea, and said :

"Oh, yes ; when Jim was a baby we went to London for a fortnight to stay with an uncle and aunt of your father's. Don't you remember them ? Uncle John and Aunt John, we always called them —why, I don't know. Uncle John was rather old when he married, and had a weak heart, and Aunt John warned me that it was safer not to contradict him. Not that it would have entered into my head to do such a thing. I was in too great awe of them both. They were a handsome couple, and Uncle John had a pair of trousers for every day of the week—shepherd-tartan ones for Sunday. Aunt was very tall, with a Roman nose, her hair parted at one side, and was always richly dressed in silks that rustled.

"They were devoted to each other, and made such a touching pair of middle-aged lovers, coquetting with each other in a way that amazed us, staid married people that we were—I suppose I was about five-and-twenty then. I overheard Aunt say to Uncle one day when she came in with a new hat : 'How do you like my *chapeau*, Jackie ? ' and always at breakfast she greeted him with a re-sounding kiss, as if she had never set eyes on him from the night before. We must have been a great nuisance to them, such a countrified couple as we were. Your father was always fit to go anywhere, but I must have been a quaint figure, in a lavender dress trimmed with ruching, and a black silk dolman and a lavender bonnet. They were the efforts of the little dressmaker in Kirkcaple, one of our church members, and we had thought them almost alarmingly smart in the parlour behind the shop; but when I saw myself reflected in long mirrors and shop windows, I had my doubts."

Ann sat forward in her chair, her eyes alight with interest.

"I had forgotten about the London visit. Had you a good time? Were they kind to you?"

"They were kindness itself. Every morning Uncle planned out things for us to do, and arranged that we should lunch somewhere with him—that was to save our pockets. And Aunt's housekeeping seemed to me on a scale nothing short of magnificent. When I went marketing with her it thrilled me to see her buy salmon and turbot as I might have bought 'penny haddies,' and she seemed to me to give a dinner-party every night. And the servants were such aloof, superior creatures. It was all very awe-inspiring to me, a timorous little country mouse."

Ann laughed. "'Wee, modest, crimson-tippit beastie,' as Charlotte renders Burns. But tell me what you saw, Mother. All the sights, I am sure. But did you do anything exciting?"

"Oh *yes*. We went to hear Spurgeon, and one evening Uncle took us to the Crystal Palace and we saw fireworks."

Ann hooted. "Mother, you are a pet! I asked you if you had done anything exciting—meaning had you seen Ellen Terry and Irving and heard Patti sing—and you tell me you heard Spurgeon and went to fireworks at the Crystal Palace!"

"I don't see why you should laugh," Mrs. Douglas said, rather affronted. "These were the things we liked to do. At least, I think what your father really liked best was to poke about in the old bookshops, and he did enjoy the good food. I liked it all, but the going home was best of all. I had felt very small and shabby in London, but when we came off that long night journey and found you all waiting for us as fresh as the morning, you and Mark and Robbie and Jim, I felt the richest woman in the world. I quite sympathized with the mother of the Gracchi, though before I had always thought her rather a fool."

"Yes," Ann said profoundly. "Sometimes things you have read and thought merely silly suddenly become true—and did the London fortnight last you a long time?"

"The next summer I had my trunk packed to go with your father to Switzerland, but at the last moment I found I couldn't leave you and he had to go alone. It was very silly, but, anyway, I always saw that he had a good holiday, and I was happy with you children at Etterick. But as you grew older and went away to school I often got away for a little. One great ploy was to go to the Assembly; sometimes we stayed with people, but we greatly preferred to have rooms in a Princes Street hotel. I don't mean to *lichtly* people's hospitality, but it is a relief when you come in tired not to have to put on a bright, interested expression and tell your hostess all about it."

" I do so agree," said Ann ; " ' a bright, interested expression ' is far too often demanded of ministers' wives and families. What a joy to scowl and look listless at a time. You know, Mums, a manse is a regular school for diplomatists. It is a splendid training. One learns to talk to and understand all sorts of people—just think what an advantage that gives one over people who have only known intimately their own class ! And you haven't time to think about yourself ; you are so on the alert to avoid hurting any one's feelings. You have to try and remember the affairs of each different member, how many children they possess, and all about them, and be careful to ask at the right moment for the welfare of each. To say to a very stout lady living alone, ' Are you all well ? ' savours of impertinence. . . . Yes, well, you went to a hotel to avoid having to look ' bright and interested,' wise people ; and what did you do there ? "

" But, Ann," Mrs. Douglas protested, having been struck with her daughter's remarks on her early training, " you spoke as if you were brought up to be hypocrites, and I'm sure that is the very last thing your father and I wanted you to be——"

" Oh, well," said Ann lightly, " the best people are all more or less hypocrites. The world would be a most unpleasant place if we had all—like Lo, the poor Indian—untutored minds and manners. Honesty is sometimes almost a crime, and the man who feels it necessary to speak what he is pleased to call his mind in season and out of season is a public nuisance.   Hold your peace if you have nothing pleasant to say.   People need encouraging far oftener than you think ; even bumptious people are often only bumptious because they are uncertain of themselves.   As the White Queen said, ' A little kindness and putting their hair in curl papers ' would work wonders for them.   But I don't know why I am chattering like a swallow when what I want is to hear about you and Father at the Assembly.''

Mrs. Douglas had taken up her knitting, and with a happy smile on her face and her fingers working busily she said :

" I remember one particularly happy Assembly. Davie was about five, and you were at home to keep things right, so my mind was quite at ease, and I had got a smart new coat and skirt—black, trimmed with grey cloth and braided, and a black hat with grey feathers.''

" A most ministerial outfit," said Ann, making a face.   " I would rather have seen you in the lavender and the dolman.''

" It was very suitable for a minister's wife, and it must have been becoming, for almost every one we met said I looked so young, and that pleased your father, though, of course, it was nonsense. We were in a mood to enjoy everything—those

May mornings when we came down to breakfast, hungry and well and eager for a new day, and sat at a little table in a bow window looking out on the Castle, and ate fresh herring ' new cam' frae the Forth,' and bacon and eggs and hot rolls."

Mrs. Douglas stopped and said solemnly :

" Ann, if I had a lot of money, do you know what I would do ? I would send fifty pounds anonymously to all the ministers—not, of course, to those with big stipends, and certainly not to the ones with rich wives—to let the minister and his wife have a week at the Assembly. It would pay their fare and hotel bill, and leave something over to shop with. Dear me, I wonder rich people don't give themselves a good time by doing happy things like that."

" It's a game that never palls," Ann said, " planning what you would do if you got a sudden fortune. I'm quite sure the real owners of riches don't get half as much pleasure out of their wealth as the paupers who have it only in dreams. And what followed after the large breakfast ? Did you spend the whole day in the assembling of yourselves together ? Attending the Assembly is like some sort of insidious drug : the more you do it, the more you want to do it. Since I have been your companion at its deliberations I have found that I can sit in it quite happily for hours. You wouldn't miss the Assembly week for a lot even now, would you ? It is odd how the sight of ministers in the mass seems to do you good.

Absolutely you get quite sleek by merely looking at them. Do you remember when you were so very ill in London you kept worrying Sir Armstrong to know if you would be better for the Assembly, and the poor doctor said to Mark, ' Your mother is very anxious to go to some assembly ; but she *couldn't dance* ? ' "

Mrs. Douglas laughed and then sighed. " I enjoy it still," she said ; " but the Assembly Hall is a place of ghosts to me now. There are so few of the faces that once I knew. I look up at my old place in the Ladies' Gallery—I never aspired to the Moderator's Gallery in those days. I always sat in the same seat, and then your father knew where to look up and smile to me during debates. I often sat very nervous, for he had a dreadful way of always being on the wrong side—I mean by that the unpopular side—and it wasn't nice for me to hear him shouted at. I thought he cared far too little for what people thought ; he had no interest in which way the cat was going to jump ; he never thought of taking the safe course simply because it was safe and would pay best. I remember after one stormy debate in which he had held the most unpopular view, a lady beside me said, ' Can you tell me who that unpleasant minister is ? ' and I said, ' I think he comes from Glasgow.' But my sins found me out almost at once, for, on his way out to vote, your father stood and grinned up at me, looking like a mischievous schoolboy who knows he's going to get a row, and

I had to smile at him—and the lady beside me glared at us both suspiciously."

" It was odd," said Ann, " that in public he was such a fighter, for in his home life, if ever man carried in his right hand gentle peace, it was my father. There was a time, when Mark and I first grew up, that we thought we knew infinitely more about everything in heaven and earth than our parents. There was a time when Father's beliefs filled me with a kind of tender scorn : they were so hopelessly out of date. I used to argue with him in my pert way that Free Will and Election could not be reconciled, and he would reply, with a twinkle, ' Ann, I sometimes think you are a very ignorant creature. Give me another cup of tea.' I remember Father's *innocence* amused us very much. He was so far away from the ugliness and the vulgarity and the idiotic smartness of modern life. He once heard Robbie singing an absurd song, and asked him to repeat the words—I forget what they were, something very silly and rather funny about :

> ' How often to myself I've said,
>   Cheer up, Cully, you'll soon be dead,
>   A short life but a gay one.'

Father listened and said gravely, ' If the wretched fellow had had any hope of an after life . . .'

" And we said, ' Isn't Father *quaint* ? '

" And when he was no longer there to stand up for his old-fashioned beliefs there wasn't one of us but would have died gladly for those same beliefs because they had been his. . . . When Robbie got the cable of his death he wrote from India : ' The best man in Scotland is gone—now he knows what his beliefs meant to all of us ; ' and Davie, that advanced young thinker, once came back from hearing a preacher of renown, and said fiercely, ' No, I didn't like him. He *sneered at the Shorter Catechism.*' "

CHAPTER XVIII

" HERE's a nice state of things," said Ann.

" Is anything wrong ? " asked her mother.

" Well, I don't know whether you would call it wrong or right. Mr. Philip Scott sends me back my MS., with his criticism of it. I agree with most of the things he says : my language is too incorrigibly noble, my quotations *are* very frequent——"

" But if they're good quotations," Mrs. Douglas interrupted.

" Oh, they're good quotations. ' It was the best butter,' as the poor March Hare said. But what he objects to most is the sweetness of it. He says, ' Put more acid into it.' "

" Into me, does he mean ? "

" I suppose so. Mr. Scott evidently finds you insipid. We must change that at once. Tell me now, about all the people you hated and who hated you."

Mrs. Douglas looked bewildered, and more than a little indignant. " Nonsense, Ann. I'm

sure I'm very glad to hear you have made me
sweet—anything else would have been most un-
dutiful ; and as for hating people, I never was
any good at that. I couldn't keep up grudges,
though I was sometimes very angry at people. I
daresay it was a weakness in my nature. But I
think, if Mr. Scott is to be allowed to criticize,
I might be allowed to read my own *Life*."

"It's so *dull*," said Ann, looking discontentedly
at the MS. "And you're not a dull woman,
Mother ! Rather a comic, really. See, read for
yourself."

Ann plumped the packet on to her mother's lap
and retired to the fender-stool with the *Times* ;
but she could hardly have done justice to the
leaders, for her eyes often wandered from the
printed page to the expressive face of her mother
reading her own *Life*.

For half an hour Ann waited ; then her patience
gave out, and she leant forward and put her hand
across the page.

"That's enough, Mums. Surely you can tell
me now how you think it goes."

Mrs. Douglas smiled at her daughter. "Why
did you do that ? I'm enjoying it immensely,
and——"

"Oh, if anybody could find it interesting, you
would ; but don't you find it rather stilted ? "

"Not stilted exactly, but if you would write
in a more homely way, it might be better. Take
the reader more into your confidence. I'm not

clever enough to explain quite what I mean ;
but I think you are writing from the outside, as
it were. Try to be more—is subjective the word
I want ? And don't say too much about me.
After all, my life was my husband and the children.
Write about your father and the boys. Never
were brothers more loved by a sister. As for
Davie—you brought him up."

Ann's eyes filled suddenly with tears, but in a
minute she said lightly :

" You see, Mother, Mr. Scott asks what I am
working up to in this *Life* of yours ; how am I going
to finish it, he wants to know. I hadn't thought of
that. I was just going to leave loose ends—like
life. I suppose there ought to be something—some
idea that binds the whole thing together. Oh, it
is all too difficult. I'd better burn all that I've
written and start again in an entirely new way.
How would it do to put your life into scenes ?
The young girl in a royal blue silk dress and a
locket and a black velvet ribbon, meeting her
future husband. The wedding. A nursery scene
—very effective this !—and then we might have
scenes from your church life—you holding a
Mothers' Meeting or a Girls' Club, or your first
address to the Fellowship meeting. Do you
remember you began (as you begin most things)
with a deep sigh, and it sounded rather like *Hooch*,
and Robbie said you reminded him of Harry
Lauder ? " Ann chuckled at the recollection, and
her mother said :

"No wonder I was nervous. It was a great ordeal to speak before you scoffing young things. No; I don't like the idea of 'scenes.' I prefer it as it is. How far are you on?"

"I've got us all at school, and I was going to write about Davie being born. It was the summer after Rosamund died, wasn't it? I was at school when I got the news, and some of the girls condoled with me, and said a new baby in the house would be a dreadful nuisance, and I pretended to be bored by the prospect, when really I could hardly contain my excitement. I had to get home for a week-end to see him."

"Poor little baby, to think that we were actually disappointed when he came. We had wanted another girl so much, and a fourth boy seemed rather unnecessary. Of course that was only at the very beginning. He was the plainest-looking baby I ever saw, and we would not have had him in the very least different."

"I thought he was lovely," said Ann. "When Mark saw him for the first time, he said, 'Hullo, Peter,' and Peter he was called for years. When I came home from school he was about three years, and he became my special charge. You were so very busy at that time with the house and church work, as well as a great scheme that the Member of Parliament for the district started, to teach working women how to make savoury dinners out of nothing. You were so keen about it that you tried all the new dishes on your family, and we nearly perished *as* a family. I can remember some of the dishes. *Stuffed cod's head*—one glance at its gruesome countenance was enough. *Mock kidney soup*, made with grated liver, which, instead of being the rich brown proper to kidney soup, was a sort of olive green. *Sea-pie* so-called, Mark said, because the sea was a handy place when you had eaten it. I once went with you to see a demonstration by the principal cooking teacher, a buxom lady with quantities of glossy black hair coiled round her head. She showed us first what she called 'a pretty puddin'.' Instead of sugar she had grated carrots in it, or something surprisingly like that. Then she made shortbread, and when the cakes were finished and ready to go into the oven she wanted something to prick them with, and nothing was at hand. She wasn't easily beaten, for I saw her withdraw a hairpin from the coils on her head and prick them with that. When they were taken from the oven, and I saw that they were to be handed round and tasted, I unobtrusively withdrew. You had noticed nothing, and ate your bite quite happily."

"Oh, Ann, you always saw far too much. That's all nonsense about the things we made. Everything was excellent and very cheap, and the women in the district enjoyed the lectures amazingly, and constantly asked to have them repeated. I enjoyed them myself. Anything to do with cooking interests me, and I read every recipe I see."

"You are the sort of guest, Mother, who would

appreciate a cookery book in her bedroom. It seems an odd taste to me. I can make porridge, smooth and soft, with no knots, and fry quite nice bacon and eggs, and I can make some rather smart meringuey puddings, and there I end. D'you remember how difficult it was to get Davie to eat when he was tiny ? I had to feed him with every meal, or I don't think he would have eaten anything. He was such a thin little slip of a thing— like an elf. At one time i got so desperate about his thinness that I took to rubbing him all over every night with olive oil. What a mess it made of everything ! We took tremendous care of him, didn't we ? He never went out in his pram with only the nursemaid ; I generally went too, in case anything happened to him. It's a wonder to me that we didn't spoil him utterly."

" He was a dear, ugly wee laddie," Mrs. Douglas said. " When Mark came down from Oxford he used to sit and study him from the other side of the table, and say, ' How has that child acquired such a Mongolian cast of countenance ? ' "

" It was too bad," said Ann, " and Davie so admiring of Mark and all his Oxford friends ! He used to amuse them a lot. I once overheard him explain to a man how he happened to live with us. ' I was playing quite quietly in heaven one day when God came up to me and said, " Peter, you've to go and live with the Douglasses." I said, ' The Douglasses ! *Good Lord !*' The weary boredom in his voice was delightful."

" Many a fright he gave me," said Davie's mother. " He picked up the most extraordinary expressions, and seemed to know when to use them with the most disastrous effect. By the time Davie was born I had grown tired of training, besides it was impossible to do anything with him when you older children, who should have known better, laughed at and encouraged him. He was a plaything to you all."

" Yes," said Ann ; " there's something about the baby of a family that's different. The youngest never grows up, and to each of us Davie seemed almost more a son than a brother, and we never lost for him—even when he was grown up and a soldier—the almost passionate tenderness that we had for the little delicate boy. He was the delight of our lives, always. I remember when I arrived in India almost the first thing Robbie wanted to be told was Davie's latest sayings. He had a name for each of us peculiarly his own. Nobody ever called me ' Nana ' but Davie, and why he christened Jim ' Ney ' no one ever knew. But, Mother, it was only as a baby that he was so very plain. Later he developed a sort of horsey look, and we dressed him in a ' horsey ' way, with a snooty bonnet and a fawn overcoat. I remember he got a very neat suit to go to a party at Anthony's house, his first real party—brown with a corduroy waistcoat—which he described, in imitation of Mark and his friends, as ' me blood waistcoat '— and short, tight trousers. As we dressed him we noticed that the shirt he was wearing had been patched at the elbow, but it was clean, and we didn't change it. When he came home he told how this one had sung and that one had recited, and ' What,' we asked, ' did you do ? ' ' Oh, me,' said Davie, ' I only took off my coat and showed them my patched shirt.' "

" It didn't matter at Anthony's house," Mrs. Douglas said ; " the Cochranes were well accustomed to the vagaries of small boys. Anthony and Davie made a funny couple. Anthony was so solemn and fat, and so ashamed of Davie's eccentric behaviour. Davie's way of telling himself stories ' out loud,' and going round the room gesticulating wildly, really shocked Anthony, who was a most self-contained child. He never showed surprise, indeed he rarely ever showed emotion of any sort. When he and Davie were very small and met outside, each took off his hat to the other and made a low bow. At the first party we gave for Davie, the child was greatly excited, and talked without ceasing, jumping up and down in his chair. Anthony was sitting next him at the tea-table in a green velvet suit, and he stood this Jack-in-the-box behaviour as long as he could, then he turned very quietly, slapped Davie's face, and resumed his tea without having said a word. And Davie bore him no ill-will ; they were fast friends from that moment. D'you remember the two going alone to a party in a cab, and they were so thrilled about it that—we were told afterwards—

they refused to do anything but sit in the hall and wait for the cab coming back ? "

" I loved Anthony," said Ann. " He took things so calmly and was so speechless. One afternoon when he was with us people began to flock up to his front door, carriages and motors arrived, and we called to him to come and tell us what occasion this was. Anthony looked at the commotion for a minute, and then said, ' It must be a party,' and not another word passed his lips. One night we said ' Anthony will recite.' He said neither yea nor nay, and we led him into the middle of the room. Still he made no protest, but stood, drooping like a candle in the sun, while large tears coursed quietly down his face. It must have been good for Davie to have such a phlegmatic friend. But I've seen Anthony wakened to enthusiasm. I came home once full of *Cyrano de Bergerac,* and, of course, told Davie all about it—I was so pleased when I heard Davie say after he was grown up, ' It was Nana made me like poetry '—and it became his favourite game. He and Anthony would crouch behind the sofa, ' behind the walls at Arras,' and then jump wildly up shouting, ' Cadets of Gascony are we . . .' Mother, I think you and I could talk for weeks on end about Davie. . . ."

The door opened and Marget came in. " It's no' nine o'clock yet," she said ; " but Mysie has rin oot doon to the cottages—what wi' the mune and the snaw it's near as light as day—an' I cam' in to speer about your *Life*, Mem. Hoo's Miss Ann gettin' on wi't ? "

" Not very well, Marget," Ann answered for herself. " I'm going to finish it, but it's a much harder job than I expected."

Marget sniffed. " I dinna see ony hardness aboot it. You hev a' the facts ; a' that you've got to dae is write them doon."

" It certainly sounds very easy put in that way," Ann said ; " but facts alone are dull things."

" But onything else wad juist be lees."

Ann began to laugh. " But, Marget," she protested, " I could put all the facts of Mother's life into one page—born, married, number of children, and so on ; but that wouldn't be any sort of record to hand down to the children. You want all sorts of little everyday touches that will make them see the home that their father was brought up in."

" Everyday touches," Marget repeated ; " d'ye mean what we hed for oor denners an' aboot washin' days ? But thaes no things to write aboot. I could tell ye some rale fine things to pit in a book. One Setterday I let in a young man to see the maister—a rale weel pit-on young man he was, an' I showed him into the study, an' what d'ye think was the very first thing he said to the maister ? "

Marget leant forward impressively. " He said that he had had a veesion to kill a man an' had been guided to oor Manse. Eh, I say ! Sic a

fricht I got when I heard aboot it! It juist lets
ye see how carefu' ye should be aboot lettin' folk
in even if they look respectable."

"And how did Father get rid of him?" Ann
asked.

"You tell her, Mem." Marget nodded towards
her mistress, and Mrs. Douglas said:

"He was a poor fellow whose brain had gone
from over-study. Your father talked quietly to
him, and said that Saturday morning was a bad
time to come, and suggested that he should put it
off till Monday. He went away quite peaceably,
and your father went out after him and had him
followed, for he was a dangerous lunatic. On the
Sunday we were afraid to leave anybody in the
house in case he came back, so we all went to
church—even Jim the baby! On the Monday we
heard that he was in an asylum. It was a tragic
case."

"We got some awfu' frichts in the Kirkcaple
Manse," said Marget; "but I dinna mind nane
in Glesgae; we had folk a' round us there. Eh,
Mem, d'ye mind the day the maister brocht in the
auld-claes wife?"

Mrs. Douglas began to laugh, and she and Marget
sat and shook in silent convulsions while Ann
demanded to know what they were laughing at.

At last Mrs. Douglas steadied her voice enough
to say:

"You know your father was always being
accused of not being cordial to people—he had

naturally rather a dry manner. One day I was standing at the study window and saw an old-clothes woman—Mrs. Burt was her name—who came regularly to ask if we had anything for her, standing at the gate as if hesitating whether or not to come in. Then I saw your father approach, raise his hat, saw him go up to the startled woman and shake her warmly by the hand, and then conduct her into the house. ' Nell,' he shouted, ' here's an old friend to see you—Mrs. Beattie from Kirkcaple ! She must have some lunch.' "

" Mrs. Burt turned to me a distressed, red face, and I stared at her wondering which of us had gone mad.

" ' Mrs. Burt . . .' I began, and then it dawned upon your father what he had done. There was a faint resemblance between the old-clothes woman and our old friend Mrs. Beattie, who had been such a help to us in the Kirkcaple church. For a moment he was absolutely nonplussed, and then he began to laugh, and he and I reeled about while Mrs. Burt looked more alarmed every minute. We recovered in time, and begged Mrs. Burt's pardon for the mistake, and saw that she had a good dinner ; but your father said he had got enough of trying to be ' frank '——"

Marget wiped her eyes. " Eh, I say," she said, " it was an awfu' set oot."

CHAPTER XIX

THE thaw came suddenly, and, almost in a night, the snow went, leaving the moorlands like some vast sponge. The air was full of the rushing of a great west wind and the noise of running water, as burns, heavy with spate, came tumbling down the hillsides.

Ann stood looking out at the wide view, at the hills purple-dark, with drifts of snow still in the hollows and at the back of dykes.

" ' As dull as a great thaw,' " she quoted. " It's like a giant's washing day—such a sloppiness and dreariness, and that horrible steamy feeling that a house gets when the frost goes suddenly and leaves everything damp, even the walls and the furniture. A new-made road is no great treat in a thaw. I stuck, and nearly left my big boots behind me this morning. I wish it would get dark and we could draw the curtains and have tea."

" I don't want to grumble," Mrs. Douglas said, turning the heel of a stocking with a resigned air, " but these last few days have been very long.

No post even! That was the last straw. I've knitted a pair of stockings for little Davie, and I've written a lot of letters, and I've tried each of the library books in turn, but nowadays nobody writes the sort of book I like. No, they don't, Ann."

" But what kind of book pleases you, Mother? I thought we had rather a good selection this week. One or two are quite interesting."

" Interesting!" repeated Mrs. Douglas. " They seemed to me the very essence of dullness. I don't think I'm ill to please, but I do like a book that is clean and kind. I put down each of those books in disgust; they're both dull and indecent. Is it easier to be clever and nasty than clever and clean? "

" Oh, much," said Ann promptly. " It's a very hard thing, I should think, to write a book that is pleasant without being mawkish, whereas any fool can be nasty and can earn a reputation of sorts by writing what Davie used to call ' hot stuff.' "

" Well, I wish some one would arise who would write for the middle-aged and elderly; there are a great many in the world, and they are neglected by nearly every one—fashion writers, fiction writers, play writers—no one caters for them. I like domestic fiction, gentle but not drivelling, good character drawing and a love story that ends all right."

" In other words," said Ann, " good print and happy ending. What about me? Why shouldn't

I become the writer for middle-aged women ? I
might almost call myself a writer now that I have
wrestled for weeks with your *Life*, and I believe
I would find it easier to write fiction than biog-
raphy—to leave what Marget calls ' facs ' and
take to ' lees.' Facts crib and cabin one. Given
a free hand I might develop an imagination."

" Who knows ? Only don't begin anything else
until you have finished the job you are at. I do
hate to leave unfinished work."

" Oh, so do I," said Ann, " and I mean to plod
on with the *Life* to the bitter end—but I had better
take bigger strides and cover the ground. From
Davie's birth—do you remember he used to say
when we complained of his accent, ' Well, you
shouldn't have borned me in Glasgow '—on till
you went to South Africa nothing of importance
happened."

Mrs. Douglas stared at her daughter. " Seven
years," she said. " Did nothing important happen
in those years ? "

" *Nothing*," Ann said firmly, " except that the
boys left school and went to Oxford——"

" Oh, but, Ann, don't hurry on so. You must
put in about the boys doing so well at school and
getting scholarships and almost educating themselves. It might spur on that lazy little Rory to
hear about them . . . and you grew up."

" My growing up wasn't much of an event,"
said Ann. " Indeed it was something of a disaster.
I had been rather attractive-looking as a schoolgirl

because my hair fluffed out round my face, but when I put it up I dragged it all back into a little tightly hair-pinned bump. The change was startling. I was like a skinned rabbit. The boys hung umbrellas on the bump and the church people came to you and asked you to make me let down my hair again because they couldn't bear the look of me. And I wore a thick brown coat and a brown hat with red in it, and I had no more notion how to dress myself becomingly than a Kaffir woman. I was a poor little object and I knew it. Then one night I went to a party—an ordinary Glasgow party, full of jokes and good things to eat—and there I met an artist; I suppose she would be about thirty—I longed prodigiously to be thirty when I was eighteen; it seemed to me the ideal age—and she wore a wonderful flowing gown, and her red hair was parted in the middle and lay in a great knot of gold at the nape of her neck. I had never seen anything like this before—all your friends had their hair tightly and tidily done up and wore bodices with lots of bones—and I sat and worshipped. I suppose she had recognized worship in the eyes of the awkward, ill-dressed young girl, for she came and sat beside me and talked to me and asked what I meant to do in the world. I hadn't thought of doing anything, I told her; I had a lot of brothers and a busy mother, and I helped at home. She told me she would like to paint me, and I was flattered beyond belief and promised to go to her studio the very next day. Margot Stronach and everything about her were a revelation to me. I thought her flat—which was probably rather tawdry and pinned together : she confessed to me that she seldom bothered to sew things— the last word in Art. Divans made out of discarded feather beds, polished floors, white walls and blue jars with cape gooseberries—what could one want more ? I felt my clothes singularly out of place in such surroundings, and I gave you no peace until I had got a long, straight-hanging white frock with gold embroideries which the boys called my nightgown and in which I felt perfectly happy. Margot certainly did improve my appearance vastly, you must admit that, Mother. She made me take a few dozen hairpins out of my poor hair, part it in the middle and fold it lightly back, and she taught me the value of line, but she turned me for the time being into a very affected, posing young person. It was then that I turned your nice, comfortable, Victorian drawing-room upside down and condemned you as a family to semi-darkness ! I can't think why you were so patient with me. The boys hooted at me, but I didn't mind them, and you and Father meekly stotted about, until Father one afternoon fell over a stool and spilt all his tea, whereupon he flew into one of his sudden rages, vowed that this nonsense must cease, and pulled up the blinds to the very top."

Mrs. Douglas laughed softly. " Poor Ann, we didn't appreciate your artist friends much, but——"

" Oh, but Mother," Ann interrupted, " Margot wasn't a real artist—not like Kathleen and Jim Strang, or any of the serious artists. She was only a woman with a certain amount of money and a small talent, good looks, and a vast amount of conceit. Even my foolish young eyes saw that very soon."

" She put me very much about," Mrs. Douglas said ; " she had such a wailing, affected way of talking. I never could think of anything to say in reply. Besides, I knew all the time she was thinking me an ignorant, frumpish woman, and that didn't inspire me. You admired her so much that you even copied her voice. . . ."

Ann began to laugh. " It must have been terrible, Mother. I remember Davie meeting Margot on the stairs, and she knelt down and began to talk to him in that wailing, affected voice. Davie was a little fellow and easily frightened, and he suddenly clutched my dress and burst into tears, sobbing ' Nana, Nana, it's the *bandarlog*.' Fortunately Margot didn't know her *Jungle Book*, so she missed the allusion."

" What happened to her ? " Mrs. Douglas asked.

" Oh, Kathleen told me she had met her some-where quite lately. She married a rich business man, stout and a little deaf—that was all to the good !—and, Kathleen said, looked very fat and prosperous and middle-aged. She said to Kath-leen, ' Still painting away ? ' and Kathleen, greatly delighted, replied, ' Still painting away.' "

'Oh yes, Kathleen would appreciate that re-mark. . . . What was your next phase, Ann?"

"I had no more *phases*," said Ann, and got up to get a paper to hold between her face and the fire. "I began to go to London for a month in the spring, and Uncle Bob took me with him when he went abroad, and Mark took me to Switzerland to climb—that was absolutely the best holiday of all—and I had a very, very good time."

"Yes," said her mother, "I remember a poor, bedridden girl in the church saying to me wistfully, 'Miss Ann's life is just like a fairy tale.'"

Ann nodded. "It must have seemed so to her, poor child! And indeed I was very fortunate; I had such wonderful brothers. But I never really liked going away from home unless we went as a family. I hated to leave Davie. How quickly we all seemed to grow up after we left Kirkcaple, Mother!—Robbie especially. It seems to me, looking back, that he sprang quite suddenly from an incredibly mischievous, rough little boy into a gentle, silent schoolboy."

Mrs. Douglas stopped knitting and looked thoughtfully into the fire. "Robbie," she said—how soft, thought Ann, her mother's voice was when it named her boys—"Robbie changed quite suddenly. Up to thirteen he was the firebrand of the household. Your father alone never lost patience with his wild laddie. 'Let him alone,' he would say, 'he'll be the best of the lot yet.' Marget used to say, 'There's naething for it but to make him a sodger; the laddie canna get his fill o' fechtin'.' I don't know what changed him. I think he just got sense. Children do, if you let them alone. He began to be keen to take a good place at school. Robbie had lots of brains, Ann."

"Oh, brains! He was one of the most capable men I ever knew. In India there was no limit to the expectations his friends had for him."

"Oh, Ann, I wish he hadn't gone to India, but his heart was set on it always. The Indian Army! How he used to talk to me about it, and beg me not to make a fuss about letting him go! I would have been so pleased if all my boys had been ministers. I used to picture to myself, when you were all little, how I would go from manse to manse, and what a proud mother I would be. I never could bear the Army as a profession; your father and I never saw eye to eye about that——"

"Poor Mother, it was too bad! You wanted nice little clucking barndoor fowls, and you found yourself with young eagles! I know. It would have been a lovely life for you to do nothing but visit manses. I can see you doing it. But even you stretched your wings a little. Was the South African trip a silver-wedding jaunt?"

"Yes; don't you remember? The congregation gave us a cheque at your father's semi-jubilee, and that was how we spent it."

"Oh, the semi-jubilee!" said Ann. "That was a great occasion. A social meeting, with tea and cakes and speakers and presentations. Eminent men brought from a distance to say complimentary things to you and Father, and all sorts of old friends from Inchkeld and Kirkcaple came with offerings, and so many of them stayed with us that the family had to be boarded out! We acquired a lot of loot at that time in the way of fitted dressing-cases and silver things, and we had a gorgeous silver-wedding cake. Robbie had thought that you couldn't have a bridescake unless you were being married, and when he found he had been mistaken he said the only reason for marrying was gone! It was a glorious cake. The boys were all at home for the Christmas holidays, and when they got hungry in the forenoon they would go and cut chunks off it with a penknife—until we had to hide it. You didn't go away directly, Mums. It was the next November before you left for South Africa, and what a business it was getting you away!"

"'There's muckle adae when cadgers ride,'" Mrs. Douglas quoted. "And it was a great undertaking. I didn't in the least want to go, but your father was as keen as a schoolboy, and I couldn't let him go alone, and I couldn't leave Davie, so the three of us went. Mark had gone to London and was settled in his rooms in the Temple. Robbie and Jim were studying, and you had invitations to fill up all the time."

"I only visited between the boys' vacations, then we were all together at Uncle Bob's. What angels he and Aunt Katharine were to us! The rest of the time I paid visits, and very nearly had a bad

nervous breakdown through having to be con-
sistently pleasant for nine months at a stretch.
You see, I stayed with such very different people,
and the effort to adjust myself to each in turn was
rather wearing. When the boys went back for the
summer term, Uncle Bob took Aunt Katharine
and me over to Touraine. We stayed at Tours,
and made expeditions all round to the lovely old
châteaux, and came home by Paris and London
and finished up at Oxford for Eights' Week.
Wasn't it kind of Uncle Bob ? Oh, I do wish all
the nice people weren't dead ! Each one that goes
takes so much of the light away with him. . . . You
didn't regret taking the trip, Mother ? "

" Not for a minute, except, perhaps, when Davie
supped a whole tin of condensed milk and nearly
perished, and your father was poisoned by a mosquito bite and was blind for two days. It did me
a world of good to come across people who had
never heard of the United Free Church of Scotland
and who had no desire to hear about it, and who
interested me enormously by the way they looked
at life. Mark always used to tell me that with me
journeys ended in Mothers' Meetings, and I was too
much like that. I hadn't, perhaps, realized that
people might be opposed to everything I thought
right and proper and yet be good people. I worried
a good deal about you children at home—it wouldn't
have been me if I hadn't had a trouble—but your
father and Davie were blissfully happy."

" You wrote splendid letters," said Ann, " telling

every detail. Father hated writing letters—we used to tell him that he would rather walk five miles than write a p.c.—and his efforts were quite short and chiefly confined to statements such as : ' What a beautiful blue the ocean is ; ' ' the veldt is much what I thought it would be.' Davie wrote delicious letters on oily scraps of paper—oily because he was generally anointed with a lotion for mosquito bites —which invariably ended : ' Now I must finch up.' He never ceased to mourn the little mongoose that died before he could bring it home, but he did fetch a giant tortoise, which snowked about at Etterick until a specially cold winter finished it. And you brought home a gorgeous fur rug and piles of ostrich feathers. How did you collect so many presents ? "

" Well, you see, part of the time your father was taking services for a minister home on leave, and the kindness and hospitality of the people were boundless. And I felt so mean about doing so little to entertain them when they turned up in Glasgow. We had a few to stay, but most of them were only asked to luncheon, and it sounded so shabby."

" Oh, but it's different out there," Ann said comfortably. " I felt I could never repay the hospitality of the people I met in India. But Robbie didn't at all take up that attitude. ' It's jolly nice for them to have you,' was what he said, and I suppose he meant that visitors from ' home ' are sure of a welcome from exiles from ' home.' You are a stranger in the land of their adoption, and they want you to see the best side of things.

It is different when they come back, then we are all at home together. Aha! tea at last, and Marget bringing it in!"

"Ay," said Marget, putting the kettle on the spirit-lamp, and carrying the covered dish of muffins to the brass stool in the fireplace. "Mysie went awa' doon to the village, seein' it was fresh again. She's young, ye ken, and juist deein' for a crack wi' some o' her frien's. There's a mune, and somebody'll see her hame I've nae doot. Will I licht the lichts the noo?"

Mrs. Douglas smiled at the old woman. "I think we'll have tea in the firelight, Marget. I'm glad Mysie has gone out for a little. It's a dull life up here for a young girl."

"Oh, her," said Marget, dismissing her niece and her possible dullness with a gesture. "D'ye mind, Mem, the maister never likit his tea in the dark. He said he couldna see the road to his mooth. 'Marget,' he would say to me, 'let's have some light on the subject.' That was aye what he said."

Marget stood in the firelight and looked at the two women at the tea-table.

"D'ye ken what I was thinkin' this afternoon when I was ma lane? I was thinkin' how queer it was that a' oor men-folk are awa' and three weemen's a' that's left."

"Marget," said Ann, "what a croaking old raven you are! We're not alone for always. Mr. Mark and Mr. Jim will be back in the spring."

Marget shook her head gloomily. "I've nae comfort in thinkin' about folk awa' ower the sea. It's a terrible dangerous thing to travel."

"Yes, Marget," said her mistress, "we've just been talking, Miss Ann and I, about our trip to South Africa. You washed your hands of us then."

"Me! I never thocht to see ony o' ye again. An' takin' wee Davie into sic danger! A' the sailin' I ever did was from Burntisland to Granton afore they pit up the Forth Bridge."

"You're as bad as little Tommy Hislop," said Ann. "I spoke to him the other day—you know he is going out with his mother to join his father in South Africa?—and asked him how he would like the big ship. 'I'm no gaun in a ship,' he said; 'I dinna like them. I'm gaun roond the road in a cairt wi' ma Uncle Jake.'"

"He's a wise laddie," said Marget. "But it was an awfu' set-oot when you gaed awa' to Africa. An' we thocht we'd better try and let the hoose for the winter and keep it fired, an' some queer American folk cam' aboot it, kin o' missionaries they were, an' the maister said they were decent folk and let them get it."

"Yes, and we knew nothing about them," said Mrs. Douglas. "They belonged to some sort of religious sect in America, and had come over here to do propaganda work. They seemed to live like the early Christians, having all things in common and taking no thought for the morrow, and they could only offer us a nominal rent; but your father talked to them and thought them sincere and liked them, so we gave them the house. We had a cellar full of coal and a cupboard full of jam, and we asked them if they would care to take them both over. They said they would have to ask the Lord, and they came back and said : ' The Lord says we may take the coal, but not the jam,' and we felt so sorry for the funny little people that we gave them the jam. They had the wildest of accents, and we had difficulty in understanding them when they asked, ' Is there a crack in the door to let the mail through ? ' and ' Has the yard been spaded over this fall ? ' "

" Wasn't it like our daft ways," said Ann, as she sipped her tea, " to let our house at a ridiculously low rent to people we knew absolutely nothing about ? You know, Mother, they held meetings in the drawing-room, and the neighbours, watching the people troop in, shuddered for our carpets. I think it was some sort of faith-healing that they did. When they left, a month before you were expected back, Aunt Agatha and Jim and I went to see what the house was like, and arrange about having it thoroughly cleaned. We found it in perfect condition. Two of the women came to see us the night we were there, and told us something of the work. I asked them how they had kept the carpets so fresh, and they said quite simply, ' We asked the Lord.' I shall never forget poor Aunt Agatha's face of utter terror—you know her almost insane horror of infection—when one of those Bible

Christians said, ' Would you believe it, we cured
a case of smallpox in this very room ? ' They had
replaced everything they had broken, so they did
very well by us. It's nice not to have to think
hardly of Christians, whatever sect they belong to."

" That's true," said Marget, " but I think the
puir bodies had leeved on cocoa. Sic a cocoa-tins
they left in a press ! "

" Ann," said Mrs. Douglas, " I've just been
thinking, you should tell about Old Christina in my
Life. She was a most interesting character."

Ann shook her head as she rose from the tea-
table. " I've too many old women in it already.
Besides, I'm not going to write just now. I'm
going to lie in the most comfortable chair the room
contains and read an article in the *Times Literary
Supplement* called ' Love and Shakespeare.' Does
that sound good enough ? "

CHAPTER XX

THE next evening, when Ann sat down with an air of determination at the writing-table, she asked: "Shall I make another stride, Mother? Go on another seven years? It's fine to wear seven-league boots and stride about as one likes among the years. What I ought to do, really, before I write any more, is to read one of the books Mr. Philip Scott sent me this morning. They are lives of different people, and he thinks they might help me a lot with yours."

"It was kind of him to send them," Mrs. Douglas said.

"Oh, thoughtful, right enough, as Glasgow people say. I shall thank him in a sentence I found in Montaigne—here it is. 'They who write lives,' says Montaigne, 'by reason that they take more notice of counsels than events, more of what proceeds from within doors than of what happens without . . . are the fittest for my perusal.' Mr. Scott will be rather impressed, I should think."

Mrs. Douglas appeared to take little interest in Montaigne. She was looking over a book that Mr. Sharp had brought her to read that afternoon.

" Mr. Sharp was telling me," she said presently,
" how good the Miss Scotts are about helping with
anything in the village. He is very keen about
getting up a club for the young men, and he told
them about it, and they at once promised to have
that empty house at the top of the village put in
order, and their nephew, Mr. Philip Scott, sent a
sum of money and is going to supply papers and
books and magazines. Mr. Sharp was quite excited
about it, quite boyish and slangy when he told me
about the football and cricket clubs he hoped to
start ; you would hardly have known him for the
shy, douce young man coming solemnly as a parson
to talk to an old woman. I hadn't realized how
young he was until to-day."

" I wish I had seen him," said Ann. " I hadn't
thought of him as caring for football and cricket.
When do his people come ? "

" Oh, not till just before New Year. And the
housekeeper has already begun to hold it over his
head that the extra work will probably prove too
much for her, and says that perhaps she ought to
go now."

" Better not tell Marget that," Ann warned her
mother. " She is so sorry for Mr. Sharp that she is
quite capable of going to the Manse and publicly
assaulting the woman. But he would be much
better to get rid of her at once ; there shouldn't be
much difficulty about getting another."

Mrs. Douglas looked doubtful. " Better rue sit
than flit," she quoted. " Unless there happened to

be a suitable woman in the district, I'm afraid it wouldn't be easy to induce one to come to such an out-of-way place. And they ask such outrageous wages now. When Marget came to me she said, 'I doot ye'll think I've an awfu' big wage. I've been gettin' seeven pound in the half-year.' And she said it in a hushed voice as if the very sound of the sum frightened her."

Ann laughed and quoted :

" ' Times is changed,' said the cat's-meat man.
' Lights is riz,' said the cat's-meat man.

The days are over when people could be passing rich on fourteen pounds in the year. Mother, are you quite sure you want to stay here over Christmas ? It is such a deadly time at the best. Won't you go and stay with some of the people who have asked us ? "

" No, I think not. I wouldn't like to be with any one but my very own at Christmas-time, and it would be ridiculous to bring the children so far—so we shall just stay quietly here."

" Very well," said Ann. Then, after a pause, " I'm asking you, Mother, but you won't pay any attention—where shall I begin to-night ? I have written about the South African trip, shall I go on another seven years ? "

" Seven years," her mother repeated. " That makes Mark thirty-one. Oh, a tremendous lot happened in these seven years, Ann. Robbie went

to India ; Jim left Oxford and had just finished his
law studies when Uncle Bob died and he had to
take his place ; Mark married ; you went to India.
And you talk glibly about writing it in one evening."

"It is rather a spate of events," Ann confessed.
"Did they really all happen in seven years, before
Davie was fourteen? First, Robbie sailed for
India. One of the church people who deeply de-
plored his going said, ' He's far ower bonnie a laddie
for India.' "

"So he was," said Robbie's mother. "It was
like cutting off a right hand to let him go."

"But, Mother," Ann said, "I don't think we
need grudge the years he was in India, for he was
never really divided from us, his heart was always
at home. People there told me that though he
loved his work he was always talking of Scotland,
his heart was full of the ' blessed beastly place '
all the time. D'you remember his first leave ?
Long before it was sanctioned he had engaged a
berth and given us elaborate instructions about
writing to every port. It was only three months
—six weeks at home—but it was enough, he said,
to build the bridge. He was just the same, the
same kind, simple boy, eager to spend his money
buying presents for every one ; then, of course,
his money went done ! I can see him now, lying
on the floor with a bit of paper and a pencil trying
to make out if he had any money to go back with.
. . . I wonder what made Robbie so utterly lovable ?
If we could only recapture the charm and put it

into words—but we can only remember it and miss
it. I think it was partly the way he had of laughing
at himself, and the funny, short-sighted way he
screwed up his eyes—when he missed a shot he
would call himself a ' blind buffer.' I always remember his second leave as being, I think, almost
the happiest time in my life."

" Yes. It was the last time we were all together
—two years after Mark's marriage. Mark took
Fennanhopes, which held us all comfortably, and
there was good shooting. Alis was a year old, and
the idol of her uncles. Davie was about fourteen,
I suppose. Robbie was particularly pleased that
Davie showed signs of being a good shot, and poor
Davie was so anxious to please that he fired at and
brought down a snipe, and then suffered agonies of
remorse over killing what he described as ' that wee
long-nebbit bird.' "

" I remember that," said Ann. " Mother, wasn't
it odd how like Robbie and Davie were ? Plain
little Davie, and Robbie who was so good-looking.
After Robbie was gone, when Davie and I were
together in a room, I used to shut my eyes and make
myself almost believe it was Robbie talking to me—
and both were so like Father. It must have been
the way they moved, and the gentle way they
touched things—and the way they fell over things !
Mark called Davie ' light-footed Ariel,' from his
capacity for taking tosses. They were such friends,
Father and the four boys, and Father was the
youngest of the lot."

Mrs. Douglas sat with her hands clasped in her lap, looking straight before her. When she spoke it was as if she were speaking to herself.

" Robbie used to say that it was a mistake for a family to be too affectionate, for when we were parted we were homesick for each other all the time. But he wrote once : ' Foreign service must be a cheerless business for the unclannish. . . .' "

" Mother," Ann said gently, " I think you can almost say Robbie's letters by heart. It wasn't so bad saying good-bye to him after his first leave —at least, not for me, for I was going out to him for the next cold weather. And Mark's marriage was our next excitement ; we were frightfully unused to marriages in our family, for you had no brothers or sisters married, and Father had none. Had you and Father proved such an awful example ? "

" It is odd," Mrs. Douglas agreed ; " but some families are like that. Others flop into matrimony like young ducks into water. Mark's engagement gave me a great shock. It came as a complete surprise, and we knew nothing about Charlotte, and it seemed to me that it must break up everything, and that I must lose my boy."

" It might have meant that, Mother, if Charlotte hadn't been Charlotte. I know young wives who have taken their husbands completely away from their own people. I don't think Mark would have allowed himself to be taken, and I am very sure that Charlotte never tried. How odd it is to remember that first visit she paid to us after she got engaged. None of us had ever seen her, and we wondered what we would talk to her about for a whole fortnight. And if it was bad for us to have a stranger come in amongst us, how infinitely worse it was for poor Charlotte to have to face a solid phalanx of—possibly hostile—new relations! We have often laughed at it since, and Charlotte has confessed that she had a subject for each of us. To you, Mums, she talked about the poor; to Jim, poetry; to Father, flowers; Davie needed no conversation, only butter-scotch; my subject was books. The great thing about Charlotte was that she could always laugh, always be trusted to see the funny side if there was one, and as a family we value that more than anything. And we are pagans in our love for beauty, and Charlotte was very good to look at. We weren't really formidable, Charlotte says. Father she loved at once. Having no brothers of her own, she was delighted to adopt Robbie and Jim and Davie. You and I were the snags, Mother."

"I?" said Mrs. Douglas in a hurt voice. "I'm sure I tried to be as kind as——"

"Of course you did, you couldn't be anything else if you tried; but you had just a little the air of a lioness being robbed of its whelps—and you sighed a good deal. Mark and I had been so much to each other always that it wouldn't have been surprising if Charlotte had disliked the person that she was, in a way, supplanting—but we both liked

Mark too well to dislike each other, so we became friends. I never hear a joke now but I think 'I must remember to tell Charlotte that,' and I never enjoy a book without thinking 'I wish Charlotte were here that we might talk it over.' We have laughed so much together, and we have cried so much together, that I don't think anything could come between us. And she has been so good about letting us share the children—What an event the wedding was! D'you remember the hat you chose for it in the middle of a most tremendous thunderstorm? It didn't seem to matter much what hat you took for we expected to be killed any minute, and it always rather solemnized you to put it on."

"It was too youthful for me," Mrs. Douglas said gloomily. "Weddings always depress me, and when it's one of your own it's worse."

"You enjoyed it in spite of yourself," said her daughter. "I know I enjoyed it—one of the seven bridesmaids in pink and silver, and I know Davie enjoyed it, flying about in his kilt. It was his very first visit to London, and we took him to *The Scarlet Pimpernel*, to a *matinée*. When we came out into the sunny street after three hours' breathless excitement, he was like an owl at noonday; I think he had forgotten entirely that he lived in the twentieth century. It was hard luck that Robbie couldn't be at the wedding. He was so amused when we wrote to him about Father kissing the bride—kissing was an almost unheard-of thing with us in those days. He wrote : ' To think of my elderly, respectable

father kissing his daughter-in-law and jaunting over
to Paris. He'll be losing his job one of these days.'
We went on to Paris after the wedding and then to
the Lakes, and all got more or less seedy. Father
and I were the only two who kept quite well, and
we had to go and buy hot-water bags for the rest
of you. Davie was in Jim's room, and in the middle
of the night, feeling ill, he thought he would go and
tell me about it, and on his way to my room he saw
in the moonlight a statue on the landing, and in his
fright he fell down a whole flight of stairs. And none
of you could eat the good dinners—it was all very
provoking."

"Yes," said Mrs. Douglas; "it is very provoking to pay for meals you haven't eaten. And
no sooner did we get home than we were all as
hungry as hunters! We had to begin after that to
get your clothes ready for going to India."

"That was great fun. I did enjoy getting all the
new frocks and the hundred and one things I needed.
My bridesmaid's frock made a very pretty evening
dress, and I had a white satin one for my presenta-
tion, and a pale green satin that was like moonlight.
Robbie was dreadfully given to walking on my train
when we went out to dinner; I was usually announced to the sound of the rending of gathers. I
wonder if other people find as much to laugh at
in India as Robbie and I did? Practically everything made us laugh. I can never be sufficiently
thankful that I was allowed to have that six months
alone with him. It is something precious to remem-

ber all my life. . . . But the leaving him was terrible.
By some wangling he managed to get down the
river with me ; that gave us a few more hours together.   He had just left me, and I was standing
straining my streaming eyes after the launch, when
another boat came to the side of the ship and a man
sprang out and came up to me.   It was one of
Martyrs' young men, Willie Martin, a clerk in a
shipping office, who had watched for my name cn
the passenger list and had come to say good-bye.
It was very touching of him.   I expect I reminded
him of home."

"His people were so pleased that you had seen
him," Mrs. Douglas said.   "You had to go the
minute you came home and tell them all you could
about him.   He never came home, poor boy !   When
war broke out he joined up in India, and was one of
the missing."

"I know.   A decent laddie he was.   When we
were in Calcutta Robbie and I invited him to tea
one Sunday afternoon, and he came, and was so nice
and modest and shy ;   Robbie was loud in his
praises because he went away directly after tea.
You see, I had got the names of several young men
from Scotland who were in business in Calcutta, and
we asked them to tea on Sunday afternoons, when
they were free, and Robbie didn't like the ones who
sat on and on making no move to go away.   Some
we had to ask to dinner because they hadn't gone
away at eight o'clock ! "

CHAPTER XXI

" . . . It was our favourite occupation, your father's and mine, when we had an hour together by the fire, to dream of the good times we would have when we retired. When we got very tired of plodding along with our faces against the wind, when people seemed indifferent about our efforts and ungrateful, when something we had taken immense pains about proved a failure, when term-time came and family after family whom we had learned to count on moved away to outlying suburbs, leaving gaps that couldn't be filled, your father would say to me, ' Never mind, Nell ; it'll be all over some day and we'll get away to the country,' and we would talk about and plan what we would do when we had no longer a congregation to tend. But, inside me, I was always sceptical about the dream ever coming true. I knew he wouldn't leave his work until he had to ; and I had visions of going on and on until we were old and grey-headed. One should never let oneself weary in this world, for everything stops so soon."

Ann sat on the fender stool sharpening a pencil,

very absorbed in the point she was making. When it was done to her satisfaction she turned round to her mother.

" Did you really ever weary in well-doing, Mother ? Ah, well ! ' Rejoice that ye have time to weary in.' But it was a pretty uphill job you and Father had in that district. There was one thing, though the congregation was small it was tremendously appreciative. You remember Mr. Gardner, the elder ? I used to like to watch his face when Father preached—it was a study. He had the nicest little doggy face, with honesty written all over it. And his friend, great big Mr. Law who sat in the seat behind him—he was exactly my idea of the Village Blacksmith."

" Mr. Law should have been put into a book," Mrs. Douglas said. " Don't you remember how he used to stand up and square his great shoulders and speak in broad Lowland Scots ? "

" I should think so. Mr. Law's addresses were our great delight. He began one on Evolution with : ' Some folk say that oor great-grandfathers hoppit aboot on the branches.' He always talked of ' the Apostle Jims,' and do you remember the description he gave us of some picture he had seen of the ' Last Judgment,' by Michael Angelo ? I don't know where this masterpiece is hung, but Mr. Law said that it depicted ' Michael Angelo creepin' oot o' a hole aneath the throne and a look o' hesitancy on the face of God ! ' And he told us one day that he was sure the Apostle Paul had never been to Scotland, or he most certainly would have put on record that Ben Lomond was the finest hill that he had ever set eyes on."

Mrs. Douglas smiled. " Mr. Law was a fine man and a most original speaker, but he felt so strongly on certain things that he was apt to upset other members."

" Ah," said Ann, shaking her head wisely, " one dreads that class of lad in a church."

" John Gardner, on the other hand," Mrs. Douglas went on, " was an undiluted blessing in the church. He was willing to do—indeed he liked doing—all the work that brought no kudos, all the dull jobs that most people try to evade. And he was always there. No matter how bad the night, you were always sure that his ' doggy ' face would beam on you. ' Thank God,' your father used to say, ' thank God for the faithful few.' "

" Yes," said Ann. " I remember I was discussing with the boys, in our usual rather irreverent way, who of the people we knew would be ' farthest ben ' in the next world. We denied admittance to quite a number of people famous for their good works ; others, we thought, might just scrape in. ' But,' said Mark, ' I back Father and Dr. Struthers and wee Gardner to be sitting on the very next steps of the Throne.' "

" Oh, Ann ! " her mother expostulated. " I never did like the way you and the boys spoke of sacred things ; it sounded so flippant. But ' wee Gardner,' as you call him, was a great gift to us.

Oh, and there were others almost as good. And the young men and women were really rather special."

"They were," said Ann. "The books they read and the wideness of their interests put me to shame. You know, Mother, it must have been very interesting for them, for they found their whole social life in the church. What fun they had at the social meetings! I almost envied them. At one social a girl said to me that she wished the men would come up—I suppose they were talking and smoking in the lower hall—and I said, stupidly, that I thought it was nicer without the men, and the girl replied with some sagacity, ' You wouldn't say that if they were your own kind of men.' A church is a great matchmaker. Old Mrs. Buchanan, talking one day of the young men and maidens in the choir, said, ' They pair *just like doos.*' There is one good thing about a small congregation— everybody knows everybody else. We were like one big family. It is touching to hear them talk now about those days ; they look back on them as a sort of Golden Age. And the presents they gave us! And they were so poor. Each of the boys got a gold watch and chain when they left home, and when I went to India I had quite a collection of keepsakes, some very odd, but all greatly valued by me, their owner. Mother, why are you sitting ' horn idle,' as Marget would say ? Have you finished your knitting ? "

Mrs. Douglas looked at her idle hands. " My knitting is like Penelope's web," she said ; " there is no end to it. I'm simply sitting idle for a change, sitting thinking about days that are past, and about people I shall never see again on this side of time. I think a great deal of Martyrs, and I feel very humble when I think of the affection and loyalty given to us."

"But, Mother, you can't have liked everybody in the church. The thing's not possible. Think of Mr. Philip Scott and the 'acid' he thinks necessary, and say something really unkind. . . . You know you never liked Mrs. Marshall, the elder's wife—she was a terrible tale-bearer, and always making mischief."

"Yes, she was, poor body. But, Ann, she was kind when Rosamund was ill, and——"

Ann threw up her hands. "Mother, you are hopeless. I'm not going to try to put any acid into you. You're just like strawberry jam. I'm afraid I've got your share of acid as well as my own, that's why I've such an 'ill-scrapit tongue.'"

But Mrs. Douglas wasn't listening. She was looking before her, dreaming. Presently she said :

"Ann, it doesn't seem a very complimentary thing to say to you, but I look back on the winter you were in India with very great pleasure. We were quite alone, your father and I, for the first time almost since we were married, and he often said, laughing, 'We're never better than when we're alone, Nell.' The letters were such a pleasure—Mark's every morning, Jim's every other morning, a curious scrawl from little Davie once

a week, and on Saturday Robbie's letter and your
great budget. Oh, Ann, Ann, why was I not de-
liriously happy? All of you well, all of you pros-
pering, my man beside me, and life full of sunlight."

" Ay, Mother, you should have been down on
your knees thanking heaven fasting—and if the
truth were known I daresay you were. But it's
only afterwards you realize how happy you have
been ! "

" Yes, afterwards," said Mrs. Douglas. " It
was when you came home from India that you
noticed that your father was failing. Living with
him I had noticed nothing."

" There was hardly anything to notice. He
didn't walk with the same light step. He sometimes wondered why his congregation always chose
to live up four flights of stairs, and one night he
said to me, half laughing, half serious : ' I'm beginning to be afraid of that which is high.' But
he was well for a year or two after that, till he had
the bad heart attack, and the doctor warned us
that it was time he was thinking of giving up
his work."

Ann got up and stood with both hands on the
mantelshelf looking into the fire.

" I remember," she went on, " the curious unreal
feeling I had, as if the solid earth had somehow
given way beneath my feet, when I realized that
Father's life was in danger. And then, when days
and weeks passed, and he didn't seem to get worse,

we just put the thought away from us and told ourselves that doctors were often mistaken, and that if he took reasonable care all would be well."

" He was only sixty-one," Mrs. Douglas said, " and the doctors assured us that if he gave up preaching he might have years of fairly good health. He had worked himself done. Twenty-two years in Glasgow had been too much for him."

Ann nodded. " He never said a word, but the fact was Father hated cities. Rosamund used to call the Park ' the policeman's country,' because of the notices to keep off the grass, and she called Etterick ' God's country.' Father longed all the time for ' God's country.' He would have been supremely happy as minister of some moorland place, with time to write, and time to love his books and flowers, and instead he had to spend his days toiling up and down endless stairs, never getting away from the sight of squalor and misery, doing the King's work through the unfeatured years. And yet he was perfectly content. He was able to find a Sabbath stillness in the noise, and from some hidden spring he could draw wells of living water to make in that dreary place a garden ' bright with dawn and dew ' to refresh a haggard world. . . . You must have felt very bad about leaving Martyrs, Mother ?—after all those years."

" Oh. . . . We felt it to be almost treachery on our part to leave some of those poor people. They depended on us. We considered whether we ought to stay on in Glasgow and still help a little, unofficially, as it were, but you were all against that, and finally we took a house in Priorsford to be near Jim. I was glad when it was settled, and glad when those last months in Glasgow were over. It was miserable work dismantling the house and packing up and saying good-bye."

"Everything has an end," said Ann, "'and a pudden has twa,' to quote Marget's favourite saying. But I could hardly believe we were finished with Martyrs, that we would tramp no more that long road, and sit no more in that back pew to the side of the pulpit, and look up at Father Sunday after Sunday—Mother, surely Father was a very good preacher?"

Mrs. Douglas sat up very straight, as if she were challenging any one to contradict her, and said proudly: "He was the best preacher I ever heard. And if he were here he would laugh at me for saying so."

"He would," said Ann; "but I think I agree with you."

"A communion in Martyrs," her mother went on; "what an occasion it was! Except for length—our services were always short—I expect it was the same service that the Covenanters held, fearfully, as hunted men. 'Following the custom of our fathers'—can't you hear him say it?—your father always 'fenced' the tables and read the warrant. Then we sung those most mournful words:

    ''Twas on that night when doomed to know
      The eager rage of every foe';

and your father took his place among the elders
round the table in the choir seat. He always
held a slice of the bread, and, breaking it, said,
'Mark the breaking of the bread,' and after the
tables were served he said a few concluding words.
I used to listen for his voice falling on the stillness—'Communicants!' It seemed to me very
beautiful."

"I know. But what will always remain with
me is the way he said the Benediction. He was
a very vigorous preacher, my father. There was
no settling down to sleep 'under' him. Sometimes he would describe the fate of those who
wilfully refused salvation, very sadly, very solemnly,
and then he would shut the big Bible and, leaning
over the side of the pulpit, he would say, 'But,
brethren, I am persuaded better things of you.'
Then came the Benediction, and I listened for the
swish of the silk of the Geneva gown as he stretched
his arms wide over the people, and his voice came
healing, soothing, restful as sleep : 'May the peace
of God which passeth all understanding . . .'
On that last Sunday—the last time he ever
preached—he gave us no farewell words, and I was
thankful, for he had an uncanny gift of pathos ;
but he offered us, as he had offered us every time
he preached in that pulpit, Christ and Him cruci-
fied. We sang 'Part in Peace,' and then he looked

round the church, slowly, searchingly, round the wide galleries and through the area. Was he seeing again all those brave old figures who had so loyally held up his hands until they had to step out into the Unknown? In twenty-two years one sees many go. Then he held out his arms—the swish of the Geneva gown—and for the last time the listeners heard that golden voice saying, ' May the peace of God which passeth all understanding keep your hearts and minds ' . . ."

There were tears standing in Ann's grey eyes as she said, " I know it's a ridiculous thing to say, but it seems to me that the people who knew Father and were blessed by him have a better idea of what that peace means—oh, Mother, aren't we a couple of foolish women sitting lauding our own ! "

" No," Mrs. Douglas said stoutly ; " we're not. If Martyrs people were in the room now I'm sure they would say ' Amen ' to all you say of your father. And I lived with him for thirty-four years and I couldn't imagine a better man. He was a saint, and yet he was human and funny and most lovable, and that isn't too common a combination. There can be nothing more terrible than to be married to a sanctimonious saint. Imagine being *forgiven* all the time ! Every time you lost your temper or spoke maliciously or unadvisedly, to see a pained expression on his face ! "

" It would drive one to crime," said Ann solemnly.

CHAPTER XXII

MARGET stood in the middle of the room pleating her black silk apron between her fingers. She wanted to be asked to sit down, for she had heard Ann and her mother talking of the removal from Glasgow, and she felt that what she had to say on the subject was of value.

" Cornel and Mrs. Moncrieff 'll be comin' next week," she reminded them. " I'm airin' the rooms an' pitten' bottles in the beds noo, for I'm never verra sure aboot unused rooms in a new hoose. Ye'll no' can write when they're here, Miss Ann. It'll tak' ye a' yer time to crack wi' the Cornel."

" Oh, but it's a long time till next week, Marget," Ann said, as she went over to the bureau to address a parcel she had been wrapping up. " I'll have finished my writing by then."

" Is that sweeties for the bairns ? " Marget asked, eyeing the parcel and sitting down as if by accident. " Ye'll file their stomachs."

" It's only Miss Smart's tablet. I never go to Priorsford without getting them some tablet at their dear Miss Smart's. Rory said to me

solemnly the last time he was here, after a very
successful visit to the shop, ' There's nobody in
England like Miss Smart.' "

" I daresay not," said Mrs. Douglas. " London
shops don't encourage small boys to poke in behind
the counter. Miss Smart is so good-natured that
her shop is a sort of Aladdin's Cave to all young
Priorsford—Ann, have you remembered to put in
my *Life* about Alis and the others being born ? "

" Goodness gracious, I have not," cried Ann.
" But I haven't got to that time yet, have
I ? You shouldn't give me unnecessary frights,
Mother. Imagine leaving out Alis ! Davie would
have been annoyed. He was the proudest young
uncle—was he thirteen ?—and Alis adored him.
' My saucy Uncle Boy ' she named him, when she
could speak ; and they were inseparable. He was
a mixture of playmate and kind old Nannie to her.
If any one made Alis cry, in a moment Davie
appeared and snatched her up and dried her tears.
' You don't know how I love my Uncle Boy,' I
heard her telling some one. ' He's my favourite of
men.' No, Davie wouldn't like Alis forgotten."

" I used to hear Alis boast," Mrs. Douglas said,
" about her young uncle to Mary Elizabeth, and
when Mary came to stay she warned her, ' He is
my Uncle Boy, you know, Mary, not yours,' and
Mary said nothing until she got Davie alone, then
she whispered to him, ' Uncle Boy, will you be my
Daddy,' and thought she had scored off poor Alis
completely."

" A' the bairns likit Davie," Marget put in.
" He had sic a cheery face an' he was aye lauchin'.
I've seen me lauch mysel' in the kitchen when I
heard him lauchin' up the stairs. He fair hated
to be vexed aboot onything. Ye mind when you
were ill, Mem, he took it awfu' ill-oot."

" All our troubles began after we left Glasgow,"
Ann said gloomily. " All those years we had
been extraordinarily healthy ; doctors would have
starved if they had had to depend on us. I know
I used to look pityingly at sick people and wonder to
myself if they wouldn't be quite well if they only
made an effort. We talked bracingly about never
having people ill in bed in our house. ' We treat
our patients on their feet,' we said, with what must
have been an insufferably superior air. And then
we had been so lucky for so long ; the boys got
everything they tried for, and everything prospered
with us, so I suppose it was time we got a downing ;
but that didn't make it any easier when it came.
We left Glasgow knowing that father's health
would always be an anxiety ; but we didn't
bargain for you crocking up, Mums."

" I'm sure I didn't want to ' crock up ' as you
call it," said Mrs. Douglas, looking aggrieved.

" Of course you didn't," Ann hastened to soothe
her mother's ruffled feelings. Then she began to
laugh. " But it was rather like you, Mother, to
go and take a most obscure disease ! We can
laugh at it now because you got better, but we put
in a terrible year. First the removing to Priors-

ford in May—taking the books alone was like removing mountains, though we gave away armfuls to any one who could be induced to take them—and we were no sooner settled down in our new house than you began to feel seedy. It began so gradually that we thought nothing of it. You looked oddly yellow, and seemed to lose strength ; but you said it was nothing, and I was only too glad to believe it. When at last we got the doctor he said you were very seriously ill, sent you to bed, and got a trained nurse."

' Eh, I say," Marget began. " I'll never forget that winter. We juist got fricht efter fricht. It was something awfu'. It was a guid thing we left the new hoose and gaed to live wi' Mr. Jim."

" It was," said Ann ; " we needed Jim beside us. Those awful attacks of fever when you lay delirious for days at a time ! We dragged you through one turn and got you fairly well, only to see you take another. It was most disheartening. No wonder poor Davie stamped with rage. Doctors and nurses walked in and out of the house, specialists were summoned from Edinburgh and Glasgow. All our money was spent on physicians, and, like the woman in the Bible, you were none the better, but rather the worse. None of them gave us any hope that you would recover. One evening we were told you couldn't live over the night, and Mark and Charlotte came flying up from London, only to find you sitting up knitting a stocking ! I really never believed that you wouldn't get better. You weren't patient enough somehow; indeed, my dear, there was nothing of the story-book touch about you at all when you were ill. What a thrawn, resentful little patient you were! You occupied your time when you were fairly well up-braiding me for keeping the house so extravagantly. You said you were sure there was great leakage. I'm sure there was, but I couldn't help it. It took me all my time to nurse you and keep things com-fortable in the house and see that Father didn't over-exert himself. Marget's whole time was taken up cooking—illness makes such a lot of extra work—and, fortunately, we had a very good housemaid. But if you didn't shine as a patient, I certainly didn't shine as a nurse. I'm afraid I hadn't the gentle, womanly touch of the real ministering angel, smoothing pillows and such like. I knew nothing about nursing, and you said I heaved hot-water bags at you."

"So you did; but you were an excellent nurse for all that. But oh, I did feel so guilty keeping you hanging round me. It was more than a year out of your life, just when you would have been having such a good time."

"Oh," said Ann, "I don't grudge the year— I've had heaps of good times. The only really bad times were when the attacks of high fever came and you got unconscious; then you wouldn't let a nurse into the room. Jim and I had to sit up with you for nights on end. But you were very brave, and you never let your illness get on our nerves. You just bounded up from an attack like an india-rubber ball. The doctors simply gasped at you. You said good-bye to us so often that we began to take it quite casually, merely saying, ' Well, have some beef-tea just now, anyway '; and Father used to laugh and say, ' You'll live and loup dykes yet.' "

" I'm sure I wasn't at all keen to live, Ann. When you get very far down dying seems so simple and easy; but I did want to see Robbie again. I think that kept me alive. When did you take me to London ? In spring, wasn't it ? "

" Yes, in March. You weren't getting a bit better, and some one told Mark about the vaccine treatment, and he thought it might be worth trying. We were told that the journey would certainly kill you, but you said, ' No such thing,' so off we set, you and I, all on a wild March morning. You stood the journey splendidly; but two days after you arrived you took the worst fever turn of all. The London doctors came and told me you wouldn't live over the night, and I really thought they were going to be right that time. I telephoned to Priorsford, and it was Davie answered me, ' Is that you, Nana ? ' I was sorry to worry the boy, but I had to tell you were very ill, and that I thought Jim should come up by the night train. But you warstled through again, and then Mark brought Sir Armstrong Weir to see you. We had seen several London doctors, very glossy and well dressed, with

beautiful cars, and we wondered if this great Sir
Armstrong would be even smarter. But the great
man came in a taxi, and wasn't at all well dressed
—grey and bent and very gentle."

"He looked old," Mrs. Douglas said; "but he
couldn't have been so very, for he told me his own
mother was living. He was very kind to me."

"He cured you," said Ann.

"Oh no," said Mrs. Douglas.

"Well, it was partly his vaccine and partly your
own marvellous pluck."

"Oh no. It wasn't pluck or vaccine or anything,
but just that I had to live more days on the earth."

"'Deed ay," said Marget, nodding in agreement
with her mistress. "Ye never did ony guid until
ye had given up doctors a'thegither. As soon as
we got quat o' them ye began to improve."

"Now, now, Marget," said Ann, "you get
carried away by your dislike of doctors. We've
been very thankful to see them many a time."

"Oh, they're a' richt for some things; but whenever it's onything serious ye canna lippen to them.
When there's onything wrang wi' yer inside naebody can help ye but yer Maker."

Ann laughed. "What a gloomy view to take,
Marget. You remind me of the old lady who
said that she gave to Dr. Barnardo's Homes
' because he has no one to help him but God.' I
won't let you malign doctors. The best kind of
doctor is about the highest type of human being.
What are you snorting at, Marget?"

" I could wish them a better job ! Hoo onybody can like clartin' aboot in folk's insides ! Doctorin's a nesty job, and I'm glad nane o' oor laddies took up wi't. They a' got clean, genteel jobs."

" Such as soldiering ? "

" Oh, I'm no' heedin' muckle aboot sodgerin' aither," said Marget. Then, turning to her mistress, she said, " As you say, Mem, nae doctor can kill ye while there's life in the cup. D'ye think it was mebbe the flittin' that brocht on yer trouble ? Ye ken ye washt a' the china yersel'."

Mrs. Douglas smiled at her. " All the years you've known me, Marget, have you ever heard of housework doing me any harm ? No. It was some sort of blood-poisoning that went away as mysteriously as it came. Though what I was spared for I know not. If I had died, how often you would have said of me, ' She was taken from the evil to come.' "

" Poor darling ! " said Ann. " Do you think you were spared simply that you might receive evil things ? Say, rather, that you were spared to help the rest of us through the terrible times. . . . Father, mercifully, had kept wonderfully well through your illness. He had accepted his limitations and knew that he must not attempt a hill road, or fight against a high wind, or move quickly ; and really, looking at him, it was difficult to believe that anything ailed him."

" But it must have been very bad for him, Ann,

all the scares he got with my illness. It's dreadful for me to think that the last year of his life was made uncomfortable and distressed by me."

"But you mustn't think that. Even in those stormy days he seemed to carry about with him a quiet, sunny peace. What a blessing we had him through that time ; the sight of him steadied one."

"And I'm sure I couldn't have lived through that time without him," Mrs. Douglas said ; "although I sometimes got very cross with him sitting reading with a pleased smile on his face when I felt so miserable."

"I think he really enjoyed his restricted life," said Ann. "To be in the open air was his delight, and he was able to take two short walks every day and spend some time pottering in the garden, going lovingly round his special treasures, those rock plants that he was trying to persuade to grow on the old wall by the waterside. We wanted him to drive, but he hated driving ; he liked, he said, to feel the ground under his feet. He never looked anything but well with his fresh-coloured face."

"He got younger-lookin'," Marget said. "I suppose it was no havin' a kirk to worry aboot, the lines of his face got kind o' smoothed oot. D'ye mind when he used to come into the room, Mem, you aye said it was like a breath o' fresh air."

"Yes, Marget, I mind well. Neil Macdonald said when he was staying with us once that when Father came into the room he had a look in his eyes as if he had been on a watch-tower, ' As if '—Neil

said, in his soft, Highland voice—' as if he had been
looking across Jordan into Canaan's green and
pleasant land.' "

Ann smiled. " I know what he meant. D'ye
remember Father's little Baxter's *Saints' Rest* that
he carried about with him in his pocket and read
in quiet moments ? And his passion for adventure
books ? I think Jim got him every ' thriller ' that
was published. And the book on Border Poets that
he was writing ? He always wrote a bit after tea.
No matter who was having tea with us, Father calmly
turned when he was finished to the bureau, pulled
forward a chair—generally rumpling up the rug,
and then I cried, ' Oh, *Father* ! '—and sat quietly
writing amid all the talk and laughter. He had
nearly finished it when he died. . . . That last
week he seemed particularly well. He said his feet
had such a firm grip of the ground now. I didn't
want him to go out because it was stormy, and he
held up one foot and said, " Dear me, girl, look at
those *splendid* soles ! ' "

Marget put her apron up to her eyes. " Eh, lassie,
ye're whiles awfu' like yer faither."

There was a silence in the room while the three
women thought their own thoughts.

At last Ann said, " What pathetic things we
mortals are ! That Saturday night when we sat
round the fire my heart was singing a song of thankfulness. You were still frail, Mother, but you were
wonderfully better, and to have you with us again
sitting by the fire knitting your stocking was com-

fort unspeakable. Jim had been reading aloud the *Vailima Letters*, and the letters to Barrie and about Barrie sent us to *The Little Minister*, and I read to you Waster Luny's inimitable remarks about ancestors. ' It's a queer thing that you and me his nae ancestors. . . . They're as lost to sicht as a flagon-lid that's fa'en ahint the dresser.' I forget how it goes, but Father enjoyed it greatly. I think anything would have made us laugh that night, for the morning's post had brought us a letter from Robbie with the unexpected news that he had been chosen for some special work and would be home shortly—he thought in about three months' time. And as I looked at you and Father smiling at each other in the firelight I said in my heart, like Agag, ' *Surely the bitterness of death is past !* ' and the next day Father died."

Mrs. Douglas sat silent with her head bowed, but Marget said, " Oh, lassie ! lassie ! " and wept openly.

In a little while Ann spoke again :

" It isn't given to many to be ' happy on the occasion of his death,' but Father was. His end was as gentle as his life. He slipped away suddenly on the Sabbath afternoon, at the hour when his hands had so often been stretched in benediction. He died in his boyhood's home. The November sun was going down behind the solemn round-backed hills, the familiar sound of the Tweed over its pebbles was in his ears, and though he had to cross the dark river the waters weren't deep for

him. I think, like Mr. Standfast, he went over
' wellnigh dry shod.' And he was taken before
the storm broke. Three months later the cable
came that broke our hearts. Robbie had died
after two days' illness on his way to Bombay to
get the steamer for home.''

CHAPTER XXIII

THEY had been talking of many things, Ann and her mother, and had fallen silent.

The wind was tearing through the Green Glen, and moaning eerily round the house of Dreams, throwing at intervals handfuls of hail which struck against the panes like pistol-shots.

" A wild night," Mrs. Douglas said, looking over her shoulder at the curtained windows, and drawing her chair nearer the fire. " This is the sort of night your father liked to sit by the fireside. He would lift his head from his book to listen to the wind outside, look round the warm, light room and give a contented sigh."

" I know," said Ann ; " it was very difficult doing without Father. He had always enjoyed the good things of life so frankly there seemed no pleasure any longer in a good dinner, or a fine morning, or a blazing fire, or an interesting book, since he wasn't there to say how fine it was. Besides, his very presence had been a sort of benediction, and it was almost as if the roof of life had been removed—and it was much worse for you, poor Mother. We were afraid you would go, too."

"Oh, Ann"—Mrs. Douglas, clasping *Hours of Silence*, raised tearful eyes to her daughter—"I'm sure I didn't *want* to live. I don't know why I go on living."

Ann caught her mother's hands in her own. "You funny wee body! You remind me of the Paisley woman who told me she had lost all her sons in the war, and was both surprised and annoyed that she hadn't died of grief. 'An' ma neebor juist lost the one an' *she* de'ed, and folk said she niver liftit her heid efter her laddie went, and here wis me losin' a' mine and gaun aboot quite healthy! An' I'm sure I wis as vext as whit she wis. It's no want o' grievin' for I'm never dune greetin'—I begin early i' the mornin' afore I get ma cup o' tea.' "

"Oh, the poor body!" said Mrs. Douglas. "I know so well what she meant. It sounds funny, but it isn't a bit. . . . Your father's death was sheer desolation to me. I remember a long time ago at Kirkcaple, going to see a widow who had brought up a most creditable family, and, looking round her cosy kitchen, I said something about how well she had done, and that life must be pleasant for her with her children all up and doing well. And the brisk, active little woman looked at me, and I was surprised to see tears in her rather hard eyes.

"The bairns are a' richt," she said; "but it maks

an awfu' difference when ye lose yer pairtner. . . .'
And then I have so many things to regret. . . ."

" Regret ? " Ann laughed. " I don't think you
have one single thing to regret. If ever a man was
happy in his home it was my father."

" Ah, but I was bad to him often. I pretended
to be a Radical—a thing I never was really—simply
from contrariness. If I had him back——"

" Now what would you change if you could ? "
Ann asked.

" Well, for one thing I would never contradict
him, or argue. . . ."

" Oh, how Father would have loathed that.
Arguing was the breath of life to him, and he
hated to be agreed with."

Mrs. Douglas went on. " And I would never
worry him to do things that went against his judgment. When people took a *tirravee* and sent for
their lines he always wanted to give them to them
at once, but I used to beg him to go and reason with
them and persuade them to remain. They generally
did, for they only wanted to be made a fuss of, but
I see now I was quite wrong ; people so senseless
deserved no consideration. And I wouldn't worry
him to go and ask popular preachers to come to us
for anniversary services and suchlike occasions !
That was the thing he most hated doing."

" I don't wonder," said Ann. " To ask favours
is never pleasant, and popular preachers are apt to
get a bit above themselves and condescend a little
to the older, less successful men who are living in

a day of small things. But I don't think any of us, you least of all, need reproach ourselves with not having appreciated Father. And yet, when he went away it seemed quite wrong to mourn for him. To have pulled long faces and gone about plunged in grief would have been like an insult to the happy soul who had finished his day's work and gone home. It wasn't a case of

> ' Better by far you should forget and smile,
>   Than that you should remember and be sad.'

It was simply that we had so many happy things to remember we couldn't but smile. We wouldn't have had anything changed. To the very end his ways were ways of pleasantness and all his paths were peace. But when Robbie died——"

Ann stopped, and her mother took up her words :

" When Robbie died we seemed to sink into a black pit of horror. We didn't want to see any one. We could hardly look at the letters that poured in ; their lamentations seemed to add to our burden. Only Miss Barbara's was any use, and all she said was, ' I have prayed for you that your faith fail not.' "

" It seemed so *unfair*," Ann said slowly. " In a shop one day the woman who was serving me asked so kindly for you, and wanted to know how you were bearing up. Then she said suddenly : ' When thae awfu' nice folk dee div ye no juist fair feel that ye could rebel ? ' Rebel ! Poor helpless mortals that we are ! "

9

Mrs. Douglas shook her head. "If there is one lesson I have learned it is the folly of kicking against the pricks. To be bitter and resentful multiplies the grief a thousandfold. There is nothing for it but submission. Shall we receive good at the hand of the Lord and not receive evil? There is an odd text that strikes me every time I come to it: '*And David was comforted concerning Ammon because he was dead.*' I don't know what it means, perhaps that Ammon fought with David, so David was glad he was dead, but it always has a special meaning for me. We had to come to it, Ann, you and I, when we tramped those long walks by Tweedside rather than sit at home and face callers and sympathy. It was Robbie himself who helped us most. The thought of him, so brave and gay and gentle, simply *made* us believe that in a short time he had fulfilled a long time, and that God had taken him against that day when He shall make up His jewels. We could only cling to the fact that God is Love, and that it was to Himself He had taken the body who seemed to us so altogether lovely."

Mrs. Douglas took off her spectacles and rubbed them with her handkerchief, and Ann said:

"Yes, Mother, at moments we felt all that, and were comforted, but there are so many days when it seems you can't get above the sense of loss. Those nights when one dreamed he was with us, and wakened. There's not much doubt about Death's sting. . . . But what kept me from going under altogether was the thought of Davie. I tried never to let him see me with a dull face. All his life the child had dreaded sadness, and it seemed hard that he should so early become ' acquainted with grief.' After Robbie's death, when he came into a room the first thing he did was to glance quickly at our faces to see if we had been crying, and if we looked at him happily his face cleared. If anybody mentioned Robbie's name he slipped quietly out of the room. Jim was the same. I think men are like that. Women can talk and find relief, but to speak about his grief is the last thing an ordinary man can do. That's why I was sorrier for the fathers in the war than the mothers. . . . I was glad Davie was at college and busy all day. I think he dreaded coming home that Easter."

" But I don't think he found it bad, Ann. He had his great friend Anthony with him, and we all tried our best to give him a good time. And at seventeen it isn't so hard to rise above trouble."

" Oh no," said Ann ; " and Davie was so willing to be happy." She laughed. " I never knew any one so appreciative of a joke—any sort of joke. When he was a tiny boy if I said anything which I meant to be funny, and which met with no response, Davie would say indignantly : ' Nana's made a joke and nobody laughed.' He always gave a loud laugh himself—' Me hearty laugh,' he called it."

" Oh, I'd forgotten that," cried Davie's mother ; " ' me hearty laugh.' We all treated Davie as a joke, and didn't bother much whether his school reports were good or only fairly good. He wasn't at all studious naturally, though he was passionately fond of reading, and I'm afraid we liked to find excuses to let him play. Only Robbie took him seriously. You remember when he was home on leave he protested against Davie bounding everywhere and having no fixed hours of study. 'We've got to think of the chap's future,' he said."

"Robbie and Davie adored each other," Ann said. "They were so funny together—Davie a little bashful with the big brother. I remember hearing Davie telling Robbie about some Fabian Society that he belonged to, and what they discussed at it, and Robbie stood looking at him through his eyeglass with an amused grin on his face, and said, 'Stout fellow!' That was always what he said to Davie, 'Stout fellow!' I can hear him now. . . . But the odd thing was that Davie seemed to take no interest in his own future. It was almost as if he realized that this world held no future for him. Mark, always careful and troubled, used to worry about a profession for him. He wanted him to go into the Navy, but you vetoed that as too dangerous; it mustn't be India, because we couldn't part with our baby."

Mrs. Douglas leaned forward to push in a falling log. "I was foolishly anxious about Davie always; never quite happy if he was away from me. I worried the boy sometimes, but he was patient with me. 'Poor wee body,' he always said, and put his arms round me—he learned that expression from Robbie."

" I have an old exercise book," said Ann, " in which Davie made his first efforts at keeping accounts—*David Douglas in account with self*. It is very much ornamented with funny faces and not very accurate, for sums are frequently noted as ' lost.' It stops suddenly, and underneath is scrawled, ' The war here intervened.' We didn't need to worry about his work in the world. That was decided for him when—

> ' God chose His squires, and trained their hands
>   For those stern lists of liberty.' "

Mrs. Douglas caught her breath with a sob. " At once he clamoured to go, but he was so young, only eighteen, and I said he must only offer for home defence ; and he said, ' All right, wee body, that'll do to start with,' but in a very short time he was away to train with Kitchener's first army."

" He was miserable, Mother, until he got away. Jim was refused permission from the first, and had to settle down to his job, but for most of us the bottom seemed to have fallen out of the world, and one could settle to nothing. In the crashing of empires the one stable thing was the fact that the *Scotsman* continued its ' Nature Notes.' That amused Davie. . . . He began an album of war poetry, cutting out and pasting in verses that appeared in the *Times* and *Spectator* and *Punch* and other papers. ' Carmina Belli ' he printed on the outside. He charged me to go on with it when he went away, and I finished it with Mark's poem on himself :

> ' You left the line with jest and smile
>   And heart that would not bow to pain—
> *I'll lay me downe and bleed awhile,*
>   *And then I'll rise and fight again.'* "

Ann got up and leaned her brow on the mantel-shelf, and looking into the fire, said :

" Do you know, Mother, I think that first going away was the worst of all, though he was only going to England to train. Nothing afterwards so broke me down as seeing the fresh-faced boy in his grey tweed suit going off with such a high heart. I don't know what you felt about it, but the sword pierced my heart then. You remember it was the Fair at Priorsford ; and the merry-go-rounds on the Green buzzed round to a tune he had often sung, some ridiculous words about ' Hold your hand out, you naughty boy.' As I stood in my little swallow's-nest of a room and looked out over the Green, and saw the glare of the naphtha lamps reflected in the water, and the swing-boats passing backwards and forwards, through light into darkness, and from darkness into light, and realized that Davie had been born for the Great War, every chord seemed to strike at my heart."

" Oh, Ann," Mrs. Douglas cried, " I never let myself think. It was my only chance to go on working as hard as ever I was able at whatever came to my hand. I left him in God's hands. I was helpless."

The tears were running down her face as she spoke, and Ann said, " Poor Mother, it was hardest for you. Your cry was the old, old cry : ' Joseph is not, Simeon is not, and ye will take Benjamin away. . . .' But our Benjamin was so glad to go. And he never found anything to grumble at, not even at Bramshott, where there was nothing fit to eat, and the huts leaked, and the mud was unspeakable, and his uniform consisted of a red tunic made for a very large man, and a pair of exceedingly bad blue breeks. When he came home at Christmas —he made me think of one of Prince Charlie's men with his shabby uniform and yellow hair—how glad he was to have a real wallowing hot bath, with bath salts and warm towels, and get into his own tweeds. He was just beginning to get clean when he had to go again ! In a few weeks he got his commission, and in the autumn of 1915 he went to France ' as gentle and as jocund as to jest went he to fight.' "

There was a silence in the pleasant room as the two women thought their own thoughts, and the fire crackled and the winter wind beat upon the house.

Mrs. Douglas spoke first. " It was a wonderful oasis in that desert of anxiety when Davie was wounded and at home. Those nights when we had lain awake thinking of him in the trenches, those days when we were afraid for every ring at the bell, and hardly dared look when we opened the hall door after being out, in case the orange envelope should be lying on the table. To have all that suddenly changed. To know that he was lying safe and warm and clean in a white bed in a private hospital in London, ' lying there with a face like a herd,' Mark wrote, with nothing much the matter with him but a shrapnel wound in his leg—it was almost too much relief. And we had him at Queensferry all summer. We were greatly blessed, Ann."

" And it wasn't quite so bad letting him go the second time," Ann said. " He had been there once and had got out alive and he knew the men he was going to, and was glad to go back ; and Mark wasn't far from him, and could see him sometimes."

" His letters were so cheery. From his accounts you would have thought that living in the trenches was a sort of jolly picnic. Oh, Ann, do you remember the letter to me written in the train going up to the line, when he said he had dreamt he was a small boy again, and ' I thought I had lost you, wee body, and I woke up shouting " Mother," to the amusement of the other men in the carriage ? ' "

" Some people," said Ann, " go through the world afraid all the time that they are being taken advantage of. Davie never ceased to be amazed at the kindness shown him. He was one of those happy souls whose path through life is lined with friends, and whose kind eyes meet only affectionate glances. His letters were full of the kindness he received—the ' decent lad ' in his platoon who heard him say his dug-out was draughty, and who made a shutter for the window and stopped up all the cracks ; the two corporals from the Gallowgate who formed his bodyguard, and every time he fell into a shell-hole or dodged a crump shouted anxiously, ' Are ye hurt, sirr ? ' You remember he wrote : ' These last two years have been the happiest in my life,' and other men who were with him told us he never lost his high spirits.''

" That was such a terribly long, hard winter," Mrs. Douglas said. " The snow was never off the hills for months. And then spring came, but such a spring ! Nothing but wild winds and dreary sleet. We hoped and hoped that Davie would get leave— he was next on the list for it—but he wrote and said his leave had gone ' very far West.' We didn't know it, but they were getting ready for the big spring offensive. Then one day we saw that a battle had begun at Arras, and Davie's letter that morning read like a farewell. ' Things may be happening shortly, but don't worry about me. I've just been thinking what a good life I've had all round, and what a lot of happiness I've had. Even the sad parts are a comfort now. . . .' "

" Mother, do you see," said Ann, " there's your text about Ammon. Out there, waiting for the big battle, Davie didn't feel it sad any more that Father and Robbie had gone out of the world—he was *comforted concerning them because they were dead.* We were thinking of him and praying for him every hour of the day, but he felt them nearer to him than we were."

" To think that when that letter came he was dead ! To think that I was in Glasgow with Miss Barbara talking of him nearly all the time, for Miss Barbara loved the boy, and nothing told us he was no longer in the world. To think of the child—he was little more—waiting there in the darkness for the signal to attack. He must have been so anxious about leading the company, so afraid——"

" Anxious maybe," said Ann, " but not really afraid. Don't you remember what his great friend Captain Shiels wrote and told us, that while they waited for the dawn Davie spoke ' words of comfort and encouragement to his men.' I cry when I think of that. . . ."

" My little boy—my baby. Away from us all— *alone*. . . ."

" No. No, Mother, never less alone ; ' compassed about with a great cloud of witnesses.' I have a notion that all the great army of men who down through the centuries have given their lives for our country's bright cause were with our men in that awful fighting, steeling the courage of those boy-soldiers. . . . And Father and Robbie were beside him, I am very sure, and Father would know then that all his prayers were answered for his boy—the bad little boy who refused to say his prayers, the timid little boy who was afraid to go into a dark room—when he saw him stand, with Death tapping him on the shoulder, speaking ' words of comfort and encouragement to his men.' I think Robbie would say, ' Stout fellow.' That was the 9th. The telegram came to us on the afternoon of the 11th. Jim and I were terribly anxious, and I had been doing all the jobs I hated most with a sort of lurking, ashamed feeling in my heart that if we worked our hardest and did our very best Davie might be spared to us."

Ann stopped, and went on, half laughing, half crying:

"Like poor Mrs. Clark, one of my women. She told me how she had gone out and helped a sick neighbour, and coming home had seen some children, whose father was fighting and whose mother was ill, playing in the rain, and she had taken them in and given them a hot meal. As they were leaving the postman brought her a letter saying her son was dead in Mesopotamia. She said to me, defiantly, as if she were scoring off Providence, ' I'm no gaun tae *pray* nae mair,' and I knew exactly what she felt."

"Oh, the poor woman," said Mrs. Douglas, weeping.

"I thought," Ann went on, "that if no wire came that day it would mean that Davie had got through—but at tea-time it came. I went into Glasgow next morning by the first train to tell you. Phœbe was washing the front door steps at No. 10, and she told me you and Miss Barbara were in the dining-room at breakfast. I stood in the doorway and looked at you. You were laughing and telling Miss Barbara something funny that had been in one of Davie's letters. I felt like a murderer standing there. When I went into the room your face lit up for a moment, and then you realized. ' It is the laddie ? ' you whispered, and I nodded. You neither spoke nor cried, but stood looking before you as if you were thinking very deeply about something, then ' I would like to go home,' you said. . . ."

" And to think," Mrs. Douglas said, breaking a long silence, " that I am only one of millions of mothers who will go mourning to their graves."

" I know, Mother. I know. But you wouldn't ask him back even if that were possible. You wouldn't, if you could, take ' the purple of his blood out of the cross on the breastplate of England.' Don't you love these words of Ruskin ? It's the proudest thing we have to think about, and, honestly—I'm not just saying this—I believe that the men who lie out there have the best of it. The men who came back will, most of them, have to fight a grim struggle, for living is none too pleasant just now, and they will grow old, and bald, and ill-tempered, and they have all to die in the end. What is twenty more years of life but twenty more years of fearing death ? But our men whose sacrifice was accepted, and who were allowed to pour out the sweet, red wine of youth, passed at one bound from glorious life to glorious life. ' Eld shall not make a mock of that dear head.' They know not age or weariness or defeat."

CHAPTER XXIV

THE December day had run its short and stormy course and the sun was going down in anger, with streaks of crimson and orange, and great purple clouds. Only over the top of the far hills was one long line of placid pale primrose, like some calm land-locked bay amid seas of tumbling waters.

Mrs. Douglas, crossing the room to get a paper from the table, paused at the wide window and looked out. Desolate the landscape looked, the stretch of moorland, and the sodden fields, and the empty highroad running like a ribbon between hills now dark with rain.

She sighed as she looked.

Ann was writing at the bureau, had been writing since luncheon, absorbed, never lifting her head, but now she blotted vigorously the last sheet, put the pen back in the tray, shut the lid of the ink-bottle, and announced:

" Now, then, Mother, that's your *Life* written ! "

Mrs. Douglas looked at the finished pile of manuscript and sighed again.

Ann got up and went over to the window.
" You are sighing like a furnace, Mother. What's
the matter ? Does it depress you to think that
I've finished my labours ? Oh, look at the sunset !
It bodes ill for the Moncrieffs ever getting over the
door, poor lambs ! Look at that quiet, shining bit
over the Farawa, how far removed it looks from
tempests ! D'you know what that sky reminds me
of, Mother ? The story of your life that I've just
finished. The clouds and the angry red colour are
all you passed through, and that quiet, serene streak
is where you are now, the clear shining after
rain. It may be dull, but you must admit it is
peaceful."

" Oh, we are peaceful enough just now, but think
of Jim in South Africa, and Charlotte and Mark in
India—who knows what news we may have of them
any day ? I just live in dread of what may happen
next."

" But, Mother, you've always lived in dread.
Mark used to say that the telegraph boys drew lots
among themselves as to who should bring the tele-
grams to our house. You used to rush out with the
unopened envelope and implore the boy to tell you
if it were bad news, and when you did open it your
frightened eyes read things that never were on the
paper. If we happened to be all at home when you
were confronted with a wire you didn't care a
bit—utterly callous. It was only your husband
and your children you cared about—ah, well, you
had the richest, fullest, happiest life for more than

thirty years, and that's not so small a thing to boast of."

" Oh, Ann, I'm not ungrateful, only——"

" Only you're like Davie when we told him to go away and count his blessings. ' I've done it,' he came back to tell us, ' and I've six things to be thankful for and nine to be unthankful for.' "

Mrs. Douglas laughed as she went back to her chair by the fire and took up her knitting. " No, I've nothing to be unthankful for, only I think so much of me died with your father and Robbie and Davie that I seem to be half with you and half with them where they are gone."

Ann nodded. " That may be so, but you are more alive than most of us even now. I don't know anybody who takes so much interest in life, who has such a capacity for enjoyment, who burdens herself with other people's burdens as that same Mrs. Douglas who says she is only half-alive and longs to depart—and here is Mysie with the tea."

Mysie lit the lamp under the kettle and arranged the tea-things. She drew the curtains across the windows, shutting out the last gleam of the stormy sunset, and turned on the lights, then she stood by the door, and, blushing, asked if she might go out for the evening, as she had an engagement.

" Now where "—cried Mrs. Douglas as the door closed behind the little maid—" where in the world can Mysie have an engagement in this out-of-the-world place on this dark, stormy night ? "

Ann smiled. " She's so pretty, Mother, so soft and round and young, and have you forgotten :

> ' For though the nicht be ne'er sae dark,
>   An' I be ne'er sae weary O,
> I'll meet ye by the lea-rig,
>   Ma ain kind dearie O.'

I haven't a doubt but that pretty Mysie has got a ' lawd.' And what for no ? I do hope Marget isn't too discouraging to the child."

Ann sat on the fender-stool with her cup and saucer, and a pot of jam on the rug beside her, and a plate with a crumpet on her lap, and ate busily.

" Life is still full of pleasant things, Mums, pretty girls and crumpets, and strawberry jam, and fender-stools, and blazing fires, and little moaning mothers who laugh even while they cry. Your pessimism is like the bubbles on a glass of champagne—oh, I know you have been a teetotaller all your days, but that doesn't harm my metaphor."

" Ann, you amaze me. How you can rattle on as if you hadn't a care in the world—you who have lost so much ! "

Ann looked at her mother in silence for a minute, then she looked into the dancing flames. " As you say, it is amazing—I who have lost so much. And when you think of it, I haven't much to laugh at. I've got the sort of looks that go very fast, so I'll soon be old and ugly—but what about it ?

" ' I may never live to be old,' says she.
' For nobody knows their day. . . .'

And I've got work to do, and I've still got brothers,
and I've got Charlotte and the children, and I've
more friends than I sometimes know what to do
with. It's an odd thing, but I do believe, Mother,
that I'm happier now than when I was twenty and
had all the world before me. Youth isn't really a
very happy time. You want and want and you
don't know what you want. As you get older you
realize that you have *no right to bliss*, and must make
the best of what you have got. Then you begin to
enjoy things in a different way. Out of almost
everything that happens there is some pleasure to
be got if you look for it, and people are so funny and
human and pitiful you can't be dull. Middle age
brings its compensations, and, anyway, whether it
does or not it is a most miserable business to be
obsessed by one's own woes. The only thing to do
is to stand a bit away from oneself and say, ' You
miserable atom, what are you whining about ? Do
you suppose the eternal scheme of things is going to
be altered because *you* don't like it ? ' "

Mrs. Douglas laughed rather ruefully. " You're
a terribly bracing person, Ann ; but I'm bound to
confess that you practise what you preach."

" But I've really no right to preach at all ! "
Ann said. " I always forget one thing, the most
important of all. I've always been perfectly well,
so I've no right to sit in judgment on people who

struggle all their lives against ill-health. It is no credit to me—I who hardly know what it means to have a headache—to be equable and gay. When I think of some people we know, fighting all the time against such uneven odds, asking only for a chance to work and be happy in working, and knocked down time and again, yet always undefeated, I could go and bury my head ashamed. Don't ever listen to me, Mother, when I preach at you ; squash me at once."

" Well, I'll try to—but, Ann, there is one thing that worries me. Remember, I will not have you sacrifice your life to me."

" No fear of that," said Ann airily. " There's nothing of the martyr about me."

" That Mr. Philip Scott——" Mrs. Douglas hesitated.

" Oh, him ! " said Ann, " or, to be more grammatical, oh, he ! I had a letter from him this morning—did I forget to show it you ? He says he is to be at Birkshaw for Christmas."

Ann stopped.

" Well, Ann ? "

" Well, Mother ? "

" Don't be provoking, Ann. Is Mr. Scott anything to you ? "

Ann turned serene grey eyes to her mother. " Nothing," she said, " except a pleasant friend. That's all he wants to be, I'm sure."

" But, Ann, don't you think . . ."

" I never think, Mother . . ."

Ann caught the Tatler in her arms and sank with it into the depths of an arm-chair.

" There's something exceedingly nice about being a spinster. Here's Marget. I shall ask her what she thinks. Marget, you don't regret being a spinster, do you ? "

Marget came farther into the room and peered suspiciously at Ann in the arm-chair with the cat in her arms.

" Ye're no' gaun to pit it doon in writin', are ye ? Weel, that's a' richt. To tell the truth I hadna muckle encouragement to be onything else. I wasna juist a'thegither negleckit, but I never had a richt offer. But lookin' roond I've often been thankfu' I wasna trachled wi' a man. Ye see, livin' a' ma life wi' kin' o' better folk I wad ha' taken ill wi' a man sittin' in his stockin' feet and spittin' into the fire. Genteel service spoils ye ; but, of course, a'body's no sae particlar. . . . Mysie, the monkey, hes gotten a lawd."

" What did I say," Ann cried. " Who is he, Marget ? "

" His name's Jim Stoddart, a dacent lawd and no sae gawky as maist o' them. He was an officer's servant in the war, and learned mainners."

" But, Marget," said Mrs. Douglas, " we're so far away from people here—how did Mysie meet him ? "

" Tuts, Mem, let a lassie alane for that. If there's a ' come hither ' in the e'e the lawd 'll turn up, though he has to tramp miles o' heather and hard road. I never kent hoo lassies did thon. I used often to watch them and wonder, but I could niver learn—I was aye a muckle hoose-end even as a lassie, an' tricks wad hev ill become me."

" It's a wise woman that knows her limitations," said Ann. " I wish we were all wise enough to avoid being arch—Marget, I've finished Mother's *Life*."

Marget immediately dropped into a convenient chair. " Let's hear it," she said.

" What! Now ? "

" What for no ? Is't that lang ? "

" Long ? " said Ann ; " like the White Knight's song, but very beautiful ! "

" Aw, if ye're gaun to haver." Marget turned to her mistress. " What's it like, Mem ? "

" I don't know, Marget, I've hardly seen a word of it, but it will certainly have to be censored before you get it typed, Ann."

" Oh yes," said Ann. " You will read it and ' riddle oot the biggest lees frae ilka page,' and then I'll send it to the typing lady Mark told me about ; if she can make out Mark's handwriting she won't be so aghast at mine. One copy for each of ourselves and some for very great friends——"

Mrs. Douglas broke in. " If you begin with friends there will be no end to it."

" Then, perhaps, we had better have it privately printed and get about a hundred copies. Have we a hundred friends ? "

" Liker twa hunner," Marget said gloomily. " To me it seems a queer-like thing to print a body's life when she's still leevin'."

Ann quoted, " That horn is blowen for me," said Balin, " yet I am not dead," then, laughing at the expression on Marget's face, she said, " It's often done, Marget, only you call it ' reminiscences.' Mrs. Asquith wrote her reminiscences, and you can't accuse her of being dead."

Marget muttered something, and Ann continued, " Mother is very fortunate to have a daughter to write hers for her."

" Fortunate ! " said Mrs. Douglas. " I'll tell you when I've read it."

" Weel," said Marget, " I hope she made it interestin', Mem, for I'm sure we hed a rale interestin' time baith in Kirkcaple and Glasgae— an' Priorsford's no bad aither, though, of course, we're no minister's folk there an' that maks a big differ : we havna the same posseetion."

" Marget," said Ann, " I believe you think a minister and his wife are the very highest in the land, higher even than a Provost and his lady ; infinitely higher than a mere earl."

Marget said " Earls ! " and grunted, then she explained, " I yince kent an earl. When ma faither was leevin' an' we were at Kinloch we kept yin o' the lodges for the big hoose, and I used to see the young earl playin' cricket. He minded me o' Joseph wi' his coat o' many colours, but, hech ! he was nae Joseph. I doot Potiphar's wife wad hae got nae rebuke frae him. I dinna hold wi' thae loose lords mysel' onyway." She turned her back on Ann and addressed her mistress. " It's

a queer thing, Mem, that the folk we have to dae
wi' now are no' near as interestin' as the folk we
kent lang syne. I sit by the fire in the fore-
suppers—my eyes are no what they were, an' I get
tired o' sewin' and readin'—an' I think awa back
to the auld days in Kirkcaple. Thae were the
days! When the bairns were a' at hame. Eh,
puir things, mony a skelp I hed at them when they
cam' fleein' wi' their lang legs ower ma new-sanded
kitchen! Thae simmer's afternunes when I went
oot to the Den wi' Ellie Robbie and them a' and
we made a fire and hed oor tea; an' winter nichts
when we sat roond the nursery fire and telt
stories. An' the neebors drappin' in: Mistress
Peat as neat as if she hed come oot o' a bandbox,
and Mistress Goskirk tellin' us hoo to mak' jeely—
we kent fine oorsels—an' hoo to cut oot breeks for
the laddies—we were never guid at cuttin' oot, ye'll
mind, Mem? An' Mistress Dewar sittin' on the
lobby chair knittin' like mad when I got doon the
stair to open the door for her, and Mr. Dewar
sayin', ' Is it bakin' day, Marget? ' An' in Glasgae
there was Mistress Burnett comin' in, aye wi' a
present, an' aye wi' something kind to say. Some
folk ye wad think tak' a fair delight in tellin'
ye things that chaw ye, they juist canna help
bein' nesty, puir sowls; ye mind Mrs. Lawrie
was like that, she couldna gang awa' wi'oot giving
ye a bit sting—but Mistress Burnett cheered up
the whole day wi' her veesit. An' Miss Barbara—
she aye cam' at the maist daft-like time so that she

wadna bother us for a meal, her that wad hae fed a' the earth! An' Mistress Lang—a braw wumman thon—she likit to come in efter tea an' hae a guid crack. An' Dr. Struthers—my! He pit us sair aboot when he cam' to stay, but I was rale pleased, it was like haein' yin o' thae auld prophets bidin' wi' us. An' the hoosefu's we had in the holidays when the bairns grew up, we whiles didna ken whaur to turn. . . . An' thae times are a' past, an' here we are sittin' an' a' the folk I've been speakin' aboot are deid, an' the Moncrieffs are comin' the morn——"

"And if you don't keep the water boiling hot, you'll hear about it," Ann warned her.

Marget drew herself up. "If the Cornel speaks to me as if I were a black oot in India I'll speir at him . . ."

"Marget, more and more you remind me of the late Queen Victoria. You have the grand manner."

"Havers!" said Marget.

Mrs. Douglas broke in. "You'll have to be very kind to Colonel and Mrs. Moncrieff, Marget. You know since we last saw them they have lost both their sons, and from what I hear they are very broken."

Marget shook her head. "It's awfu' hertless work leevin' now that sae mony o' the young folk are deid. A' ma life I've been fear't to dee, an' at meetings I never sang at 'O for the pearly gates o' Heaven' for fear I'd be taken at ma

word, but the ither nicht I hed sic a bonnie dream.
I thocht I was in an awfu' neat wee hoose, an'
it was Johnnie Johnston's hoose—ye mind him,
Mem, at Kirkcaple ?—an' I said, ' My, Johnnie,
ye're awfu' comfortable here,' an' he says, ' Ay,'
he says, ' Look oot o' the windy.' An' there was
a great sea, a terrible sea wi' waves an' a' kinds o'
wee boats on it, some o' them gettin' an awfu'
whummlin. An' I says, ' Eh, is that Galilee ? '
an' he says, ' Na, it's the Sea of Life.' An' he says,
' Look oot at the other windy noo,' an' here was
anither sea, but it was a wee narra sea an' awfu'
quait, an' I says, Is that the Jordan ? ' ' Look
ower at the ither side,' he says, an' I lookit,
and there was the Golden City. It was the
bonniest place I ever saw, the *very bonniest*, an'
I said, ' Eh, I wad like awfu' weel to get ower
there, Johnnie Johnston, an' he said, ' No the
day, but there's naething surer than that ye'll
get ower some day.' An' wi' that I wakened. . . .
I was that vexed I fair grat, but I'll mind ma
dream an' it'll help me when ma time comes to
gang."

Marget wiped her eyes and then, as if ashamed
of having shown emotion, stalked majestically
from the room.

Ann and her mother, left alone, sat looking
into the fire. For a long time they sat. The
logs burned through and fell together, but
Ann did not seem to notice that the fire needed
mending. The Tatler playfully clawed her hand

to entice her to a game, but she pushed him away.

Mrs. Douglas was the first to break the silence. "Dear me, I've never begun my 'reading,' and it will soon be dinner-time. Give me my books over, Ann."

Ann rose and fetched the pile and put them beside her mother. "Biggest first," she said, and handed her *Hours of Silence*.

Mrs. Douglas put on her large tortoiseshell spectacles and began at once to read, but presently her eyes strayed from the printed page to her daughter's face, and she said, "Why are you sitting looking at me, Ann?"

"Because you're such a queer little mother sitting there, with your owlish spectacles and your devotional books."

Mrs. Douglas sighed, and then she smiled. "Poor Marget, with her 'bonnie' dream! I was sitting thinking just now how well off I am having her to go back with me to the old days. As she says, it is heartless work living now, and yet there is something very heartening about the continuity of life. When I stay with Mark and Charlotte and see Mark rushing, the moment he gets home, to his garden, and watch him among the flowers, one hand behind his back in his father's very attitude, it might be my Mark with me again. And Rory, who came into the world the day his grandfather went out of it—one Mark Douglas going and another Mark Douglas taking his place—Rory sidles up to me and puts his head on my shoulder when he wants something just as his father did thirty years ago—I think they should stop calling him Rory now and call him Mark."

"Well, it's a little confusing for Charlotte to have two Marks in the house unless she does as Marget suggests, and 'ca's Mr. Mark Papaw.' But I know what you mean about the feeling of continuity. Last summer Alis and Rory, greatly condescending, were allowing young Robbie to play some game with them. I came upon them suddenly, and the years seemed to roll back when I saw the earnest absorbed face of Robbie as he padded about—it might have been my own Robbie. He, too, played with his whole might. . . . Oh, look at the fire going out rapidly."

Ann knelt down and mended the fire with great care, sweeping in the ashes and making the hearth clean and tidy.

"I spend my life tidying up this fireside. I might as well be a vestal virgin in a temple. There, that will be a fine fire when we come back. Have you finished your reading, Mother? We must go and change. It's a good thing the Moncrieffs are coming to-morrow. You and I have been living so much in the past that we are like two little grey ghosts."

"I've enjoyed it," said Mrs. Douglas. "But think a long time before you decide to print what you've written."

She gathered up her devotional books and built them in a neat pile on a table.

" I wonder who you think could possibly be interested in such an uneventful record ?   All about nothing, and not even an end——"

" I *wonder*," said Ann.

THE END

PRINTED IN GREAT BRITAIN AT
THE PRESS OF THE PUBLISHERS

NELSON CLASSICS

SELECTED VOLUMES

GEORGE ELIOT : Adam Bede ; The Mill on the Floss ; Romola ; Scenes of Clerical Life ; Silas Marner

MRS GASKELL : Cranford ; The Cage at Cranford and Other Stories, Introduction by Paul Beard ; Mary Barton

OLIVER GOLDSMITH : Essays and Tales ; The Vicar of Wakefield, with Sir Walter Scott's Life of Goldsmith ; Poems and Plays

J. C. HARRIS : Uncle Remus

NATHANIEL HAWTHORNE : The Scarlet Letter ; Tanglewood Tales

ROBERT HERRICK : Poems. Introduction by Sir John Squire

HENRIK IBSEN : Four Plays—Ghosts, The Master Builder, The Wild Duck, and A Doll's House. Introduction by Desmond MacCarthy

RICHARD JEFFERIES : Amaryllis at the Fair

CHRISTOPHER MARLOWE : Three Plays. Edited and with an Introduction by John Hampden

CAPTAIN MARRYAT : The Children of the New Forest ; Masterman Ready ; Mr Midshipman Easy

SIR HENRY NEWBOLT (Editor) : Devotional Poets of the Seventeenth Century (Donne, Herbert, Crashaw, Herrick, Vaughan, Traherne ; with an Introduction) ; New Paths on Helicon

EDGAR ALLAN POE : Tales of Mystery and Imagination

WILLIAM SHAKESPEARE : Complete Works (in 6 volumes)—Comedies (2 vols.) ; Histories, Poems (2 vols.) ; Tragedies (2 vols.)

STEVENSON, R. L. Works in 18 volumes

FRANCIS THOMPSON : Poems

WILLIAM WORDSWORTH : Poems. Introduction by Viscount Grey of Fallodon

J. R. WYSS : The Swiss Family Robinson

CHARLOTTE M. YONGE : A Book of Golden Deeds

Established 1798

T. NELSON
& SONS, Ltd.
PRINTERS AND
PUBLISHERS